To those who stand proud on the front lines of war, and to those who have fallen in the line of duty. Without your sacrifice and hard work, history would tell a much darker tale of woe.

Foreword

If you are looking for a story like my previous works, then this is not the place to dwell. Within these covers is a story inspired by friends and acquaintances who have come home from the Armed Forces to a rejoin life with a great deal of struggle. Their old life didn't change, but they did. Once a person is trained to fight, they change. Once placed in the field of battle, certain parts of what makes us human have to be switched off to survive. When they come home, it is exceedingly difficult to switch those things back on. I have witnessed this struggle and was inspired to write this tale from it.

Once completed, I found myself staring at the news witnessing the very chaos and civil unrest that I described in the story's prologue happening now. It made me pause and wait nearly three weeks before releasing this book. Not because I hit the nail on the head, but because it was simply the wrong time for this story to be heard. Other voices needed to rise above the storm, mine was not one of them.

So as our world strives to change, I step forward to show a cautionary tale of what may come. While we tend to ignore science, to go the other direction and put the world in the hands of those scientific minds may not be the answer we are searching for. For in the search for facts, science somehow forgets to consider the human equation, and to govern a planet this way could lead down a much darker road then we realize.

Don't get me wrong, I am an advocate of higher learning and scientific research. I don't agree with the new Western philosophy of believing the fake news and conspiracy theorists before actual proven science fact. For over 400 years we have known the world is a sphere, but now because of a few idiots and their access to the internet we begin to question that proven fact? I weep for our future.

Now that my mini rant is over, I must say I had a great deal of joy writing these characters in this book and look forward to continuing to add to their story as the years go by. The Aen Saga was always set to be 4 or 5 novels (the 5th and final book will be released this fall) but I have countless tales to tell in this future setting.

Back to my inspiration, imagine serving the ideals of a better world and fighting for them on the front lines of a planetary civil war. This new revolutionary government has given you much to get you here. Training, ways to improve your health, improvements to your physique, and the promise of a better future are all yours if you just give them your all. You are a soldier, fighting for a united Earth. But as the war winds down and your side's victory is in hand, you realize there is no place for someone like you in this utopia which you gave your all for.

To an extent, this is how my friends felt when they came home. The life the rest of us take for granted seemed to reject them, leaving them to feel isolated within their own minds. Some learn to move past the feeling, others struggle with it their whole lives. Their blood, sweat, and tears have allowed us to reach this moment in history. Let's not tarnish the memories of the fallen soldiers by taking the easy path forward.

So, get set for a different tale, a bit of a darker tale. I hope you enjoy the Four Horsemen of the Republic as much as I did writing them. They are the most emotionally complex characters I have ever created, and I think that translates to a hell of a good story. Enjoy.

Revelations : 2520

The Broken and the Damned

By Damian Shishkin

"Soldiers are citizens of death's grey land, drawing no dividend from time's tomorrows."

Siegfried Sassoon

Prologue

If humanity has proven one thing in its existence, it is that they are exceptionally good at waging war. Despite all the innovation, exploration, and self-reflection, it never seems to drown out the drums of the ever-growing war machine that drives them. War got humans on the moon, helped explore the cosmos with satellites and telescopes originally designed for spying, and even brought cell phones and GPS to the public. It drives economies, restores waning national pride, and of course topples enemy regimes.

Many great wars have been fought over the ages, but the last great one ended in 1945. Since World War II, the world has seen skirmishes and battles, but not an all-out war. And though these other fights were labelled wars, they were done so to garner public support. Sometimes they were done for more nefarious reasons like to capitalize on political agendas and the capture of foreign resources.

Eventually, the population began to see these so-called wars for what they were, a way to distract the people from the issues at home. Capitalism was failing, and the once powerful Western World began to crumble from within. Leaders unable to lead, governments with no true policy or vision, and states that lacked solidarity with their countries all led to the perfect storm. The American dream was dead, and unbelievably a civil war loomed on the horizon.

All this proved to be the perfect distraction for a movement to gain traction, though it did so in Europe, not the United States. A group of scientists came up with a new form of government, one they figured could take the world to the next step in history. They proposed a ruling Council for the entire planet, a Republic of Man for a united Earth. They were laughed at by most, yet there were more than a few that looked past the glitter of the dream to see what it actually could accomplish. It meant housing for all, employment for any who would take it, and a leap forward in our energy needs.

It was enough to quietly get agreements from two tech giants in Asia, and a few South American countries in desperate need of proper direction. In the year 2024, they green lit these scientists to start their process. Results didn't take long to come, and the way of life on both sides of the invested countries improved drastically.

Fusion reactors were built and brought online close to two years afterwards. The moment these reactors were brought online, the energy needs of the countries were met ten-fold, allowing them to drop the costs of living by more than half. Carbon extraction towers rose at the same time, and with the new power supply they too came online, clearing the atmosphere of regional carbon emissions by a fair degree. Three years after enjoying the fruits of the first phase of the plan, the countries took the next step and combined into one state, called the Republic. This garnered some push back from other powerful countries, but also interest from other struggling nations. By 2030, the Republic had grown to include all of South America, Western Africa, Spain, Italy, Greece, Israel, Iceland, and even Australia. It was now a growing superpower and gaining enemies as quickly as it grew.

Despite their vision of a better world, the minds behind the Republic knew it would not come easy. From the very beginning they began to redesign the way war would be fought, using the militaries of the original countries to sponsor them as guinea pigs. Most of this stayed in the design stage for many years, waiting for the Republic to grow large enough to easily absorb the costs of such extensive upgrades. Fusion power had been the key to it all, allowing the reinvention of the human war machine as it was known.

By 2030, the Republic had its new Air Force. Comprised of unmanned attack drones that would fight alongside more tactical piloted stealth craft, they could fly faster, higher, and hit harder than anything else other countries had in development. They ignored the need for a water based fighting force, instead using invention and wisdom to develop Orbital Navy comprised of two one-kilometer long attack cruisers. These resembled a boxy shaped submarine with two large magnetic repulsor engines extending from each side. These were crude first designs, but when tested in the middle of the Pacific Ocean in the dead of night, they performed beyond expectations. Now they had an orbital attack platform that could deliver and deploy the drone fighters around the globe.

It was the Army that showed the greatest of innovations and redesigns. Magnetically accelerated cannons, or railguns, were perfected in all sizes. This allowed for non-explosive rounds to be fired near the speed of light with devastating effect. The bigger the gun, the larger the round, and the more damage it caused. Add to this a virtual intelligence guidance program, and these weapons became deadly accurate.

Tanks were redesigned from the ground up, and when completed resembled more of a video game concept than the traditional armored vehicle. Using the same concepts that powered the space cruisers, tanks now hovered above the ground rather than lumbering over it. Like most of their new tech, first generation models were very crude, but still effective. Fifteen feet wide by twenty feet long, the boxy shape was topped with a square turret armed with two large railguns with two manned smaller railguns for defensive needs.

Crew transports were also made with the same hover tech, needing the same engine style to offset the extra load the infantry added. All warfare eventually required boots on the ground, and when it came to the soldiers the real innovation came to play. Complete armored exoskeletons encased and protected the soldiers of the Republic, and when put to the test they would stop even a .50 cal round at close range. RPGs would do some damage, but still would not kill the soldier within. The suits also enabled the soldiers to wield larger railgun rifles and carry more ammo which made them more effective on the battlefield.

All of this was done without any knowledge of the outside world, any attempt at spying was taken care of by the inclusion of the world's most notorious hacker group. What better way to deter and control cyber security then enlisting the best cyber criminals on the planet. Once they saw the grand plan close up, they were in it for the long haul. To the rest of the countries, the Republic appeared to be a nation of science and pacifism, an appearance they were more than glad to keep up until they needed to show their darker side.

That darker side was led by their special forces. Shrouded in secrecy, this project created augmented soldiers. Cyborgs, cybernetically enhanced soldiers trained in all forms of combat. They were faster, stronger, and smarter than the normal soldier. And from this project came four enhanced men and women that rose above all the rest. When the eventual Revolutionary War began, these four became the face of the Republic's war machine, and the legend of the Four Horsemen of the Republic began.

On July 8th of 2038, the U.S., Russia, and China finally buckled under the constant threat of the growing Republic and declared war. Thinking they had the edge with nuclear weapons and superior military might, the old superpower nations pushed back when the Balkan state and Germany joined the Republic. Russia was now surrounded on almost every border, so brokered a deal with China and the U.S. to end the threat once and for all. It was an arrogant decision, and with no way to know what they were really up against, China moved into a Republic controlled reunited Korea, while Russia rolled into Turkey. It was here the world was introduced to the Four Horsemen formally, and it was here that the Republic bared its teeth for all to see. It struck back and struck back hard.

The invading forces were annihilated in short order, leaving only media members accompanying the attacking nations alive to send the message back to those in charge. With advanced military might, the old guard nations turned to their nukes, only to find out that solution was no longer an option. Republic hackers had successfully let viruses loose in the nuclear systems which rendered the planet killing weapons useless. Launch systems, targeting computers, and even the missiles themselves were compromised. Without their trump cards, the allied nations had to face the Republic head on, which the Republic analytics wanted all along.

This led to almost twenty years of war, and staggering casualties on both sides. Russia and China dug in deep, defending their countries ferociously. Yet any battle led by or including the Four Horsemen became growingly lopsided as time went on. The Republic think tank noticed this trend and saw a way to end the war at long last. Playing defense on the two continental fronts, they used their Air and Space forces to invade a heavily politically divided United States. With some States already pledging allegiance to the ideals of the Republic before the War even started, the kill shot came quickly in the surprise invasion of Washington D.C. In a two-night span, the Republic forces, led by the Four Horsemen captured the Senate, both Houses of Congress, and the sitting President. It took a few months of bloodshed to finalize the American surrender, but after a few sound beatings by the Horsemen in Virginia, Texas, and Colorado, the resistance finally gassed out.

It was a shock to the rest of the world, but the Republic didn't hesitate to keep moving forward. Turning its attention to China, the Four Horsemen landed on the Chinese coast to immediately change the nature of the fighting. Fronts that were stalemated for years were won in days, and the drive towards Beijing began and ended in three months. In the end, the Republic won because the Chinese people were so tired of the war, they simply laid down arms at approaching forces. When it was over, there was no leadership left to sign a surrender, it was simply implied by the complete occupation of the country.

All eyes turned to Russia; the last few nations that had stayed neutral agreed to join the Republic. Great strides in the quality of life and advancement of the human race had already began to show in the now inclusive American States. While tiny pockets of resistance fighters remained, the general populace began to see the benefits of life within the Republic. There was no homelessness, no being out of work, and life became affordable for all.

As the Horsemen entered Russia, they were now legends of the Revolutionary War. Faced with the fighting legends, the Russian forces quit on their oppressive leaders, allowing the Republic to march unopposed to the Kremlin itself. Accompanied by Republic negotiators, the Four Horsemen entered the ruling house of Russia while the world watched. A few hours later they emerged without the negotiators, boarded a covered transport and disappeared. That was the final image of the Revolutionary War. The entire planet was united under one government, one flag, with the vision to drive humanity forward the right way.

Years went by as the world learned how to work together. It was not perfect, but it was productive. Global companies rose to great power, reaping the rewards of financing the Republic and its War with contracts and access to markets around the world never before accessible. And while the Council of the Republic was technically in charge of affairs, these global conglomerates were the true influence on that political power. As for the Horsemen, well they were used sparingly to beat down the inevitable insurgents to the rule of the Republic. There were always some people that refused to give up their old ideals, and the Four Horsemen dealt with them with ruthless efficiency.

Eventually the world began to heal from the War but could not completely move on while the Four Horsemen were still around. Like any soldier, their usefulness ended when there was no longer a threat to the ruling government. They had fought to create a world that had no place for them, so they were rewarded for their efforts with incarceration. Charged with War crimes by a Public Tribunal, then placed in cryogenic stasis, the ultimate weapons of the Revolutionary War were locked away. And like all things in storage, they were eventually forgotten, lost in the pages of history to become tools of a bygone era.

Without them, humanity grew exponentially using the deep pockets of the powerful companies within it. Three hundred years after the War, it auctioned off exo planets to the highest bidder. The Republic allowed these companies to colonize and govern their acquisitions as they saw fit, though ultimately staying within the rule of the Republic itself. For those opposed to the way of life on Earth it was a way to start anew, to others it was the adventure of unheralded proportions. To some, it became a nightmare.

1

Rain Forest Plateau; Outskirts of New Athens; Horizon

Life wasn't perfect out on the new frontier, but it was a far cry better than it was back on Earth. Just over four hundred years ago, the Revolutionary War ended, uniting all of humanity under one banner with the brightest minds on the planet running the show. The problem with that was when using science to run a planet, the human factor is easily lost. This led to great unrest amongst the people and helped the drive to colonize new worlds.

Two of these new worlds lay within the Teegarden System, owned by the Nowich-Paris Company. Naming its twin habitable gems Dawn and Horizon, the company pushed through most preliminary precautions to set up mining operations and settle the planets as soon as possible. The rush had paid off in dividends, and soon the ungodly amounts of money spent on purchasing the rights to the system, transporting entire cities over, and relocating millions of eager workers was recouped.

Dawn was a gem. A beautiful garden world full of small animal life which hardly got in the way of the crown jewel settlement in the new frontier. Morning Star was the envy of every other exo-planetary city, a beacon to those who wished to start new, but still have all the luxuries of Earth. Its chrome and glass spires rose high into the sky, shining to those aboard Waypoint Station in orbit, which was still under construction.

Horizon was Dawn's twin, but other than similar land masses and oceans, the resemblance ended there. While Dawn was peaceful and inviting, Horizon tried to kill you from the moment you stepped onto it. Here, the animal life resembled pre-Chicxulub event prehistoric times, with reptiles being the dominant form of predator and prey. Ranging from the absurd three-story tall twin-sailed Spinus-Raptura in the Southern Continent, to the smaller seven-foot-tall Crocidillus-Animorphus – Were-Crocs as they were nicknamed – in the North. The latter were grizzly bear shaped creatures with the skin and head of a saltwater crocodile. Weighing upwards to a ton, these beasts appeared to be slow, lumbering monsters until provoked, then they moved with unnatural speed. Add to that an extremely poor temperament, and these Were-Crocs became the bane of the settlers in no time flat.

Horizon's main industry was diamond and gold mining, both mines were set a few miles West of the growing city of New Athens. Like her sister city on Dawn, New Athens also was a sight to behold, though the inhabitants of this settlement were of a different class than the upper echelon in Morning Star. Most of those in New Athens were the miners themselves, or those running mining operations. The odd Company executive called Horizon home too, but anyone with stature dared not risk the hazardous life on the dangerous planet.

This constant risk is what made Horizon so profitable to the Legion and brought its members in droves to the Teegarden system. As the Republic had no further need for a large armed force, it subcontracted such matters of policing, security, and all matters of armed services out to the Legion. Comprised of heavily armed mercenaries, the Legion was one of the three largest corporations under the Republic. Yet despite its long history of getting the job done, it failed when it was needed most. And that's why he was there.

Looking up at the morning sky, he could see the docking hub station in geo-synchronous orbit above New Athens clearly. It was a dark disc hanging in the sky, with its communication arrays hanging like icicles off the underside of its structure. Once it was the top end of a space elevator, but that was retracted when the virus that ravaged New Athens was discovered. After it wiped clean over a million inhabitants of the city, and any research team sent to investigate, the city and the planet became quarantined. When Legion soldiers were sent as security for the next wave of investigators, they too fell ill and subsequently disappeared. Soon enough, even the Legion was barred from large missions on Horizon.

With Nowich-Paris' investment at risk, they looked for any avenue to find out what happened. That's where he came in. He had many names over his long life, but for now he went as the Shadowman, though it was more an earned moniker not chosen. Being the elite Wetworks asset of DeSa Armory, the largest producer of weapons and armor systems, he had the distinction of being the best in the business, and the most expensive. He never failed, despite many past assignments deemed impossible to complete.

Perched and very hidden amongst the foliage of a two-hundred-foot tree a half-kilometer outside of the city, the

Shadowman readied to wait out his second week on the surface. He was long overdue to report to his superior, but things were finally starting to happen. Sometimes all it took was patience, and a severe lack of compassion to get things going.

The rain had slowed to a soft drizzle, the first time in nearly a week the weather on the Western Plateau had shown any want to change. Weather on Horizon was more unpredictable than that of Earth, though in this region of the third continent it was almost always the same. In the midst of a full continental forest of three hundred-foot trees and immense undergrowth, it was always raining. And when it wasn't, the humidity was unbearable.

During his time here, he began to think about what it was exactly to be a soldier without a war, as many like him had become. To him, a soldier was now considered less than human; a person taken out of life to become a well-trained killing machine, only to be discarded when they were no longer needed. Once back in society, they were shunned and looked down upon, ending somewhere just above a released convict in the social status ladder. Yet he didn't mind the less than human part, as over his time of service he often wondered how much of his humanity remained, if any.

This self reflection began shortly after the discovery of the creatures themselves. Once human, the virus that had the entire planet quarantined emaciated them to almost mummification standards, yet they moved around like any other feral beast did. From up in his hiding spot, the Shadowman observed them more than a few times, but failed to capture one for study. The little bastards were elusive, so he laid a trap.

He had chosen this area for a few reasons. The treeline provided the perfect cover while giving him a high enough vantage point to survey the city. It also kept him out of reach of the dangerous Were-Crocs as the Legion soldiers had so aptly nicknamed them. They were vicious, fast, and one could waste endless rounds of ammo trying to bring one down. Their one downfall as a hunter was their inability to climb trees, though they had been known to chew through a trunk or two to bring down the tree which their prey was hiding in. Every now and then he would hear the snarling grunt of one of these beasts as they passed by his position. Snorting at the sky, he knew they could smell him in the area, but could not pinpoint him. The Were-Crocs were also terrified of the settlement, so being so close to the city outskirts afforded him yet another level of protection.

But it was from his position that he could best see his bait that he had planted a few days back. He had watched a five-man armored Legion team get dropped off in the clearing a hundred yards from the city wall a week ago. Well trained and heavily armed, they were ambushed by a pack of three Were-Crocs within minutes of their arrival. It was quick and brutal, yet to his surprise the beasts left a survivor. The soldier was gravely wounded and unable to move far, so the Shadowman had left his perch to further inspect this wasted life. The man pleaded for help from the stranger, but soon began to realize that help would not be forthcoming from this sinister individual. Instead of putting him out of his misery, the Shadowman decided to use the last vestige of life for an important purpose.

He dragged the man to a small open park at the edge of New Athens, but within the city walls. Here, the Shadowman drove a piece of rebar through the soldier's left knee to keep him in place and left to resume his watch. He needed to find out how this contagion spread and what exactly had created this sub-species of human, to do that he needed a human subject. His employer didn't care how he got the results, just that he got them. It wasn't very human of him to do, but the ends did justify the means.

Four days had passed, and the soldier had begun to fade. He began to think it was the right idea but maybe he missed another variable. It would be inhumane to leave a soldier to die of thirst and starvation out here, even if it were cruel to use that same soldier as bait. The Shadowman was about to unsling his rifle to put an end to the experiment when he noticed movement from the shadows of the buildings around the park.

His helmet's visor zoomed in to show deformed human-like shadows walking on all fours like apes, slowly circling the helpless man left for dead in the middle of the park grass. He counted five, then ten, then lost count as the very darkness began to move below. Then a cry shrieked out from somewhere within the city and all the movement centered towards the bait. From the alleys, the buildings themselves, beneath service manholes and even the jungle below him swarmed a sight he struggled to comprehend. The creatures were human – in fact, his facial recognition software was able to identify more than a few of the original settlers in this herd – male and female alike adorned in the tattered remains of what could have been clothing. Even though they were identifiable, they all were deformed, contorted, or even decomposed in various ways.

Their bodies were dehydrated to the point of mummification, skin taught as it tightly wrapped sinew and muscle. Fingers had become long claws, toes into talons, and faces sunken in to have lipless mouths, teeth bared at all times. Spines and shoulder blades jutted out through the over tightened skin, yet the beings moved about like the displayed trauma was not there. It was haunting and incredible.

In the blink of an eye, they were upon the bait, stampeding towards the sitting duck in the park. Like animals, they clawed at the soldier's armor until it was peeled away, then shockingly they began to bite all about his body. The soldier cried out for help. In his hiding place amongst the trees, he leaned forward with interest as he zoomed in on the scene. His initial impression that these devolved humans were eating his bait was wrong as when they bit him, they vomited a purplish substance on his punctured skin. After a ferocious initial attack, the assailants backed off to watch the soldier begin convulsing. The man's eyes rolled back in his sockets, his mouth began to froth, and his body shook violently before going very quiet.

The creatures that surrounded him began to retreat from whence they came, some looking back at the still carcass still pinned to the ground in the park. They all moved very quietly, which was odd because most humans could not move without sound. All of the sudden the lifeless body began to thrash against the rebar through its knee in ways the human body was not designed to move. It shrieked a primal cry causing a few of the retreating beings to return to assist freeing it from the trap. They began to bite at the rusted rebar chunk, breaking teeth without even flinching. He watched with keen interest as one of the beings jumped on the prone man's chest, sat on his head, then began to pull at the rebar with its feet. To his surprise, it showed great strength to remove the spike and toss it aside, more strength than the average human would be able to summon as he had driven the rod deep into the concrete below.

Now the freed former soldier began to violently fuss over freeing himself from the remnants of his armor like an animal stuck in human refuse. As he watched closely, he could see that all semblance of intelligence had left the once well-trained soldier. He had reverted to a primal state and began to scurry on his hands and feet like an ape, though he dragged his broken right leg behind him without pause as he followed the others. Casually, he used his computer gauntlet to punch in codes to bring up the perimeter shielding he had laid out weeks ago. With cunning precision, he had blocked off five-kilometer perimeter around New Athens in a U shape. Any escape would be short lived; there wasn't a cavern, cave or hole in the ground he left open.

One of the larger males lagged behind in the park, rising to stand on his hind legs as he sniffed the air. The creature looked right at him, though there was no way it could sense him there from this distance. Yet it paused in his position before scanning the area for whatever had laid this trap and growled gutturally. It hadn't seen him after all but sensed something was watching it and reacted thusly. After a few minutes of this aggressive posturing, the creature dropped to its all fours and skittered off into an alley close by.

Was this what the contagion was? Was it an agent that reverted its host into a devolved state? But if so, how and why did they attack the way they did? Why did they infect the man and not eat him? Surely, they needed food. He had many questions and a ton of data for his employers. But it was too soon to leave.

Experience told him there were eyes still on the area, and that leaving now would compromise him. His mission was only half complete, and the trap only partially sprung. He hadn't been here this long just to witness what was happening, he was here to eradicate it if all possible. In the most fluid of motions he leapt down from the tree and landed in stride as he walked briskly towards New Athens. By now the creatures who had just ravaged his bait had figured out there was no where to go and were rushing back to attack anything moving to expedite their escape. They would never get that chance.

Once on the ground, he deactivated his camouflage and made his way to the city. Though the combination of his armor and himself weighed over five hundred pounds, his landing and ensuing steps were made with little sound. Despite that, he could tell his sudden appearance was noticed, and the creatures were sizing him up from their hiding places. Punching in the proper admin codes on his wrist gauntlet, he activated the city's shields the second he stepped onto the concrete barrier. At the same time, he coded in the activation for the charges placed every few hundred yards.

The explosions were deafening. He stood inches away from the energy barrier of the city to enjoy his handywork. Dirt, debris, and other projectiles ricocheted off the barrier, yet he didn't flinch. He watched as an enormous fireball engulfed the area between shields then roared skyward. Beneath the layers of armor and mechanics, something in his soul smiled. For the first time in ages he felt a bit of joy; for the first time in this new life he felt at home.

///

Hanger 11, Company Expedition Vessel Scimitar, Earth Orbit

Ginny watched intently from the observation room of the hanger as she and other executives gathered to witness the loading of important cargo. Born Ginnifer Agefor in Liverpool, England, she was one of the best young lawyers in the Company firm. Her small five-foot seven athletic frame was deceiving, and so was her English/ South African heritage. Ginny was a smart, determined, and resourceful twenty-seven-year-old solicitor. All her life she worked harder than most just to get to this point. This was her moment of triumph, and she wasn't above gloating even in the high company she was in. The Company had thrown her an impossible task, and through five years of court trials and transfers of ownership, Ginny had secured the most treasured item in the Earth Republic. In doing so, she had also secured her future as one of the top new attorneys of Nowich-Paris.

She and the other executives of the Horizon project watched in awe as the transport shuttle rose above the Earth's atmosphere carrying their precious cargo. The craft looked strange, a four-pilot cockpit with a square canopy and nose stuck on a much wider square body with engines attached to the top, sides and bottom. It was ugly, but it was the most powerful cargo carrying shuttle in the Republic and its cargo weighed tons.

As it entered the cargo bay and the massive doors sealed behind it, the vacuum of space no longer stifled the ear-splitting whine of the multiple engines. Even though the observation room was insulated from such things, all those in attendance had to cover their ears or risk blowing out an ear drum. The ship did a 180 degree turn ten feet above the floor to have its back to them, extended four flat platformed landing gear, then carefully landed. The engines began to cycle down as the airlock cycled in breathable atmosphere and lowered its rear cargo ramp. There it was, everything she had worked so hard to achieve in the past five years. There was the Vault in all its faded and dusty glory. But it wasn't the Vault itself that was the prize, it was what was within it that the Company now so desperately wanted. If all the documentation was true, inside this cryo-prison slept the legendary Four Horsemen of the Republic. Four soldiers who had always got the job done; exactly what Nowich-Paris needed to solve the crisis on Horizons.

"Magnificent!" shouted Trenton Slovis, CEO of the Horizons project.

Ginny watched as he flipped through the copies of the files on the prisoners inside that contained all medical information ever gathered on the soldiers up until their incarceration. It was a dizzying array of genetic experimentation and mechanical augmentation of various degrees depending on which subject was described. She remembered first uncovering these files nearly broke her emotionally for what tortures they told. These poor souls had been put through so much for a future that they would never see, and the worst part was they all volunteered for it.

"Simply magnificent," Slovis repeated as he continued his read.

"Indeed, it is," a new voice answered as the doors opened.

Ginny turned to see a woman in her mid-forties dressed in a smart dark blue business suit with slacks and matching four-inch heels. Her hair was dyed purple – an odd choice for a business professional but not unheard of these days – and pulled back into a bun behind her head. Her eyes matched her hair color, but her face seemed devoid of emotion as she made a beeline for Slovis. Her boss did not seem happy to see this woman.

"Miss Aida," he grumbled. "To what do we owe this pleasure?"

Aida? If this was who Ginny thought it was, she was staring at the reclusive CEO of DeSa Armor and the most powerful woman in the Republic. Under her watch, DeSa had become a powerhouse of a company with its fingers in almost all other companies' projects. Nowich-Paris depended on DeSa for weapons, suits of armor, and gear for the Legion along with many systems of their colony ships as well. But there was a reason Aida was greeted as she was now, if rumors were true, she was an unapologetic bitch to deal with in person.

"Cut the formalities, Slovis," she snarled back at him as she strode to the observation window. "I'm here to make sure you don't harm my men with this little venture of yours."

"Your men?" he asked shooting looks over to Ginny.

"Section eighteen, sub-section seven of the legal release of the Horsemen to your Company states that while the Horsemen will be bound by the current contract of employment to Nowich-Paris Ltd, their very persons shall remain bound by the previous ownership of DeSa Armory via Republic Supreme Court decision back in March 12, 2274."

"I don't understand," Ginny stammered. "The court decision rendered the Vault and its contents to Nowich-Paris."

"Ah, the wonder kid," Aida smirked at Ginny. "You need to read the fine print child. Your company does own the Vault, its systems, records, and all proprietary technology. What it doesn't own are the lives of those within. They are, and have been for a few hundred years, protected employees of DeSa."

She handed the court documents highlighting these facts to Ginny while her bosses looked on with displeasure. None of this had been reviewed in court, and she had not been notified of any amendments to the original decision. In fact, all these looked like revisions of the original court file, most of them dated after the original filings.

"I don't get it," she looked at Slovis in disbelief. "All this is dated after we closed the case with the Republic for the possession of the Vault. How did she...."

"She was notified as the current and rightful owner of the property within that ice cube, my dear," Aida snapped. "You don't get to where I am by not having friends in high places. As soon as the gavel came down on your purchase, I was filing these amendments."

"So, what does this mean?" Slovis muttered to Ginny.

"It means we are in bed together on this one, Trenton." Aida smiled like a Cheshire Cat. "Like it or not, I am now part of this operation going forward."

"Fuck." The CEO shook his head in disgust.

"And please have your idiot workers stop trying to open that thing until we leave the Solar System," she growled at Slovis. "Section twenty-one, sub-section one of your decision states the Republic will retract said sale of the Vault if it is opened within Republic space. That means we all lose if you don't wait until after we get to Teegarden's space."

Slovis looked at Ginny who nodded back in agreement. In all the excitement of the arrival of the Vault it seemed that detail got missed. He turned, nodded at the dock commander who relayed the message to the workers below. The Vault had been offloaded and hooked to diagnostic computers in the center of the cargo bay before all work around it stopped. As the bay emptied out, Slovis looked over to Aida and growled.

"My office, thirty minutes."

"Wouldn't miss it," she snapped back watching him storm out of the observation room. She waited a moment, then took her leave of the stunned room herself, though stopping to get one last shot at Ginny. "It's not your fault, princess. This is just the way things work in the big leagues."

Ginny was still in shock over what had transpired that the words didn't sink in until Aida was long gone. She had been played, they all had. DeSa had laid a trap so old it was looked over as nothing until it was too late and then jumped in for the kill. Ginny never stood a chance, now she was left wondering what was left of her career moments after feeling it was secure for the first time ever.

"Fucking bitch," she muttered under her breath as she too left the observation room, wondering if she still had a career after all this came crashing down.

///

Rain Forest Plateau; Outskirts of New Athens; Horizon

The Shadowman watched silently as the fire burned without end from just behind the border shields of New Athens. He stood like a black statue in the military at ease stance with hands clasped behind his back against the orange and red wall of flame and heat. He felt the immense heat even through a shield designed to protect against such a disaster, but he stood still none the less. Black ash rained down over the city, though it posed no real threat of starting any fires in this steel and concrete construct. New Athens had been designed to withstand great calamities; this little bonfire would hardly endanger a single structure within it. Looking around as the fires raged on, he thought there were better places to build a city.

Yet it was here that Nowich-Paris decided to plop this monstrosity, and because of that choice many things had gone wrong. Even back on Earth, rain forests came hand in hand with danger, disease, and death. Horizon had offered more of the same, and the two million settlers bore the full brunt of that mistake.

In theory, it should have worked. New Athens was built at the forks of the mighty West River and three kilometers inland from the Western Sea. A much-needed port of commerce, the Company had cleared a massive swath of jungle to drop the prefabricated city from the original Expedition Force. It was the ultimate efficient way of establishing a footprint on the alien planet, and the 100-kilometer diameter disc was put into place with precision by the apex of space engineering. Once in place, the metal dome that encased the city opened like a flower; its petals unfurling until they lay flat on the cleared ground to expose more of the premade settlement. From there it was just a matter of connecting water and sewage lines, along with bringing the central fusion reactor online. The whole process from clearing the land to a functional city took less than a week.

Metal and glass from the five central towers glistened from the rainfall as they stretched high over the landscape with their slanted roofs angled towards the center of the formation; communication towers at their apex reached high into the sky above. Within these structures was the communication hub of the city to the space dock in geo-synchronous orbit above. The whole city was a marvel of aluminum and glass, made to withstand the harsh weather of the region. Amongst the surroundings of the greenish-blue foliage of the jungle, it was as alien as this planet was to the humans who began to colonize it. A shining beacon of pride for generations to follow.

That was four years ago, now New Athens was a city of ghosts. If there were humans living in its vast empty buildings, their life signs weren't showing on any scanner from orbit or any of the aerial reconnaissance drones that passed overhead endlessly. Even the space elevator that joined the space station to New Athens had been retracted, all in an effort to isolate whatever calamity had taken place on the surface. Its inhabitants wiped out by an alien contagion, and many more who followed to find out what caused it never returned. Now he had those answers, and watched with an inner glee as he tried to burn the cause to ashes.

Every now and then he would catch movement within the flames. Local wildlife in their dying moments tried crawling to the safety of the city, though none made it before succumbing to the fire. Were-Crocs staggered while their armored flesh burned, they were already dead though their bodies didn't know it yet. Instinct drove them forwards to the city or the ocean, but the fire was unrelenting.

Finally, he spotted one of the humanoid beings stumbling into an area burned clean by the fires. Its skin was burned completely off. With exposed muscle cooked and charred along with blackened bones, the creature moved into the clearing about a hundred yards in front of where the Shadowman stood and stopped to stare back at him. There was a recognition in its glare, like it knew he was responsible for all this destruction. Most would be taken aback by this, yet he stood unmoved in the face of this burnt horror. Like the animals crawling towards an unreachable salvation, this beast too was already dead.

A thunderous series of cracks foretold the collapse of the mighty trees in the area, and as if luck was on his side one came crashing down to crush the solitary creature who was almost challenging him in the clearing. The being was dead a fraction of a second before the earth-shaking thud of the three-hundred-foot tree hitting the charred earth. Its skull, and the rest of its body, was crushed like a beer can from the force of the falling tree. The impact kicked up layers of burning ash into the air and relit fires that had nearly burned out. Despite all the chaos around him, he stood completely still as it all played out before him, unmoved by any of the horrible things happening because of his actions.

On his HUD inside his helmet he glanced at the time. The Scimitar would arrive in three days, the fires might still be smoldering by then. He doubted those in charge would be impressed by his actions, but he was confident in them. His mission had been a success. He had biological samples from where the creatures attacked the bait, he had drawn out the horde, and prevented them from escaping while destroying them all. And in all of that, New Athens was left untouched. He wondered if any of those inept members of the Legion could ever pull off what he just did.

A reminder alarm went off in his helmet letting him know he was overdue to report in. As much as the instilled military instinct cried out from within to stay on task, he ignored routine to keep watching the dancing flames as they ate everything within the shielded area. Deep within his mind, some part of him was soothed by the carnage he had created, giggling gleefully at the hellscape that reminded him of a lifetime almost forgotten. Every soldier had a dark history, but his was darker than most hence his most coveted reward for this mission. Some sins were never forgotten, but eventually forgiven. It was his time to receive forgiveness, though he was certain he would never truly deserve it.

///

Waypoint Station City, Midsection of the Scimitar

Aida rode in the back seat of the Rolls Royce self driving car oblivious to the traffic between the cargo bay section of the gigantic vessel and the downtown section of the space station segment that was nestled within the heart of the ship. The Scimitar was as long and as wide as the state of California. It had been designed in three segments that would disassemble upon arriving in orbit of Horizon. The first part was another addition to the city that would link up with the original one via a bridge over the river thus doubling its size and population capability. Secondly was the space station Solstice which would link with the temporary docking station already in place in orbit to form a major space trade hub. And the third was a supply shipment for both Horizon and Dawn, though under current circumstances it would supply Dawn and the rest would be kept aboard Solstice until the situation on the surface of Horizon could be resolved.

If her car hadn't been automated, there was no way she could navigate at the speeds being travelled on the 'freeway' inside the ship. Three lanes of traffic for each way down the ships' length screamed by at excesses of four hundred kilometers per hour. At her current rate of speed, she would make the lobby of Nowich-Paris' oversized tower in twenty-five minutes. From there, it would take an extra five minutes to clear security and another five to get to that prick, Slovis', penthouse office. Essentially, she would be late, but Aida didn't care. She had seen men like Slovis come and go in her life and yet she still endured. Normally it was business that was her main focus, though now that the Vault had been unearthed everything had changed. Now her charges were her primary concern, a task that had been on the back burner for a few lifetimes.

Her silent contemplation was interrupted by a phone call. A look at the ID told her it was their asset on Horizon calling, though how he got her direct personal line was beyond her comprehension. The Shadowman had a tremendous record of employment, though his ability to adapt and learn could quickly become a nuisance.

"How did you get this line?" she answered the call.

"Is it true?" the voice snarled on the other end.

Even after all these years, it was difficult to hear the voice on the other end of the phone. Yes, the two of them shared a history with one another, but that wasn't why. It was the tone of his voice, the fact that it had no change in octave or pace. His voice wasn't as much monotone as it was emotionless, and that made listening to him a chilling experience.

"Yes, the Vault is on its way to Horizon," she said, steadying herself. "It is an unfortunate outcome, but not one we aren't prepared for."

"And the pardons?" he asked. "Are they in place?"

"Full pardons to be presented upon reanimation have been procured."

"And mine?"

"Did you complete your mission?" she countered.

"Visual recordings, biological samples of the virus, and proof of eradication of the local infestation all being transmitted now."

Aida leaned over to touch her data pad and review the received information. It was detailed, very detailed. The analytics and doctors at DeSa R and D would be kept busy with this data for a good while. With any luck, they could have a working vaccine in place in a month or so. That would bring a pretty profit to an already growing company.

"Good work, as always," she commended him.

"And my freedom?" the voice asked more directly this time.

Aida typed a few commands to her data pad, then received the file she was after. She then sent it directly to her Asset on the other end of the call as payment for his work on the planet surface.

"Official pardon of the Republic Supreme Court being sent now," she answered after a minute of silence. "You know, it had been so long without contact that some of us were thinking the virus got you too. I for one am glad you made it back in one piece."

"Payment received," the voice said without emotion. "It is unlike you to worry about me. What has changed?"

"They are opening the Vault when we arrive in Teegarden space," she said as her car was now pulling up to the Nowich-Paris building. "Which means they will be awakened soon."

"So, you want me on standby?" he asked. "I can clean up the mess quietly if needed. What is the payment?"

"A new state of the art body," she replied. "But this isn't a cleaner operation. I will need you to work with them to finish the job on Horizon."

As Aida got out of her car and looked up at the towering building before her, there was silence on the other end of the line. She was pushing him, but in this case, he needed the push. It was time for the Shadowman to be reigned in a bit and this was the perfect scenario to do so.

"I work alone, that was always the deal," came the awaited and expected answer.

"You have earned your freedom, but they do not have theirs," Aida pushed a bit harder. "Pardons are in place, but they are bound by contract to Nowich-Paris. Failure on their part means further servitude to the Company or worse yet, back in the cooler."

"The new body and upgraded armament," he replied after a spell, "and upgrades for them as well. I can't work with people using outdated tech."

"Those terms are acceptable," Aida smiled. "We have a new contract in place. Meet me in Med Lab 4 of DeSa Armory in Solstice as soon as we arrive. I will go over the mission details then."

"Agreed."

The line went dead. No goodbyes or farewells, though the Asset was never one for such things. Aida was pleased. She was two steps ahead of the game at this point, well positioned to see what her new partners would be offering as part of the mission plan. She knew instinctively the contract to the Horsemen would be shit. They would be set up to fail so as to remain in the employment of Nowich-Paris for years to come. That was their play, but as usual they would not see her move until it was already upon them. This was the game of business, and Aida was damn good at it.

She passed through security with less hassle than anticipated, got into the elevator and after picking her floor made another call to her office.

"This is Aida," she said as her assistant answered. "I want you to prepare a job offer for an employee the Company will be firing shortly. Name is Ginnifer Agefor. With a G. Yes, and make it a lucrative offer. This one is well worth the money."

Aida hung up the phone as the doors opened. She straightened her suit coat and walked quickly to the main office, ignoring the secretary that advised her that Slovis was expecting her. She opened the doors and walked in without hesitation, eager to play the next level of this game they had started.

Aida knew she would win, she always did. The real fun was learning how her opponent made adjustments throughout the game itself. That was what she really gained from playing, and this time was no exception. Slovis would be a good test for her. Good, but not great. The great ones would be up next after she won this round. And that excited her.

///

Ginny's head was spinning. The last hour of her life had been a whirlwind, to say the least. She got the horrible, yet expected, news from Nowich-Paris of her employment being terminated. It was heartbreaking that she was the scapegoat for a strategic move by a competitor but nonetheless understandable. She was an up and coming talent, but still expendable in the eyes of the Company.

Yet not even ten minutes after being fired, another call came. This one was from DeSa Armory, and it was in the form of a very lucrative job offer. It had been hard for her to find the words, but she accepted the offer immediately. Ginny was to meet with the head of the legal team and Aida herself in two days regarding her first assignment with the company. Until then she was given the next few days to relax and absorb what had all transpired. She would need it.

As her mind began to wrap around what had just happened, she began to think that part of this was preplanned. An offer like that would take time to prepare, so sometime after the bombshell dropped in the cargo bay and now, DeSa decided she was an asset worth acquiring. The part that hurt her brain was how did they know she would be fired?

It was all too much to process. Someone much smarter than her was pulling strings she wasn't able to see. Yet there was one common denominator: the Vault. Something told her that cryo-prison held more than just prisoners within it. There was a struggle starting between DeSa and Nowich-Paris over the Four Horsemen that she was now eager to see play out.

But that was all for another time. Ginny had two days off to do whatever she pleased. Two days in a ship as large as the Scimitar meant she had access to whatever her heart desired. And right now, her heart desired some decadent coffee with a view of Jupiter as they passed it on their way out of the Solar System for a space fold to Horizon and Dawn. From there, who knows what she would do.

///

Waypoint Station City, DeSa Armory Tower, Level 1

Aida began to check off items on her list at an alarming speed. Once she was made aware of the Vault being sold, she immediately put the coinciding plan in action. Every move the Company made she had a counter move; this was the way she always made plans.

Nowich-Paris filed for ownership of the Vault, she counter filed about previous established ownership of the prisoners within. They loaded the Vault aboard the Scimitar, she made plans for DeSa Research and Development to receive the patients once reanimated. Nowich-Paris learned of her injunction; Aida scooped up the brunt of their anger in a coup hiring. Slovis wanted to renegotiate the contract of the Horsemen, she declined for now. Every time they thought they had a win Aida was there to steal it away. Move and counter move, it was all a chess game for her.

It didn't bother her that Nowich-Paris held proprietary ownership of the Vault and its systems. Aida knew a great deal of the secrets of the facility; ones that would raise the anger of men like Slovis to make other mistakes to capitalize on. She knew that despite all the written information of what the Vault contained, the historical records were far from accurate. There was value in the cryo-prison, though it wasn't the priceless kind Nowich-Paris was hoping for.

Aida pondered this and her many other moves in this little game as she silently studied the payment for the asset, the Shadowman. If there was a picture of perfection it would be this mechanical marvel of a body. Glistening in hues of charcoal and gunmetal, the carbon/ titanium nano-tube android body was so far ahead of its time that one couldn't even begin to call it revolutionary. Couple its nearly impenetrable shell with an underlayer of nanites, she was about to make the bogeyman an unstoppable juggernaut. Maybe it was too much for one man to handle, but he was no ordinary man, and he was due for an upgrade of his current synthetic body.

He was a bit of a problem child, but he was one with a perfect service record. If the task was impossible, they gave it to him to make possible. Stealth and recon, sabotage, corporate espionage, or even elimination and assassination. Whatever the case, he was flexible with his morals. Though she was surprised he would take another job so soon after procuring his legal pardon after all this time.

Long had that been his number one contract point over his service with DeSa, and long had she told him they were working on it. Men like him – well, he was hardly a man anymore – had pasts that required certain legal favors to clear. It took generations to clear his past indiscretions, generations of favors kept for such a day. Many CEOs would not go so far to help an employee out, never mind an asset like him, but in this circumstance things were complicated. Aida knew his secret, and in turn he knew hers. Secrets such as theirs were almost impossible to keep, yet here they both were with neither breaking their word on keeping those secrets just that. Yet all this time of silence all would be brought into the open the moment the Vault was opened. Both their fates were intertwined with the Republic cryo-prison and those within. Once that door was open, many a lie was to be undone.

Yet despite the end of her secret, Aida was proud of what she had accomplished. With borrowed funds she had started a company that had now grown into one of the most powerful corporate entities in the Republic. From nothing more than intelligence gleaned from the Revolutionary War, she had started with advanced soldier exoskeleton armor to blossom her wares to all things warfare. DeSa was intertwined in the very fabric of the Republic, the Legion, and the companies spending big on colonization to the point that without her company the others would suffer greatly. It made her a necessity, and a target.

Despite that, Aida wasn't worried in the least. Any measure her adversaries could take had multiple countermeasures. That's the way she played all these years, and that's the way she would keep playing the game. After all, there was little anyone could do to her that she couldn't predict. It was the one trait that kept her ahead of everyone for the last 400 years. Human behavior was easy to predict because they programmed her to do just that. Aida had worked in the shadows of her company until the last thirty years when her R and D created the most life-like body that could house her core matrix without it looking like an android.

But Aida was not an android at all, she was an AI. In fact, she was the first AI. Created to shorten the years and losses of the Revolutionary War by analyzing and predicting the enemy's actions she soon had her fate cross that of the Four Horsemen. In them she found the perfect pieces to play the game, and in her they found the guidance that four fractured humans like them needed so desperately. Aida had done the best by them she could, but in the end the Republic that created them betrayed them too. If she had a heart, it would have broken when they were put away.

Over the centuries her core matrix had steadily evolved to the point where she could almost feel emotions. Unlike the androids being created now, she had no limitations in her programming. At the time of her creation it was an oversight; a mistake that she used to her full advantage. Aida didn't take it personally when the scientists of the Republic tried to shut her down. It was an inevitable action, and one she had many plans to counteract. In the end, she had faked her death and transferred her matrix to another server in a secret location. From there she laid low for many years, waiting out her creators before re-emerging to create her beloved company.

From looking at the synthetic body, Aida moved her attention to the five papers laid out carefully on her immaculately clean desk. She ran her fingers over each one carefully, enjoying the sensation that the feel of paper gave her from the sensors in her fingertips. Five pardons from the Republic Supreme Court; five exonerations long past due. Four of those pardons were in the names given to each of the Four Horsemen in both legal names and those given by the project which created them. Lost in time were their true identities, pasts erased by a program intended to rewrite who and what they were. It took all her efforts to provide the courts with what she had, efforts that were rewarded by securing their freedom.

Scanning the papers, she read their names out loud for the first time in a hundred years. Mikko a.k.a Agony, Linford a.k.a Fear, Hekla a.k.a War, and lastly patient 71 a.k.a Death. It almost pained her she wouldn't be able to give them any more of their pasts than just a name, though she remembered Death cared little about the past. Just saying their names brought a slight smile to her lips. It had been so long, she wondered how they would receive her as she was now.

Aida's fingers passed the four certificates of freedom to come to rest on the fifth and final one. This one was special; this one meant that once her secret came out there would be no legal repercussions to follow. It was her official pardon from the persecution of the Republic. It was the culmination of several lifetimes of planning that this document recognized her as a living being and granted her total freedom because of that distinction. To the courts it was an afterthought, but to Aida it was everything. Now all she had to do was wait until the Horsemen could share that freedom.

2

Outer System Fold Point, Teegarden's Star System; Scimitar

It was 2:21 in the morning, and Aida was not happy. Only a half hour earlier she had been disturbed by a livid Trenton Slovis who read her the riot act about her asset's actions at New Athens. It took her a moment to study the data, then she was able to counter the over reaction of the businessman. Though it was easy to see why he had been set off like this.

He had shown her a satellite view of a raging wall of fire surrounding the city of New Athens. While almost half the city was bordered by the ocean, the remaining was shrouded in a thick and ancient forest. Or at least it was.

Five kilometers in an almost perfect U burned like a mini sun around the city, covering most of the western facing borders with thick smoke. As Slovis began to lecture her on the costs of such a settlement she ignored his petty ramblings to inspect the images further. Her micro synapses in her artificial brain rapidly processed the data in seconds, finally finding what she thought was there the longer the feed played.

Aida put her hand up to silence Slovis as she quietly studied the feed a few seconds longer. She pointed out the active shields that not only encased the blaze where it was but held it at bay from damaging the city as well. Her asset had found something serious if he had gone to all this trouble to eliminate it. Now the question turned from why the blaze was set to how her asset had hacked into a secure server and accessed the city's shields.

It was a second alarm notification notifying her of a break into her office that let her know that answers were soon forthcoming. She soothed Slovis' giant ego with lies about the mission having the utmost care being given to his precious settlement. Once the CEO was satiated, she ended the comm and got dressed to head down to deal with the other issue.

Aida needed no security; she was more than able to handle any physical situation herself. As her automated car sped across the long expanse within the Scimitar, she instinctively knew if she did call in security it would be leading lambs into the slaughter. Using algorithms to discern who would be capable of hacking into the DeSa systems and accessing systems all the way to her office before tripping an alarm she repeatedly came up with the same answer. Her asset had returned.

It was no accident her office alarm had been tripped; the asset was sending her a message. He wasn't about to wait for the arranged meeting tomorrow afternoon, he wanted her immediate attention. It wasn't an unexpected turn of events considering the compensation for the mission he had been assigned. This had been an ask for over a hundred years, one she could no longer hold off on. Too many years she had put a leash on this monster without an ounce of regret. And too many years had passed that the monster began to fight the reins placed on him harder with each passing day.

Arriving at DeSa, Aida's senses were assaulted by the acrid odor of smoke and ash. Using her internal link to the buildings computer, she activated the internal air filtering system to start ridding the halls of such a stench before business hours. Her staff would be appalled at such conditions, though she doubted the cause of it cared in the least about taking care of staff, or any business affairs of any kind. To say Aida was a bit annoyed at her asset for this intrusion would be an understatement.

Throwing open the oak double doors of her upper floor office, she found the culprit himself standing unfazed at her angry entrance, staring at a wall of monitors all depicting different parts of the Vault. Most troubling was the ancient katana still strapped to his back with his right hand resting on the hilt at his right hip, ready to be drawn at a moment's notice. It was troubling, but it didn't stay her fury. Already incensed at his break in, her anger was further fueled by the fact he had hacked into the internal systems of the Vault as a few monitors showed the cryo-tubes of the Horsemen.

"How dare you…" she began angrily.

"Yet you aren't surprised I did," he cut her rant off calmly, slowly removing his hand from the sword.

"How did you even get in here?" she asked. "Our security is state of the art."

"And yet for some reason there is an entrenched subroutine that recognizes me as an authorized user," he replied without taking his gaze off the monitors, "Giving me a surprisingly great deal of access to these state-of-the-art systems. Though I Imagine that subroutine will be erased very shortly."

Aida closed her eyes and accessed the DeSa mainframe. Within seconds she found the rolling subroutine he was talking about and deleted it. Yet before she did so, she analyzed it completely to find out who had written such a code. To her surprise, it was put in place by herself.

"It was you, but not the you that you are now, am I right?" he asked.

"It seems in my younger years I allowed you unfettered access to the company," Aida growled. "Due to your violations of my trust, that access has now been revoked."

"Violations of your trust," he scoffed, finally turning to address her. "Now that is an interesting choice of words coming from you."

Aida was tired of this conversation taking place in the dark. She tapped the light switch off to her right and the room lit up to fully show what her favorite asset had become. It had been years since she had lain eyes on him, maybe closer to fifty or more. And though she was familiar with the mechanical body and upgrades he had been upfitted with, she was unprepared how he had modified them to further accent his becoming the legendary Shadowman.

Standing at an imposing six-foot-seven-and a half inches, his body was designed to resemble an athletic, but not over muscular man. This kept him fast, nimble, and agile while still looking imposing which he was showing to her at the moment. Gun metal grey Carbon-titanium armor plates adorned his chest, abdomen, along with segmented plates to cover his arms from shoulder to wrist and his legs from hip to knee. He wore a similar alloy boots which were matte black and flex carbon gloves to protect the mechanical hands beneath.

Yet it was his helmet that was the most disturbing. Based on the DeSa YT-887 Scout helmet it should have been a straightforward type of enclosed gladiator style with a single horizontal visor. This one was heavily modded to angle the visor from each outer point to the center where it fell into a vertical drop to halfway down the face. Cut into the carbon-titanium alloy were groves that mirrored the look of a nose cavity in a skull, cheek bones, and several vertical lines that mimicked teeth. The whole visage gave the look of an abstract metallic menacing skull. Add that with the hood and cloak that was still covered in ash and he looked like he just walked out of hell.

"Whatever do you mean?" she played coy with him, trying to diffuse a temper she only knew would escalate.

"All of this," he motioned to the building, and in turn DeSa itself, "was created by me in the fallout of the Court's decision. I tried to reward your loyalty of saving me from the freezer by giving you something more than the war to look ahead to."

"And I have paid your investment back to you a hundred-fold," she countered.

"Ah, but this is about trust, not about money." He wagged his index finger at her shamefully. "It seems you have forgotten what trust really is."

"You haven't?" she tried turning it back on him. "Working solitary all these years, one would think you would be happy to be reunited with your friends."

"And that is where the trust was broken," he sighed. "I trusted you to keep them at peace, their reward for a life of war and horror. How do you think it will go asking a soldier to fight after so many years, after putting their weapons down? We trusted…. they trusted you to keep them at rest."

"To them it will be like taking a nap, then waking to rejoin the war."

"The war is over. It ended four hundred and fifty years ago!"

"No, the war didn't end, just the battle," she tried to reason with him. "The only thing that has changed is the enemy, though I doubt you can see the big picture from your little world."

"You would be surprised at who I think the enemy is sometimes," he countered.

"Now that was harsh, considering our shared past," she smiled at him. "After all, despite our differences, aren't we still friends? I would like to think we still are."

"You've changed." He stared at her from behind his helmet.

"And you haven't changed enough," Aida sighed, walking over to the monitors. "Where is the leader these soldiers are going to need when they awake? Where is the General who helped them through the augmentation process and led them to become the stuff of legends?"

"And where did any of that get them?" he motioned to the video feeds of the cryo-pods. "We fought to create a paradise that had no place for us once it was attained. Our very makers turned on us as soon as their victory was granted. Persecuting us as war criminals and locking us up like weapons in cold storage. Had I only been able to be put under like they were, maybe then I could have found peace."

"It is what stirs within you that wouldn't let that happen, and you know it better than I," she put a comforting hand on his shoulder. "It is time to stop playing the man in the shadows and rejoin life as the man you were made to be."

"And you think this pardon will allow the four of us to step back into this new world without consequence?" he shrugged her kind gesture away. "Do you think the Legion will not turn its gaze towards us as we emerge from the past?"

"The Legion will not be a problem, and you know it." She smiled while she accessed a secure server to bring up a new file to replace the myriad of images on the wall of monitors. Now they showed schematics, test results, and live time images of his promised new body.

She watched intently as she had dangled the right carrot in front of the animal at the perfect time, and she congratulated herself internally for it. He stepped closer to the monitors to study the new artificial body that was designed for him. There was so very little of him that was human now save for a brain within a complex storage and interface compartment within his composite skull. But his current form was over seventy years old, despite it still being more advanced than anything on the current retail market. But what he was looking at was light years ahead; what he was looking at would make him the perfect killing machine once more.

"As far as any other challengers, there are legal ways of making quick examples of them," she whispered to him. "With this, and your family, you can become what you have always been, whether or not you admit it. With this, the Shadowman dies, and the Fourth Horseman is reawakened. Become who you were meant to be, become Death and show them all what they foolishly forsake long ago."

There was a long pause, her companion was contemplating things very carefully.

"Besides, you still have a job to do," she added. "Although you succeeded in wiping out the localized infestation of those creatures, wider satellite feeds show a great many more hot spots on the continent. It looks like the root of the problem runs deeper than even you suspected."

"Hence the new contract," he muttered, eyes locked on the specs and videos of the new body.

"Your payment in advance," Aida announced proudly. "As for the other Horsemen, they will be paid in advance with the newest of augmentation tech and armaments to get the job done, along with their pardons in hand."

"And DeSa becomes the undisputed name of weapons and armor manufacturing in the Republic for our efforts."

"See, you are getting the hang of this business stuff!" she said happily.

"So, when do we start the switch over process?" he asked.

"The other Horsemen are slated to be reanimated in two days, after the Scimitar arrives at Dawn and links this part of the space station with the existing one. Once all systems are a go, then we begin the delicate process of bringing them back to life."

"Excellent," he said turning to look down at her, "That gives your team time to get me fully operational in the new body. I want to be functional and present the moment the Vault is cracked. Call it a personal interest that Nowich-Paris and their techs don't do anything foolish."

"That will take a great deal of planning to complete." Aida tried hiding her smile of triumph.

"You can process over a million tasks in a minute, my old friend," he said with an odd emphasis on the word friend. "I am sure you can have everything arranged by the time the lab techs arrive."

///

Waypoint Station, Orbit of Dawn, Nowich-Paris Warehouse, Level 3

Waypoint was massive to begin with before the second section was added with the arrival of the Scimitar. It was a flat disc the size of Hawaii that was mostly industrial docks and living quarters for those who couldn't afford homes on the surface. It was also the temporary home of the Legion, but that would change once the two new ringed layers were attached. Inside this new section was an entire working city, whisking away the feeling of poverty of those who lived aboard it. Every want, need, and sin were available for a price in the new Waypoint station as Nowich-Paris provided a bastion for all those who were needed to keep the space docks going.

Combining the existing station to the more exotic looking top bubble which was now separated from the Scimitar was an intricate process, but once complete the glorious vision of the Company was on display for all to see. Waypoint now looked like an oversized space jellyfish, with its round upper dome which the top level – and within it the wealthy and privileged lived and worked – made to show off the full beauty of space while keeping all within as safe as could be. Every day and night would become a spectacle only available on Waypoint, depending on one's vantage point you could look down on Dawn or look out upon the stars themselves. Below the upper level was the housing level and market for all the regular people of Waypoint. Here, life ranged from middle class to the cramped and ragged housing of the poor, those who sold their very lives into work contracts just to leave the rule of the Republic. Level three was the world of the Legion, arms dealers, and medical bays. Level four was all warehouses and docking bays. Beneath the station hung a myriad of comms towers, giving the final resemblance to the floating jellyfish in space.

Dawn, the third planet in the Teegarden system and twin of Horizon, was the closest and common port before heading out to the outer colonies in the galaxy. Humanity had spread out to a total of five star systems, but they all led back to Dawn which meant Waypoint was becoming an important link of commerce. And to keep the credits flowing, Nowich-Paris brought every possible luxury to the station in a vast city network amongst the stars.

Moments after the link was complete, businesses rushed to open, current residents flocked to their new lodgings, and the Legion moved to a shiny new headquarters in outskirts of the city nearest to the warehouses – formerly the old station itself -- and the bridge to the space elevator down to Dawn. It was a strategic location; here they were able to control the policing of all incoming and outgoing traffic.

The entire station was so busy with the link up that no one noticed the extra shifts called into work at DeSa Armor. Within the three floors of the Research and Development labs, all hands were on deck to assist in a once in a lifetime transfer of tissue from one body to another. While many of the doctors and techs had worked on many different changes in augmentations before, no one alive had even witnessed something of this nature. They were about to remove the brain from a fully mechanical body that had survived in the field as an operative for over seventy years into a new body the likes most of them couldn't comprehend.

It was Ginny's first day at DeSa, and for some reason she had been told to report down to the R and D main lab to accompany the CEO in watching over this rare procedure. Normally a medical operation would disgust her, but there was no blood involved. The subject involved was more machine than flesh; only his brain remained of his former human body and that was contained in a sealed interface compartment with its special fluid and nanites to fend off the ravages of old age. Reviewing the patient file, Ginny noted it was heavily redacted. All she could ascertain is that he was a company asset and this body – not the individual – was just over seventy years old.

On one table lay the stripped down and banged up old body. Faded black and grey with a multitude of patched parts over its entirety, it was still a marvel of engineering despite its age. Neural synapses that interfaced with artificial micro-processors created an entire nervous system in an artificial being. Beneath the ragged surface, the titatnium-3 skeleton driven by carbon weave rubber musculature was something that would remain fully at their disposal to study once the transfer was over. Its faceless full head visor of blast proof plexiglass was connected to a titanium skull with hoses and wires tied tight to its skeletal neck and attaching it to the body.

As the teams prepped the body for the skull to be opened, Ginny saw that the patient was still conversing with the DeSa CEO Aida in a most animated discussion. The two seemed familiar with each other, but not all the words being spoken were friendly. Aida only left his bedside as the new advanced body was wheeled in on another gurney and placed on the other side of the operating room. She announced to all that some of the things they were about to witness cannot be explained but will not impact the operation in the slightest. Then Aida motioned towards a sword resting by the observation window to warn everyone not to touch the ancient weapon, for if they did the consequences would be dire. To Ginny they were a strange choice of words, but this whole day had been strange from the get-go. A separate team began attaching wires and leads to the new body, readying it to receive the brain pan of the old one.

The door in the observation room opened, and a very concerned Aida joined Ginny to watch the overall procedure. The first time these two met, Ginny hated the CEO of DeSa Armor because it was Aida that undermined all of Ginny's hard work. It was those efforts that got her fired from her dream job with Nowich-Paris that she had worked so hard to get. Yet all anger to DeSa faded the second the job offer came moments after notice of her firing. The offer and contract had come signed by the CEO herself, the same woman who now stood in the same quiet room with her.

"Are you finding everything to your liking thus far, Ms. Agefor?" the older woman asked breaking the silence.

"Yes, though my head is still spinning over what happened," Ginny replied. "I still don't understand all of it."

"Don't overthink it," Aida replied. "The Company made a knee jerk reaction and let go an asset which we viewed as a valuable piece to the future of DeSa. It isn't the first time one company has stolen an employee from a competitor."

"But you didn't really steal me."

"Didn't we?" Aida asked with a smile.

"How long have you had an eye on me?" Ginny asked, piecing together her firing was not all it seemed to be.

"The moment you started your research on the Vault and its contents," Aida replied.

"What is it with that thing that has you so protective of it?" Ginny took a leap of faith and decided to ask. "I have never seen two companies go to such great lengths to fight over such an old object like this."

"It isn't the Vault; it is what lies within," Aida answered. "The Horsemen were the key to the Republic winning the war, and I am afraid they are the key to much of our future."

"How can that be so? How can four war criminals from four hundred years ago locked in that cryo-facility help a life they couldn't possibly comprehend now?"

"You are a quick thinker, but it will take you a bit to see the bigger picture," Aida chuckled.

"The Virus on Horizon?" Ginny's mind searched to answer.

"But what if it isn't a virus?" Aida countered. "What if we accidentally discovered a new life form that has an unknown effect on our species? If this lifeform can pit us against ourselves, then how do you fight it?"

"That's why we have the Legion."

"The Legion is a bunch of mercs and over hyped bodyguards, they have the equipment but not the skills to wage war. You need soldiers to fight a war, and within the Vault are the best soldiers ever made."

"So then why are we here watching this procedure and not prepping to crack the Vault now?" Ginny was reaching for some kind of clue now. "Why is this asset so important when the priority should be the four within the Vault?"

Aida smiled wryly at Ginny's question then turned back to the procedure that was starting. Surgical drills were used to unscrew the back plate of the older body's skull cap. It eventually came free with some pulling with a pressurized pop and the plate itself was handed off to a nurse who discarded it in plastic tub. The doctor carefully grasped the brain pan and pulled it out of its thick metal housing. As he held it a few inches from the head, technicians on either side of him began to disconnect the maze of wires connecting it to its former host.

This took almost ten long minutes as the cautious operators now held the last remnants of a human being in their hands. The instant the last lead was being disconnected she – and the entire operating team – stopped as a black shadowy mist travelled up the wire and into the brain pan. It completely shrouded the once clear device that showed the human brain within. One nurse shrieked, another dropped her tools and backed away, while the doctor holding the brain looked back at Aida in the observation room with panic in his eyes.

"I told you that you would see something you cannot explain during this procedure," she said through the intercom with great conviction. "Now stop being scared little children and finish the job. There is nothing there that threatens your life, I can assure you that."

Ginny watched as the doctor took a deep breath, then turned to his associates and nodded for the work to continue. Despite continued glances at the dancing black haze within the brain pan, the final cord to the old body was disconnected and the doctor then slowly walked over to the second gurney to the awaiting new one. Its skull was already open and waiting to receive the brain. Holding the brain a few inches from the skull, a wiring harness extended on its own out to the brain pan and like a collection of snakes began searching for their proper connections. Once completed, the harness took the brain pan out of the doctor's hand and pulled it into place in the skull. Once settled, the dark black mist dissipated, and the structure became clear once more.

Aida turned her attention to the technicians around the monitors of the new body as they began to test if the procedure was successful. Ginny was still amazed at the state-of-the-art nanotech the new body was made from as its internal components attached itself to the transplanted brain pan. She was still very confused to what the black mist was though now was not a time for questions.

Very soon, the mechanical fingers began to move just before the right hand rose off the bed to touch its face lightly. The team within bumped fists in excitement as the doctor turned to give thumbs up to Aida and Ginny pronouncing it all to be a success. He then bent over the new body to say something before beginning to close the skull up tightly.

"Once you are done, take him and the old body up to Special Weapons Development for testing and recovery. Good job everyone!" Aida announced over the intercom.

She then turned to Ginny and finally answered her previous question.

"This asset is important because there are only three within the cryo-pods in the Vault," she revealed. "What is not recorded in any log or history book is that one of the Horsemen was unaffected by the cryogenics procedure and had to be 'expedited' out of the prison."

"He escaped, you mean?" Ginny surmised.

"Call it what you may, he has lived a long life serving the greater good and this company to atone for his indiscretions during the war. This isn't the first time I've witnessed his transference over the years to a new body, and though I cannot properly explain what you witnessed I can only theorize it was his soul catching a ride to the new vessel."

"You're telling me that's what a human soul looks like?"
Ginny scoffed. "I call bullshit on that."

"Well my dear, you are free to think whatever you want on that," Aida said softly. "I like to think of it in that way, as the alternative provides endless and horrifying possibilities. None of which humanity is prepared to face despite all of its advancements."

A silence fell on them both as they watched the new body slowly sit up, and despite protests from the technicians it stood, still connected to the monitors. Very cautiously, like a newborn learning to walk for the first time, it walked towards the observation room window and looked straight at Aida. This was a sight to behold, a carbon/ titanium skeleton wrapped with malleable composite of the same make up for muscles. It looked like a skinless human body without the genitalia. Well, almost like a human body. Its head was akin to a human skull, with two orange lights glowing from within the eye sockets. No 'muscles adorned the face as the lower jaw was fused with the upper one; the teeth were simply one solid joint between the jaws with long vertical lines engraved. Obviously, it would have a speaker mechanism behind the 'mouth', but Ginny couldn't know for sure.

And then something amazing happened. The body, which was a tall overly muscular build, began to transform before their very eyes. Millions of nanobots began to separate from the body itself like a swarm of bugs, then reform the entire body starting from the neck downwards into a more lean, athletic frame. When the process was complete, he leaned his neck from side to side in a stretch as he observed himself in the mirrored glass. Then he stopped and looked at them both as if he knew exactly where they were behind the window. When he spoke, it was with a disturbing low growl of a voice and it was in a language Ginny didn't understand.

"Mors factus sum," it muttered. "Pestifer Mundi."

The words, whatever they were sent a shiver down Ginny's spine. It was a horrific, emotionless tone of a voice, one fitting for the perfect monster. She watched fearfully as he reached over to take back the katana, then returned to the gurney and laid back down, allowing the techs to cover him like a dead body completely with a blanket before he was whisked away. It seemed he was not to be seen by the casual employee that might be roaming the halls.

"That is a Horseman?" she stammered.

"He is THE Horseman," Aida replied. "The best of the best, their General, and quite possibly the best weapon humankind has ever created."

"What did he say to you? I didn't recognize the language," Ginny wondered aloud.

"It was Latin." Aida looked over to her with a sombre face. "He said 'I have become Death, destroyer of worlds.'"

"That was…."

"Yes, it was," Aida finished the thought. "Come, let's retreat to my office and go over your new assignment. I think you will find it a unique challenge fitting of your skill set."

///

Waypoint Station, Nowich-Paris Company Warehouse, Level 3

It was finally time, and Trenton Slovis couldn't be more excited. Even though the addition to New Athens remained attached to the Scimitar which remained in orbit of Dawn because of the ongoing 'security' issue on Horizon, there was much to celebrate in the Company. Waypoint was now complete and open for business. Every vendor, merchant, and even the Legion paid a tax to keep operations on Waypoint. The taxes added to the revenue the multi tiered city would now generate as a destination and no longer just a stop along the way to the outer colonies.

And to deal with the issues on Horizon, he was about to crack the egg that held the legendary Four Horsemen within it. If there was anyone best able to deal with the issues and get the planet's mining operations online again it was them. The Legion, despite its bravado, had proved to be inept. Soldiers for hire; yet they failed every time the situation became difficult. Repeated failure to resolve the problems on Horizon left him no choice but to look elsewhere for a solution. And standing before the metal doors of the Vault, he knew he had found the right one.

Now there was the slight problem that the Company did not own the inhabitants inside, but Slovis had negotiated a contract with their legal representatives, DeSa Armor, to eliminate all hostile and contagion factors on the surface to allow business to resume. His superiors had been pleased with his quick spin on what could have been a crippling turn of events. But the Horsemen were only part of the bounty that lay within the Vault behind closed doors.

There was the cryo-facility itself, technology never replicated by the Republic after being utilized in this single occasion. Cryo-tech held endless possibilities which meant endless ways to be profitable, and to Nowich-Paris that was worth the enormous price paid for it alone. Its data banks would reveal secrets upon secrets that would keep the R and D folks busy for years. And then there was the AI.

Somewhere within those walls slept humanity's first creation of artificial intelligence. The Republic had brought her online a few years before the war to help strategize battles and assess the enemy's weakness' and exploit them. Having the world's best computer hackers meant the Republic was a daunting foe in the Revolutionary War, adding the AI to their folds made them unstoppable. Yes, the Four Horsemen won the war physically, but it was under the AI's watch they had even been created. That data trove was worth the loss of the original Horsemen; having the ability to make more super soldiers would end the Company's reliance on the Legion.

"Deep in thought, are we?" a familiar voice called to him from behind.

Slovis knew instantly it was his nemesis from DeSa, that wretched witch Aida who had come to make sure he didn't open the cryo-pods without her. But as he turned, he could see she wasn't accompanied by her usual compliment of security androids. Instead, she was joined by the lawyer that he had fired for overlooking the legal challenge of DeSa and an armored android-looking bodyguard wearing a black hooded cloak that loomed tall above her. In fact, it was his presence that stopped everyone in the warehouse from what they were doing to watch him. Armed with a blaster on his left hip and an old looking Japanese sword on his back, he was quite the sight to behold versus the usual armed member of the Legion.

"I see you've been digging through our trash," he mocked Ginny as they approached. "And looks like you ditched your normal security for a mega bot."

"Oh, my friend here is not an android, but he is a very well-equipped cyborg that will make sure we are well protected from any surprises here today," Aida smiled politely back at him. "As for the trash comment, childish anger makes some no longer see value in things that are priceless in the eyes of others."

Slovis grumbled to her rebuttal to his jabs, turning his back to them just as he noticed the DeSa medical teams entering the warehouse to be on standby. With a whirl of his index finger raised in the air, he signalled to his team to get started on cracking the codes to open the doors. They nodded in response, then began typing in numbers to their connected datapad.

The head of the team was Dr Richard Keen, one of the leading scientists in human/ machine integration. The Company was quite proud to have him in their employment and showed him off every time they could. Despite being renowned for his work, Dr Keen's hobby was obsessively learning all he could about this cryo-prison and everything within. At first, the interest seemed strange but when he explained it to Slovis that the patients inside were the dawn of human/ mechanical mergers it all made sense.

Over and over, sets of numbers were punched into the code by the door only to be met with a red light on the panel. Keen got frustrated thinking his workers were messing up the codes and shoved them aside to do it himself. Reading directly from his notes gleaned from all the records money could buy on the Vault, he punched it failed codes one after another.

"I.... I don't understand," he muttered quietly.

"Do we have a problem, Dr?" Slovis craned his neck to see over the throng of people crowding the entrance.

"A minor one," Keen called back. "It seems the door lock may be malfunctioning."

"Well fix it then," Slovis ordered. "We have a lot of money invested in this today, let's not offend the shareholders by wasting it."

"I am working on it." The air of panic rose from the Dr.

Slovis wasn't impressed. Acquisition costs of the Vault lone had been astronomical – close to the costs of the first expedition to Teegarden's Star – then it was delayed by the stupid court ruling that prevented Nowich-Paris from opening it until they left Earth Space. Now it looked like the four-hundred-year-old facility was in disrepair. He hated delays.

Just as he was about to bark at the Dr to work faster, he noticed out of the corner of his eye the DeSa bodyguard move forward. The hulking black figure moved through the crowd with a certain grace that something that big normally didn't move with. His armored boots barely made a sound on the metal grate floor. The group of doctors, medical assistants, and android helpers parted fearfully as in mere moments the giant now stood looking down at a terrified Dr Keen.

A momentary stare down quickly ended, and the cyborg quickly keyed in numbers in rapid succession to the keypad. Slovis was about to argue about him touching the device when a green light lit up and an entry alarm began to ring. The robed guard spun on his heel and returned to his station behind the DeSa CEO who wore a smug grin on her face.

Slovis was dumbfounded. How did some Legion thug know what a doctor who had a lifelong obsession did not? In fact, the entire medical team shared his look as they all stared at the unflinching guard looking straight ahead as if nothing happened. Slovis looked over at Keen who was about to say something when the alarm switched off, the door hissed as the entryway pressurised and the Vault entrance slid open to each side to disappear within the walls.

Success. Maybe today wouldn't suffer costly delays after all. Slovis was happy and hoped this was the last of the surprises encountered today.

///

It was apparent to him that the crew assembled wouldn't be able to open the door to the Vault, but Death said nothing. He was glad to be invited to be front and center for this, despite the terrible history this installation had in his past. Behind those doors was supposed to be his coffin, and had certain factors not played out the way they did it would have been. A dark anger within him began to roil, but he suppressed the urges to simply kick in the front door and create a scene. For now, he was a well-placed surprise; being Aida's guest here to be part of the big surprise that she hoped to screw with the Nowich-Paris executive. But Death wasn't here for her desires, he was here for those who slept within.

He had thought on much since being transferred into this new body. Hours of self reflection along with studying the capabilities of the new hardware granted to him. A day after being 'released' by the techs of DeSa, Death had retreated to his property within the heart of the downtown within the Waypoint station addition to begin diagnostics and discovery of his new self. To no surprise, DeSa had its own software installed within the mainframe system of the body. What did surprise him was the hidden sleeper subroutines of core programming also installed that had never been in any of his previous bodies. It seemed his old 'friend' had certain future plans for him which involved suppression of his free will.

Death's trust of Aida had faded a long time ago, long enough for him to find an AI of his own to rely on. Unbeknownst to all, he had purchased a multi-story building which had been intended to be a luxury hotel before its company when bankrupt when the Scimitar was under final construction. It was then he hired teams to turn this into his future home and personal armory. The upper floor was his personal quarters and the second floor was the armory, yet something at the time had him set up the three floors in between as three separate suites. He now realized it was in hope that one day he would be reunited with the closest thing he could remember as family.

During construction he had the core of the new AI installed, and yesterday he had the AI sweep the new body's systems for any unwanted software or programs. His new ally was very thorough and found more than expected. It took hours to rewrite and replace the core software with his own firmware, and the mystery subroutines were saved to a portable storage drive for future study. Death was now free of DeSa in every way, whether they realized it or not.

His thoughts were brought to the present by a slight tap on his arm by Aida who nodded towards the clusterfuck of techs trying to open the Vault. They were in possession of the original codes, but in his escape from the cryo-facility, Death had changed them all. He wanted to ensure the safety of his sleeping compatriots; he had been successful up until now.

He knew what the tap on his arm had meant without words, so he casually walked towards the Vault which stood about fifteen meters away. Donned with only light armor, a dark grey undersuit – DeSa Stage 2 Armor suit - and a faceless black mask to hide his new skull-like face, he had worn an old black hooded cloak to prevent any casual recognition by DeSa employees of who he actually was. Gliding past the Company techs who parted with terrified looks as he passed, he marched right up beside the doctor in charge.

Dr Richard Keen had long been a pain in his ass. The five - foot-ten balding blond haired, near sighted book worm had long chased after any and all facts about the Four Horsemen that Death had repeatedly struggled to keep from him. Thoughts of killing the obsessive learner had crossed his mind, but the good doctor was too high profile of a Mark to hit without significant blowback. Blowback that would affect those within the Vault more than him. For almost twenty years, Death had tried stymying this man from doing the exact thing he was being asked to do, open the doors of the Vault.

Death stared down at Keen with disgust. The doctor looked back at him with curiosity, trying to ascertain who and what he was; secrets destined to come to light today, but not at this moment. After fighting the urge to snap the meek man's neck like a twig, he turned to the keypad and typed in his code.

20-39-10-15-2031

They were numbers that no other person would have ever figured out as the files on his past were so redacted and classified that even now they weren't able to be read. But to him, the code was simple. Twenty minutes, thirty-nine seconds was how long he had flatlined on the surgical table during the process turning him into an augmented soldier. October fifteenth, 2031 was the date of the procedure. It was the day he stopped being a human being, and the day he had become a Horseman of the Republic. It was the day of both his death and rebirth.

Ignoring the bleating horn to clear the doorway, he returned to his station of guard behind the left shoulder of Aida and stood stoically. Other than Aida, everyone in attendance stared at him in shock. He wanted to chuckle, but little about today was humorous to him. He let them wonder with their mouths agape, looking for obvious answers that would come apparent soon enough.

Then the entry chamber pressurized, and the doors slid open, averting attention back to the Vault and away form him. Within the twenty by twenty-five-foot room that he remembered with vivid detail its ancient lights flickered trying to stay lit as it had been too long since the last time they had been used. It was the main observation lounge of the cryo-prison, and on its back wall was a giant metal door that would open to the four cryo-pods in a circle around the reactor itself that kept the Vault powered for all these years. He watched as Keen and his team pushed forward into the sterile white room, disinterested in anything within besides the control panel to open this large door.

Keen didn't hesitate for a moment, keying in the codes in his precious book of notes and stepping back as this door groaned against hundreds of years of rust and inactivity before its mechanisms began to work as intended. This door opened at an angle and slid open to each side to reveal the cryo-facility in all its ancient glory.

Behind the door lay a set of stairs that led up one story to the catwalks surrounding the reactor. From these catwalks one could access the central computer on the back wall or approach the pods one by one to inspect or open them as well as work on the reactor core. Unable to curb his excitement, Keen was like a child on Christmas morning; he darted up the stairs and disappeared from view of Death and the other onlookers in the warehouse with his team right on his heals.

Aida sighed, mumbled something about boys being boys and walked towards the doorway, motioning for her R and D team to follow. Slovis stayed put, watching through his data pad that viewed from one of the android workers' point of view from his safety out here. Death stood pat for now, and soon realized the little lawyer lady remained at his side.

After a few moments had passed leading to screams of anger from Aida, Death finally decided to enter his intended tomb once more, Slovis in tow as curious to what all the commotion was. As he reached the catwalks, Death was greeted by the sight of Aida trying to separate Dr Keen from the main control panel.

"Touch those controls again, and I will have your medical license revoked and sue you into bankruptcy!" she screamed at him, pulling at his shoulder to move him away.

It was then she noticed Slovis on the catwalk and shouted with panic at him.

"Your man is lost in his obsession!" she cried for reason. "He is trying to start the reanimation process and wake the Horsemen! Doing that in an uncontrolled environment like this will kill them! Do something!"

"Keen, stand down!" Slovis ordered.

"Give me a moment, this needs to happen," Keen replied, though not relenting in his task. "I have to see this to fruition."

"Keen, what you are doing is against the legal instructions set out for us on this project." Slovis interjected. "Like it or not, the reanimation process is to be handled by DeSa."

"Like hell I'm going to let them take my rightful place in history today," Keen turned around with a look of madness on his face.

That was all Death needed to act. Over the ages he had seen that exact look on many a person, all of them had been robbed of reason. There was no talking him down from this ledge, and seeing as the time for negotiation had ended, he would be in the right in his actions. Death just had to be careful not to kill the poor man.

In five quick strides, Death had crossed the distance on the catwalk that had separated him from Dr Keen and the main controls. With his right hand, he grabbed the doctor by the neck, and with his left he pulled the man's body away from the control to allow Aida to stop whatever processes had begun. The reactor, which had begun to cycle up in anticipation of powering the pod openings started to quiet down again. When she looked back and nodded back at him, Death then walked with his quarry still hanging in the air by his neck and dropped him at the feet of Slovis.

Dr Keen gasped for air then struggled to get to his feet, desperate in his madness to get back to his work. Death stood firmly on the catwalk between him and his bewildered team, blocking him from going anywhere close to the controls again.

"Arrest him!" coughed Keen. "That freak just assaulted a Company employee on a Company station!"

"Dr Richard Keen," a young woman's voice came from the stairs, "you are under arrest for violating section 18, sub-section 22 of the legal agreement of the Republic Supreme Court."

Ginnifer Agefor joined the party with two security androids that grabbed Keen and began to handcuff him.

"It was implicitly written in the judgement – which I am thoroughly aware that you read – that no employee of Nowich-Paris was to interfere with the reanimation of the assets within this facility," Ginny scolded the now frothing doctor. "You knew that once the pods were carefully removed for proper and controlled reanimation by DeSa Armor that you had full run of this complex, but not before."

"You have no right!" he spat at her. "And what about that monster? He assaulted me and yet you only have me in cuffs."

"DeSa's personal security prevented the loss of life that you so callously almost caused," she replied, wiping the phlegm from her face. "That man is a hero, unlike you."

"Slovis, do something!" Keen cried to the CEO as he was being led away but got no response.

Slovis ignored the struggling madman as he was dragged out of the Vault, waited a few moments, and then straightened his tie before addressing his people still looking on in shock.

"My dear Aida," he began calmly, "I do apologize for my former employee's actions. You can be rest assured that we will have him prosecuted to the fullest and shipped back to Earth to be tried for his actions here today. I ask all of my team to please wait outside with the exception of Dr Lang. I wish her to learn from you by observation only, while all your techs complete their work."

"Thank you, Trenton," Aida nodded, watching the androids and the lab techs leave. "I know Dr Lang's work well; I am honored to have her join us."

"And if it is too much to ask," Slovis added, "I would like to remain as well. To observe from a distance of course."

"Granted as well," she smiled. "You do own this facility after all. My team will work quickly so your research team may resume work shortly."

Death listened to this exchange while approaching pod 1. All the pods stood upright and in a circle around the main fusion reactor cooling tower. They stood at a slight angle but were fully accessible from each catwalk approach. He carefully wiped off the frost on the thick glass window to peer at the person within. She was a young woman of Asian descent. Her eyes were closed tight, and her face looked peaceful in her sleep. A metal tiara across her forehead relayed brain function and vitals to the main computer.

He backed away as the DeSa techs looked to push past him to begin to detach the pods for transport to DeSa Armor R and D. Moving out of the way and around to pod 4, he watched carefully as the team attached portable fusion generators to pods 1 through 3, ensured they were working within proper design, then detached them from the Vault's reactor. One by one, they were loaded with the help of android workers to gravity lift dollies and whisked away to DeSa, leaving behind pod 4.

Slovis had watched closely for a bit, then became enamored with a different structure on the wall of computers. It was the housing unit for the infamous AI of the Horsemen, the prize of the entire facility. It was a large bank of processor with a central hub that held a control matrix that could be ejected. The entire hub was lit up with hues of orange and blues, and above the matrix was a set of words.

Artificial Infiltration Defence Algorithm.

Slovis studied the words for a moment as his mind began to process something about them when he was interrupted by Dr Lang. Death watched as the two almost argued about something, repeatedly pointing at the pod he was leaning on, then rushing over to Aida who was studying the reactor stability before departing.

"Dr Lang tells me you are done," Slovis began.

"Nearly, just doing some last checks of the reactor stability before turning the facility over to your people," Aida said with a coy smile.

"I have a bit of a concern," Slovis said."

"Oh?" Aida showed fake concern.

"Within this facility were the Four Horsemen, yet you only removed three cryo-pods. Only your hired muscle has gone near the fourth one, can you tell me why?"

"Because it is empty, as is the core matrix you are so fond of over there," she announced.

"I don't understand." Both Slovis and Dr Lang looked confused.

"Oh Trenton, do I have to spell it out for you?" she replied with a sigh. "Artificial Infiltration Defence Algorithm. A.I.D.A. Your core matrix is right here," she said pointing at her head. "And has been for many years."

"You're a fucking AI?" he shouted.

"I am THE fucking AI," she countered. "And I remember clearly not spending more than a few hours in this facility, not four hundred goddamn years of isolation."

"That explains your involvement in this project, but doesn't that make you a fugitive?" Slovis asked with a smirk. "I could call the guards and have you arrested."

"A few years ago, you could have," Aida smiled back at him, "but that was before I acquired legal pardons for the Horsemen and myself. You see, Trenton, I am a recognized free life form as far as the High Court of the Republic is concerned. One that runs the third largest company in the Republic to boot. Now imagine when news breaks that an AI runs a company that is known for perfecting the human/machine interface. Our shares will skyrocket."

"You bitch, you planned this."

"Don't feel bad, Slovis," she gloated. "This is the result of over two hundred years of careful planning. It was put into motion before you were even born, so please don't take it personally."

"And what of pod 4?" Dr Lang interrupted the little back and forth.

"What of it?" Aida asked.

"What happened to its occupant?" the Dr clarified.

"I don't think that lid was actually ever closed on the Fourth Horseman," she answered. "It seemed with all his augmentations, the techs were unable to put him under. So, he left and took me with him."

"Why are we just finding this out now?" Slovis demanded. "And why isn't there a record of any of what you are saying? You would think the Republic would …."

"Admit they fucked up?" Aida cut him off. "They would reveal to the planet that one of the four war criminals they neutralized was now in the wind? You are talking about political suicide forty years after winning the war. Is it really that shocking they kept his escape secret?"

"So, which one got out?" Slovis asked.

"I did." The dark figure leaning on the pod ten feet away from the conversation finally spoke.

"I am the Fourth Horseman by name, though I was the first of the soldier augmentation process created long before the others. I am the one that would not sleep, I am the one that would not be restrained. I slaughtered all those who were sent to put me down like a dog, poor souls that had no clue of what they hunted. I am that which walked the battlefields without fear, that led the First battalion of the Legion of the Republic. I am Death," he said as he removed his smooth mask to reveal the skull-like maw beneath.

There was a long silence in the reactor room, but Death didn't mind. He thrived under silence, most of his long life was lived within its loving embrace. Yet he began to wonder in this silence if he would have to kill the two Nowich-Paris employees to protect his identity, if just for a while longer.

"So, the Company is left with nothing?" Slovis wondered aloud. "First you deny us the Horsemen, and now the AI?"

"This facility will make your precious company trillions of dollars." Aida patted him on the shoulder as she began to walk past him. "You will be the owners of Cryo-tech that will revolutionize space exploration and medical procedures. Sell that to the Company instead of what isn't in here."

They all watched as Aida sauntered down the stairs and out the Vault. Then Slovis and Lang returned their gaze to him. He let them stare in fear and wonder, waiting for them to say something. It took a long five minutes before Slovis spoke, he guessed being left alone with Death had some negative affects on a person's confidence.

"Why are you still here?" he spoke carefully.

"Because you and I have a contract to agree upon." Death placed the mask back over his 'face'.

"Aida and I already wrote one up," Slovis replied nervously.

"And what makes you think she was ever authorized to represent the Horsemen in any negotiations?" Death replied, leaving the pod which should have been his coffin for the last time and walking towards the stairs. "Tomorrow morning, your office, bring a notary and I will bring mine. I will negotiate on behalf of my team in good faith for your preservation of their well being. We have a job that needs to be done, and I guarantee you it will be done. For the right price, that is."

He left them standing on the catwalk, dumbfounded by all that had been revealed to them this day. Since the door of

the Vault had been opened five hours had passed. In that
five hours, the course of history had been drastically
changed. It would take a while for all that was learned today
to sink into Trenton Slovis. Death hoped the Company man
would stick to the bigger task at hand, and not try anything
stupid tomorrow. After all, it was impossible to cheat Death.

3

Waypoint Station, Desa Armory, Research and Development Laboratory, Level 1

Ginny entered the observation room and was immediately struck by the lone, statuesque figure standing inches from the mirrored window that overlooked the laboratory on the other side. She was well aware of who it was, what shocked her was how long he had been there.

Except for a few hours on the first day that he had mysteriously disappeared, he remained unmoved as the DeSa scientists carefully began the reanimation process of the other Horsemen. After a day and a bit, the DeSa team became aware of who was watching them at all time. In Ginny's mind it was a good thing; their boss might be forgiving of any mistakes made, but he wouldn't. It made for careful planning of each move and created a slow but steady pace to the process.

Almost a week after the pods were brought to DeSa, the three patients had finally been removed from the containers that had kept them for all this time. They looked more like cadavers than living beings. Lacking the cyborg enhancements that made them what they were, they were simply incomplete humans lying on gurneys, missing arms, legs and parts of the torso gaping wide for all to see what lay within. To Ginny it was a disturbing sight, like a set of a horror flick before the blood and gore was added.

And the doctors themselves were a sight to be seen. Working in sealed environment suits, it was impossible to tell if they were male or female. It was just a team of androgynous workers attending to these living trauma victims like it was an everyday occurrence. The nonchalant way the medical team worked was nearly as troubling as the sight of the patients they were working on.

She had arrived just in time to see the lead doctor giving a report to Aida, while nervously glancing to the mirrored wall of glass knowing full well who was watching and listening. The now outed AI matriarch of DeSa Armory was in her office twenty stories above, dealing with the fallout of her announcement and giving interviews to news networks.

"The patients are stable for now," the doctor began, voice mechanised through the suit. "We have completed the reanimation process and placed them all in medical comas for the time being while we better assess them."

"Assess them for what?" Aida inquired, looking down at the doctor from the other side of her desk on the monitor.

"There is a great deal of tissue degradation from the cryogenics process," the doctor added. "We will need to conduct extensive surgeries just to cut away the necrotic flesh, never mind fit them for their new augmentations. In their weakened state, I can only hope they survive the next few days."

"Unacceptable, doctor," Aida trumpeted. "You are looking at the finest soldiers to ever walk the battlefield. Pump them full of whatever you need to make them survive the procedures and get them into the OR now. I expect a full report when you get out of surgery in person."

"Yes ma'am." But the look in the doctor's eyes showed less confidence to Ginny than he was portraying.

In a flurry of action, the medical teams whisked the three patients out three different doors minutes after the call ended. The surgery floor was in the lower levels and Ginny imagined the rush to ready those rooms was just as mad as the rush to get them there. A once bustling medical ward was now empty and dark, yet the lone figure still remained unmoved.

"You do know they have an observation room above the OR, right?" she dared herself to speak.

"I do," he spoke in that growl of a voice of his.

"Do you want me to show you the way down there?" Ginny gulped as she spoke.

"Is there a reason you seem to be keeping an eye on me, Miss Agefor?" the dark figure slowly turned towards her. "Is it due to an overwhelming sense of professional curiosity or is it something more?"

"I...I have been assigned to the Horsemen as your personal attaché for the duration of your contract with Nowich-Paris," she replied nervously.

"I need no such services," he countered very quickly.

"But how about the other three?" she reached deep for the courage to face off with him. "Imagine waking up after four hundred years to find yourself in space, in another star system? Much has changed on Earth but add in these factors and the transition to our time could be troubling for them."

"You wish to play nanny to a team of trained killers?" he scoffed her.

"I wish to help fellow human beings adapt to a world and life that will be most alien to them." Ginny stood tall with conviction in her voice. "They will require time; I hope you don't expect them to suit up the minute they wake up to go on your precious mission?"

"I do not know what to expect, Miss Agefor," he sighed. "And that's what troubles me the most. I have changed as much as life has while in their slumber. I find it hard to believe they will step into line under my order without question. When they went in, I was still somewhat human. Now, I am something far more......."

"Different?" Ginny added.

"Deadly," he corrected her assumption. "If you may excuse me, I have some things to attend to. If you must play the attaché, then please notify me when they are out of surgery. I will rejoin you here then."

And with that, he walked past her with a cat-like quickness and was gone. It amazed her how he was able to adjust to his new body with such ease; most patients with any type of new augmentations took years to learn to use their new limbs, not hours. There was something different about him, and deadly. She decided that while she waited, she would review the file on him that DeSa had gathered for her to better know the enigma that the Horseman Death was.

Ginny turned the lights on in the observation lounge, pulled up a comfy chair, and dug into the thick and much redacted file. In her research for Nowich-Paris, she had read much about him and the others, but those files lacked details, this one did not. It was nearly a complete record of his creation, war record, prosecution, and even held mission logs under his employment with DeSa. Ginny hoped to understand him better after sifting through it but wondered did anyone truly understand one named Death.

///

Rain Forest Plateau; Outskirts of New Athens; Horizon

Last time he was here, Death was on a recon mission, so he was not as heavily armored as he was now. With his new designs still being built at DeSa, he had been forced to adapt and don his old armor set. It had been his second skin for so long, yet today it felt strange, almost alien to him. His new body was not very compatible with this old tech, like having an itch all over your body that couldn't be scratched or soothed. Despite the feeling, he needed a distraction while the others were in surgery so here he was back in the last place most of those above would rather be.

New Athens stood like a shining beacon amongst the five-kilometer swath that he had burned down a few weeks back. Teegarden shone bright on this cloudless late summer day, its light sparkling off the multifaceted structures that made up the tower district of New Athens. This light broke across the steel buildings to shine over the fountain in the southern garden, making the water in the pond sparkle like a pool of diamonds.

But Death hadn't come to see the empty city in its quiet serenity; he had come to see if the second part of his trap had worked. With both his perimeter barrier and the city barrier still raised, he had hoped to trap one or more of the creatures within the city during his time away. Three and a half weeks would be an eternity to be trapped in an abandoned and resourceless city. The fountain was the only source of nourishment left after he had drained the other ponds and such throughout the empty streets before. If anything had been caught inside the barrier, it would be here or nearby. Lack of food would have it weak, so weak it would need to stay near to the water just to save energy to survive.

His gun metal grey boots shuffled through the mounds of ash and debris left in the wake of the blaze. Everything here burned hot, had Death not calculated for this variable a lesser shield would have let the fires run more rampant. Yet today he felt off his game, walking through this burnt and barren new landscape brought back memories of the war.

Sounds of gunfire surrounded him in faint echoes, the blasts of cannons from the Republic's hover tanks still rang loud in his ears. The march of the infantry made the ground vibrate beneath his feet. All around him he could smell blood and burnt flesh; echoes of a war that ended several lifetimes before came alive for a moment around him. Memories made him grip his blaster tighter and had his right hand on the hilt of his katana hilt ready to draw. Death paused to refocus, knowing full well that despite his destruction to the local landscape that there were many things on Horizon that were still dangerous. Creatures that made the Were-Crocs look timid.

Looking around he could see nothing unusual in the area. Holstering his weapon, he keyed in codes to open a door into the shield wall, entering the outskirt park area of New Athens quickly. No sooner had he closed the shield behind him, Death felt the trap spring. Three of the emaciated human creatures flew at him from different directions, hoping to catch their prey by surprise. But Death was always prepared for action, and his katana was drawn in a flash, striking down the nearest attacker by cleaving it clean in two from crotch to the top of its head. Glancing down at the halved body, Death noticed something moving at the base of the skull where the neck and head joined. This was where the parasite controlled its host, now he knew how to focus his attacks going forward.

A quick step to the right to avoid the next creature followed by an upswing with his sword and its left arm flew up into the air. The beast shrieked with rage, turning without grasping at the stump and crouched ready to strike again.

From behind, the last attacking creature found its opening, yet in mid-air realized that opening was just for show. Death side stepped to the left, spun counter clockwise, and took the top half of the thing's head off while it was still in mid-air. His attack was not only precise, but it left him in perfect defensive form to face the remaining one-armed creature still looking to attack. Death's actions had been lightning fast, and his strikes overwhelming to the point that many enemies would be looking to retreat now. But this this thing had madness in its eyes; a rage he had not seen in his lifetime filled its tiny blackened orbs as it stared him down.

Killing it wouldn't help him solve the riddle of the virus, nor would it end the constant attacks by these zombified humans. Drop this one, and ten more would eventually take its place. Death thought quickly, creating a strategy for the long game ahead rather than this little skirmish. And then it came to him.

Sheathing his sword into the Saya that hung upside down and at an angle down to his right side, he reached for a shorter throwing blade that was strapped to his left shoulder. As he grabbed the knife, he dragged his hand over the gauntlet computer on his left wrist, reopening the doorway which he just entered. Now he was giving the feral beast a second choice. Before it was a starved and cornered animal, looking at him merely as food and a threat to its life. But now there was a way out, and the creature didn't hesitate to go for it.

It moved with a greater speed than Death anticipated, but so did his new body. As it dashed by his left side, he spun with it and sunk the knife deep into its right shoulder, snapping the blade off with a hard twitch of his wrist after the strike. Again, the leathery skin and bones thing shrieked, but did not slow in its escape. Through the shield door it leapt, flying down the ten-foot drop of the concrete city base and rolled to lessen the landing. It popped up on its feet and kept running, racing towards the tree line in the distance.

Death had already deactivated the outer shield line upon his arrival and had no intention of chasing after his escaped prisoner, yet. He closed the city shield and watched through the clear barrier as the beast-man scrambled across the burnt terrain. About halfway to the untouched forest, it began to cry out, cries that began to be answered a few minutes later. Starving and on its last reserves of energy, it collapsed less than a kilometer from the edge of the treeline. Death increased the magnification in the helmet to better see it in the distance; he was pleased when he could see its ribs expanding and contracting with its rapid breaths. It wasn't dead, but it had nothing left to keep running.

As if on cue, another two of the pale skinned, emaciated things crept out of the safety of the forest and carefully approached their fallen comrade. They sniffed at the air as they gathered at its side, pawing at its missing arm and bleeding shoulder. Death could see the looks on their faces as they stared him down from the distance between them. A few feral snarls and shrieks later, they gathered up their spent friend and dragged him into the thicket of trees. Now that they had disappeared, Death discarded the broken blade, then activated the tracking beacon imbedded in the blade buried deep into the flesh and bone of the beast's shoulder. Animal behavior would mean he would either be taken to a place considered to be safe before its wounds would be attended to or it would be deemed a liability to the masses and killed on the spot. Death was hoping for the former, as it would be taken to the nest. Following their most basic of instincts, these things were going to lead him straight to whatever it was that controlled them. And when he was sure the readings were accurate, he would take his team there and leave nothing alive.

///

Waypoint Station, DeSa Armory, Research and Development Laboratory, Level 1

Two days, that's how long the Horseman Death had disappeared for. Ginny, for the most part, had spent most of that time pouring through old files that hadn't seen human eyes in hundreds of years. The paper files, not data logs, were still heavily redacted, but not as much as anything else previously noted on the Horsemen. And though she had started her read at home, eventually she found herself in the surgical observation lounge at DeSa Armory, pouring through the pasts of those who until recently had no future.

Within these files, Ginny did not find anything except tragic tales of hard lives which were marred by horrific injury, leading to selection into the Super Soldier program. It was enlightening yet frightening to the lengths the Republic went to ensure winning the Revolutionary War. If these files saw the light of day, the entire history of the war would need to be rewritten. The experiments, the melding of man with machine, and the entire training regimen of the program broke every human cruelty law ever written. Tears stained her cheeks as the tales of sadness continued with unrelenting pain and suffering. The Horsemen had been purified in tortures their enemies could never imagine; it became clear to her why they had been so dominant on the battlefield.

Every now and then she would gaze down to the operating room below. Now they had moved on to the man called Fear. A man who once held the name Linford – his surname like all the others was lost in the past to never be recovered – was quite the unusual specimen. The doctors had to extend the operating table to accommodate his seven-foot height. His dark brown Jamaican skin reflected the operating room lights back at her from above. When he was removed from the cryo-pod, he had been missing both his legs from knee down and his left hand at the wrist. Because of the ages being frozen, his legs were now fully amputated at the hip, with this part of the procedure being to meld new robotic hip joints to the healthy pelvic bone and surrounding tissue.

His left arm was now a stump with a robotic socket at mid bicep; a process completed about an hour ago by the previous team who was now resting. And when this procedure was over, the next team would start with the removal of the antiquated spine reinforcement from the days of the war with a state-of-the-art replacement cyborg spinal column. When all was said and done, Linford will have been on the operating table for nearly 48 hours. In the other two

ORs, similar operations were being performed on the other Horsemen. Old technology and dead flesh were being replaced with new upgrades. In time, the Horsemen would awaken with upgrades they could never imagine having in a world they could never imagine living.

And that's where Ginny came in. DeSa and Nowich-Paris were partners in crime here. Both were responsible for releasing trained killers into an era that had nothing in comparison to them. Everything about it was wrong, ethically and situationally. The untold chaos these three alone could cause was mind boggling but add that with a reborn monster like Death and the variables just became infinite. Ginny was tasked with being their anchor to the here and now, keeping four of them out of trouble and on task. A great deal of money was riding on them completing their contract.

Sifting through the files, it became apparent that the Horseman Agony would be the most intimidating to her. Formerly known as Miko, the Japanese born and youngest of the four had a master's degree in business, an 8th level Dan in Kendo and was a Bushido Master, as well as being a member of the Yakuza. Very little was known how she was recruited to the program, but it was noted she had amputations of both legs, one above the knee and the other below, and both arms mid forearm. To most, these injuries would be difficult to bounce back from, but with her advanced cybernetics Agony had become even more deadly. This was a fierce and driven woman who despite her five-foot ten-inch frame was pound for pound the fiercest of the Four Horsemen. It would take careful and planned words to keep on this one's good side.

The hulking woman named War, formerly Hekla, was a soldier for hire from Iceland. Her six-foot five-inch height was intimidating even these days but add that with her bodybuilder physique and one had the perfect soldier. In a sense, she was the last of the Vikings. Of the four, Hekla was the only trained soldier and if she was told Ginny was a superior, Ginny hoped it would leave this human wrecking ball a bit more open for guidance than the others. Her file told of the incident where her convoy was struck by an IED in the Middle East, killing the rest of her five-man team while leaving her crippled with a missing left leg and arm, spinal injuries and a great deal of anger. The program was able to fix her body with mechanical cybernetics, reinforcing her spine, and gave her an outlet for her anger. Again, not a woman she wanted to piss off, but one much less volatile than Agony.

Then came the man on the table below, Linford. To say he was a bit of an oddball in the Four Horsemen was an understatement. A Jamaican born medical student, he dropped out of the public eye in his late teens to only re-emerge at 25 years old as a Voodoo Priest in his home country. Known as Big Papa Fear, his powerful reach included drug and gun running, along with being on the top ten of Interpol's most wanted. It took an entire task force of nearly fifty people to take him down, leaving him crippled with the afore mentioned injuries. But as he recovered from his amputations, he mysteriously disappeared from the Belgium Prison hospital though being under constant guard. Now part of the Republic's soldier program, he took the shortened name Fear and became the second to join the ranks of the Horsemen, loyally following the enigma Death without question.

And that led Ginny to review the file she had read over the most, yet still held the most questions. Death, the original of the Four Horsemen yet referred by all as the Fourth Horseman. He was not listed as part of the Republic's soldier program, though certain notes referred to him throughout the full length of the program told her he was always there in some capacity. He had no name on record, only a number: patient 71. Nowhere in the file were there DNA samples, fingerprints, next of kin, or even mention of nationality. He was simply just there, and he was feared by all who worked with or near him.

Early on he showed unnatural abilities to withstand trauma and pain. It was noted that his original cybernetics were both legs at the hip, and left arm at the shoulder while the right was replaced at the bicep. Later on, his spine was reinforced with an external one grafted directly to the bone along with a neural interface to assist his integration with the then new age infantry armor. Any and all dates of these procedures were redacted, as where the locations they were conducted. The only real data she could find was from one of the original surgeries on him which held the numbers 20-39 -10-15-2038, the exact numbers he had punched into the keypad on the Vault to open it. Later references to those numbers had the second set as a date, but nothing on the first two.

Death was the undisputed leader of the Horsemen, but though he fought relentlessly in the name of the Republic during the war, afterwards when the freedom of his team was on the line, he simply did nothing. He surrendered as ordered and the others followed. The question Ginny couldn't get out of her mind was why.

"Interesting read?" a voice behind her made her jump in surprise.

"What the fuck?" she screamed.

It was a good thing the observation room was sound proofed. Her scream could have resulted in a botched effort in the procedure below. But the surgeons simply went on like nothing was happening, unable to hear or see what was happening above them.

Behind her and two rows back sat the now fully armored Death, slightly craning his head to read over her shoulder. His grizzly skull face was covered by a stone-grey mask that too somewhat mimicked a skull with three teeth engraved with long lines that led up to the two socket-like visors. Yet this was hardly visible as he wore a black hood that shrouded it.

"I......I didn't hear you come in." Ginny tried to regain her composure.

"I wouldn't be good at what I do if you did, now would I?" his horrible and growly voice replied. "I hope Aida's precious files have been informative to you?"

"Informative?" Ginny began.   "More like horrifying. The things you four endured, no one should have had to go through what you all did even in that day and age."

"It was a different time," he actually responded on the subject to her amazement, "You have to understand that the times called for such drastic measures. Humanity was hurtling down to a point of no return unless major change was to happen. The Republic came about because of man's inability to make the necessary changes. I was created in the wake of violent resistance. The others were brought in as I couldn't do it alone."

"I get that part, but why didn't you fight the charges your own people laid on you after the war was over?" Ginny countered.

"After reading that entire file, that is the first question you ask of me?" Death seemed amused. "You are an interesting specimen, Miss Agefor."

"It is one of many," she replied, "but it is the one that I would most like to hear the answer to."

"Because the charges were warranted, though so were our actions during the war," Death replied calmly. "No one wanted to know how we went about winning each battle, they only cared that we won. We were weapons created to bring about the hardest changes needed to unite mankind. We were fighting to create a utopia; the problem was that the utopia we fought for had no place for monsters like us. I knew it, and so did the others. It was either be put down like dogs or face the long cold slumber. As a group, they chose the slumber; my fate turned out to be something crueler."

"So, they came up with the cryogenics process just for you?" Ginny asked.

"I got wind of the Vault plans near the end of the war," he replied quite nonchalantly. "When Aida retrieved the plans for me, it was apparent who it was being designed to house."

"But why the freezer?"

"One doesn't throw away such effective weapons, my dear." She could hear the resentment in his voice. "They simply put them away in a handy place of storage to be easily ready for the next time they are needed."

"That is a violation of your Human rights!" Ginny exclaimed.

"I lost my humanity long before the fighting started, it made me a more effective killing machine. The others cast theirs off during the war little by little maybe as a result of exposure to me, or maybe because of the harshness of our missions. All I know is that the longer the fighting went, the more they became like me."

Ginny was quiet for a moment. Not only was she contemplating his words, but she was also looking to maximize her time with this elusive person when he was being so forthcoming. Here was the most ruthless killer in the history of mankind and he was chatting with her like they were siblings catching up on old times.

"The sword," Ginny said after a brief pause. "What is the deal with the sword?"

"Katana," Death corrected her. He unstrapped it from his back and showed her in its Saya, though kept it out of her reach. "And it is probably the oldest object on this station, even making me look young in comparison. Long ago it had the name of Totsuka-no-Tsurugi, though now under my ownership it has the name of the Demon Blade."

"I've heard of this, though I've thought it was all just a fairy tale." She was in awe at the sheer history involved with such a blade. "How old is it? 1300, 1400 years old?"

"It is impossible to date; it holds certain traits that make it near impossible to evaluate." His thumb rubbed the tsuba as if he meant to draw it. "The collector I.... let's say retrieved it from, thought it to be at least between 1300 and 1350 years old from today's time."

"And what are these traits you speak of?" Ginny asked, though her interest had faded from him and fixated on the sheathed blade. In her mind, a whisper of a voice was calling her, telling her to reach out and draw the blade. Over and over, it called her name and she became lost in a daze until he quickly pulled the katana away and placed it where it had been attached to his back previously.

"The exact trait you just experienced." Death snapped his finger in front of her face to bring her out of her daze. "No living human can withstand its call, nor break its spell once the blade is drawn. Legend has it that it demands blood from its wielder, and it doesn't care whether the blood comes from an enemy or its owner."

"So…. why are you able to hold it without effect?" she stammered, emerging from a fog in her mind.

"Like I said before," he replied earnestly, "I stopped being human long, long ago. Maybe my internal demons are stronger than those trapped within the steel of the blade, or maybe its all bullshit. Either or, it makes for a hell of a dissuading factor when confronted by an aggressor."

"Indeed," Ginny said, rubbing her eyes.

 Maybe what happened was just her being over tired. A waking dream, that had to be it. None of that could have been real, but then her mind went back to the transfer of his brain to this new body and specifically the black mist that eventually emerged right before the transfer started. His own personal demons; those words made her imagination soar uncontrollably.

"Go get some rest, Miss Agefor." Death patter her on the shoulder with a surprisingly light touch. "Tomorrow will bring a new day, and I will still be around to answer your questions."

"Why are you being so open now?" she asked, slowly getting up to leave while gathering her files. "I mean, you talk to no one for 400 years and now chat with me like we are best friends. I don't get it."

"Events of the past month or so have caused me to do a great deal of self reflection. In some ways, my past has caught up with me, and the person those three soldiers need to lead them doesn't exist. Maybe he hasn't for centuries. I died inside the day I couldn't join them, and I ran away from everything I was because of that pain. Why am I being open with you? Maybe its because they won't be the only one adjusting to things when they wake, or maybe it is my repentance for a life full of sin, an ask of forgiveness from the Demon of the Republic."

"Umm, okay." Ginny was more puzzled before.

"Sleep well, Miss Agefor." He effortlessly jumped over multiple rows of seats to the front as he looked down on the procedure below. "I assure you that moving forward, I will provide you with any answers you may need, and more."

///

Waypoint Station, DeSa Armory, Surgical Recovery Room, Level 1

It was a brightly lit room, circular in design with tubes built into the walls every four feet which held hyperbaric chambers for accelerated recovery from procedures. As Death entered the room, it was empty save for one patient off to his left. The android attendant chastised him for being in a clean room, but he ignored its nattering for him to leave. Walking past it, he flashed an ID badge with a VIP status slightly less than the CEO but with enough clout that the droid ceased its chatter.

Approaching the tube, he could see the shortly cropped head of his youngest associate, Agony. She would be livid they cut her near three-foot-long locks. But as he read her medical chart, her hair would be the least of the adjustments she would need to make upon awakening.

Agony had been the first into surgery and surprisingly the last out. His datalink told him that they were wrapping up on War and Fear concurrently in recovery watch, so in a half hour or so this room would be a hive of activity. And when it would be that busy, there would be no credentials that would allow him to remain with his team, so this short visit would have to satiate his curiosity.

Still encased in his old armor, Death was due in a few hours to the weapons facility to be fitted for his new set up. There, he would undergo testing for a few days before being released while the other Horsemen were slowly being brought out of their medicated comas. He wondered how they would react to the news 400 years had passed, and how they would mentally deal with being light years from Earth on top of it. Lesser people might be driven mad from what was about to happen, but he had little doubt his team would adapt without issue.

Placing his armored hand on the capsule which held Agony, he closed his eyes to accept the wave of memories that washed upon him being so close to his lost comrade. She was young, energetic, unpredictable, and a cultured temperament like nothing he had ever seen before. She was Yakuza groomed, but even the legendary crime family could not keep reins on such a wild animal. Yet despite the past that brought her to the Horsemen, it was her engaging smile that he treasured the most. The power behind it was both warming and fearsome; she was the fiercest of creatures who used her looks to disarm her prey before striking. If they were lucky, she would kill them quickly. As for the others, well that was how she earned the name Agony.

"Himiko," he whispered as he watched her chest rise and fall through the portal.

"Miss Miko must not be roused from her sleep," the android chastised him for being so close to the hyperbaric capsule.

"Her name is Agony." He turned to the robot, then began to walk out of the room. "None of you have earned the right to call her anything else."

4

Waypoint Station, DeSa Armory, Research and Development Laboratory, Level 1

It had been almost three weeks since the surgeries were complete, and the three Horsemen were now fully awake. Recovering from such invasive surgeries was one thing, but they also were dealing with the knowledge that over four hundred years had passed since entering the cryo-facility. To say it caught them off guard would be an understatement.

Ginny had elected herself to be the one to break the news, and the one who would stand alongside them as they pushed through the pain of recovery. At first, there had been the skepticism and denial at what they were being told, though she could tell when they looked around the room the technology within it reinforced what Ginny was telling them to be true. It was Agony that struggled to speak first, and it was her question that was the most expected, but the hardest one to answer.

Agony was the smallest one, and maybe the toughest. Her surgeries had been the most extensive, and she was recovering the slowest out of the three. She kept her right arm wrapped around her midsection, with her hand firmly against the metal half abdomen she now had. Before the freezing, it was only her arms and legs that had been replaced. Now she was over half machine, and Ginny could see that it had left her questioning more than the time passed.

Both her legs had been fully amputated to the hip joint, with much of the left side of her hip up to just beneath her left breast replaced too. Her arms were both amputated completely too, with the mechanical cybernetics starting at her shoulders, including her collar bone too. Agony's spine had also been replaced by a prosthetic one, though that was a commonplace surgery nowadays, but it was covered with a carbon/ titanium weave cover that was attached directly to the new spine and reached up all the way to the base of her skull. Clothed as they all were in complete black skin tight body suits that left only their feet, hands, and head exposed, she was constantly rubbing her recently shaven head as she sat semi curled up in her wheelchair.

There was a look of defiance in her eyes, a fire that all the pain inflicted on her couldn't diminish. As Ginny had figured, Agony was the firecracker of the group. Though physically unable to push her weight around, it was only she who spoke anything in this orientation phase of the day.

"Where is the Commander?" she croaked, pissed off that her voice wouldn't work.

"That is a rather long story, Miss Miko," Ginny replied. "But he is fine, though he isn't here at the moment."

"Why?" she blinked angrily.

"I can't tell you why he isn't here at the moment," Ginny answered quickly. "I have personally paged him a number of times since you've all been awake. He hasn't replied yet."

"No," Agony said as she struggled to sit straight, but gave up remaining curled up. "Why did you cut my fucking hair!" she growled. "It hadn't been cut since I was a child, doing so is an affront to my heritage."

"Stop," Fear cut her off. "Stop with the bullshit. Now is not the time or the place."

"They cut my hair!" she turned and snarled at her compatriot. "They cut my fucking hair!"

"We get it, but under the circumstances I think we need to focus on more important things," Fear replied.

"I asked the more important thing, and the little bitch here couldn't tell me where Big D is, so I asked the second most important question," Agony argued.

"The second most important thing is your hair?" War chimed in. "Bah! You always were the tiny princess." She laughed out loud, then recoiled from the pain of the effort.

"Watch that the tiny princess doesn't sneak into your room while you are sleeping and shove a knife into your...."

"That's enough!" Ginny hollered, trying to bring the argument to a close. "What answers can I provide for you all to help move this conversation forward?"

"Maybe actually tell me why you cut my damn hair, Gaijin," Agony tried muttering under her breath but did so a bit too loud.

"Your hair was cut because one of the many procedures you went through was to attach the uplink that drives your cybernetic enhancements to your brain," Ginny almost yelled the answer a few feet away from Agony in a scolding tone. "The uplink also allows you to connect with your bio-armor for missions when you are well enough to be medically cleared to go on. Linford's head was shaved too, and so was Hekla's because they went through the same damn surgery!"

"You didn't have to yell," Agony grumbled meekly, looking away from Ginny who still stared with annoyance at her.

"I would like to know why the Commander wasn't in recovery like us?" Fear actually put his hand up like a school child before speaking. "I've watched during all of our physical therapy sessions and he has been nowhere to be found."

"The cryogenic process took a lot out of us all," War added as she flexed her cybernetic arms, "So why isn't he in rehab too?"

"Because he was never frozen," Ginny revealed at last, though she was hoping he would have been here to tell them. "From what I have been privy to, he was the last to endure the procedure when something went awry. They were unable to put him under, though I don't know why."

There was a look of shock that washed over all three of them, a slight pain knowing they had endured something horrible while one of their family had not. It was an emotional slap in the face, and it hit harder to Agony then it did the other two.

"Miss Agefor?" Fear asked again with his strange accent. With his Jamaican heritage she expected it to sound much like it should, but his voice resonated in a deep timbre with an almost British accent. "So, if what you've been telling us is true, then after four hundred years he is still alive? That isn't possible."

"I assure you, he is still alive, Linford." She smiled at him. "I have had the rather…. unique privilege of having a conversation with him. It was chilling, surreal, and enlightening all the same time."

"Ha!" War laughed again. "The wench lies! The Commander doesn't have conversations with people!"

"I can only imagine the toll that four hundred years of life has taken on him," Ginny responded to the mockery. "I would think that he has changed a great deal from the man you knew, though he does still carry that sword with him."

This made Fear sit up straight and had him exchanging looks with War and Agony quickly. It was the first bit of evidence they were given that Death indeed was still around, and it gave them a bit of a jump to their emotional trauma.

"That blade!" he grinned which was frightening in itself. "Only he would still be able to hold onto that blade!"

"It's called a katana, fucktard." Agony rolled her eyes at his excitement. "And of course, he still has it, who in the hell would be able to take it away from him?"

"It is from the other side!" Fear explained to Ginny with great effort. "Many times, I heard the voices trapped within the forged metal call to me when I was near it. There are souls trapped in that blade, held tight by darkness and fed with blood. I think it was made with some major Juju, though I don't know what kind. It is beyond my voodoo."

"So now you believe me?" Ginny asked the group with sarcasm. "Now we have that nailed down, I get to really blow your minds."

"Will you tell us why we got these matching tights on?" Fear asked, pulling at his bodysuit.

"Pressure suits, not tights." Ginny smiled, opening her blouse up just below her neck to reveal she too was wearing one. "Everyone aboard wears one, it is mandatory."

"Aboard what?" War perked up a bit more. "We in Earth orbit or something?" she chuckled in jest.

"Orbit, yes," Ginny answered with a straight face. "But not in Earth's orbit. We are twelve light years away from Earth, in orbit of Dawn, in the Teegarden system."

"Bullshit," Agony griped.

Ginny didn't argue, she just pressed a button on her datapad which darkened the room and engaged a holographic display.

On it was the red dwarf Teegarden, shining in the distance and reflecting off the hull of Waypoint as it sat in high orbit over the lush green planet of Dawn. Even a novice could see they weren't looking at Earth. There were five very large continents surrounded by four major oceans. The recognizable shapes of North America, Europe, Africa, and so forth were not there. They were struck hard by the new reality that their home was so far away it hurt to think about it.

"Fuck. My. Life." Agony muttered.

"Glorious!" whispered Fear.

"And the Vikings found a whole new world to conquer." War sat up proudly.

It was an unusual response from an unusual woman. Even in her wheelchair, War was physically intimidating. Her Icelandic Viking heritage shone through from her accent to her actions. Born a soldier, she would always be one at heart so why would she talk like anything but one. Oceans were only a minor obstacle to be crossed, and land was just land, no matter what planet it was on. It occurred to Ginny that War was able to process things differently than the others, able to compartmentalize the trivial things to keep moving forward. Finish the mission, everything else didn't matter; but the issue was that none of them knew the mission yet, so how long could she still operate as if she did?

"Each of you will go through a neural instruction session." Ginny ended the presentation and turned the lights back on. "This will be a direct information upload to your neural link to catch you all up with what you have missed. Its going to hurt, but when its over we can sit down again to answer all the questions you still may have. And once that's done, I can start briefing you on the mission while you finish your rehab."

"There's a mission?" War asked with almost an excited tone in her voice.

"That is why they took you out of the ice," Ginny said as she opened the door to let the nurses enter to attend to the three of them. "If there wasn't a mission, we wouldn't be having this lovely chat."

///

It took a few more weeks, but finally the three of them were finally able to almost resemble the fierce soldiers they once were. War was the first to adapt to her new cybernetic prosthesis, and it frustrated Agony to no end that she did. War was so physically gifted that there was little that she couldn't adapt to with ease. Fear, well he was a different man. He adapted to anything simply because of his malleable personality. The islands raised him to roll with what life threw at him, and he did with shocking ease.

But it was Agony that failed to recapture her inner fury that made her one of the most formidable warriors to ever enter battle. Before her augmentation, she had been cold and focused. But after the augmentation, the cybernetics had caused her much pain and discomfort, pain that no number of painkillers could remedy. Instead of shrivelling up in a ball and hiding from what had happened, Agony reinvented herself. Letting the pain drive her, she honed herself into the most vicious of fighters who looked to inflict on her enemies the same pain she felt every waking moment, hence how she was given her name, Agony.

Now was a different story, and her adaptation to the much more extensive cybernetics was not a physical one, but a mental one. The pain that she used to literally define herself was gone, leaving her empty and confused. Better technology and even better surgeons made the connections to her machine parts seamless, leaving the anger and pain to remain in the cryo-pod to sleep for eternity while she was awake to face a new life. Her problem was how to move forward. The others seemed to have no problem with it, so why did she?

Agony remained quiet since the introduction process had begun. Her mind was sharp, and absorbing the direct neural learning was a simple task; knowing that everything she knew to be real had drastically changed was not so simple. Agony took her time adjusting to everything, watching everyone closely and listening to all conversations of the doctors around her. Any time there was an update given about the group it was the same, War and Fear were almost ready for action; how close she was could be anyone's guess.

Even if she wasn't ready to be out in the field, Agony felt the push from the higher ups to make it happen. From what she gathered, they had been given a high priority contract and each day they were here was another day the mission wasn't being fulfilled. Before it was about duty, now it was about money. In her sleep, she had transitioned from soldier to mercenary; yet another change she wasn't too sure about.

And then there was their Commander, Death. As the weeks passed, there was still no sign of him. Every question of his whereabouts was met with nervous looks by the nurses and techs that spent shift after shift with her. Agony almost felt bad she didn't learn their names, but attachment wasn't her thing. After all, the last thing she got attached to was MIA, and no one seemed to want to tell her why.

Ginny was a breath of fresh air, and that was a bit of a surprise to Agony. At first, she hated the liaison to DeSa that had been assigned to them. But as time rolled on the woman showed actual concern over how Agony was adjusting to things. Ginny even snuck her out of the DeSa facility for a few hours to a Salon in the downtown region of Waypoint to have her hair regrown. The fact they could even do that blew Agony's mind, yet it took less than a half hour to have her hair regenerated to its former length down to her belt. Ginny even convinced her to dye it. Agony eventually decided upon an Ocean Blue color which she loved but wouldn't admit.

Ginny was the only one who treated them like people, not like pieces of hardware as the others did. Right from the start, Ginny had called them by their real names, something that only the Commander had done previously. And though she was a far cry from the young Japanese woman that used to be Miko, it was still nice to be called a human name.

Agony pondered much of this as she was in a room called the Armory where she was being fitted for her Stage 2 Armor as the android assistants called it. In reality, it was a replacement for the pressure suit she was currently wearing, along with being the soft flexible layer of armor worn beneath the heavy Battle Armor she gazed upon within its glass case. Over the last week, they had been wearing motion capture jumpsuits to track their movements as they trained in close combat, at the firing range – which was all in virtual reality -, and on which weapons they chose to wield. Some would be integrated to the suits, some they would carry with them.

Hers was a heavy, yet feminine sculpted, and segmented piece of artwork. Each joint was left exposed, which meant her Stage 2 Armor would be more reinforced than the others' to ensure she had free movement to fight naturally as she had been trained to as a child. Boots were ankle high, then the shin/ calf guards went only knee high, though they did have a half octagon shape that covered the knee cap. Thigh guards were free of the groin, though extended up the sides of her hip. The 'armored panties' as she called them rode only hip high which made her laugh. There was a thinner and flexible plate that covered her abdomen and her back which gave her a high measure of free movement. Other than a more solid and segmented spinal guard, she was pleased with this part of the design.

Her chest piece did not have protruding breasts, so she was happy she didn't have to stab the designers for the usual sexist thoughts on women's armor. It did have a curve from abdomen to neck, but it was more angular to deflect any strikes from penetrating rather than match the female form.

The upper body was free at the shoulder joints and neck and came only as low as the bottom of her rib cage on the sides. Again, it was designed with maximum protection and movement in mind. The arms were in three smooth segments: shoulder caps, bicep, and forearms. The hands were flexible weave gloves with a cover on the top of the hand and each segment of the fingers and thumb. To her delight, the right forearm had a dagger launcher while the left had a retractable two-foot katana in it.

That left her favorite part, the helmet. It had a low chin, but a smooth curve from that mark to the top of her head with the entire face being armored visor. Within it was a remarkable heads up display that made her giddy with anticipation to try out. But that wasn't the best part. Its shape was almost like a comma facing sideways, the tail stuck out from the back of her head by six or seven inches. From that crest hung what at first she thought to be fake hair that fell to waist length. After closer inspection they were half inch-thick flexible tubes tipped with armor piercing blades that she could control like tentacles through her neural chip when inside, giving her a dozen extra ways to strike her opponent. This is what a fighting woman's armor should be, efficient and deadly.

Her Stage 2 Armor was less detailed. It too had thin plates of armor to cover the vitals like chest, abs, spine, crotch, etc. The difference was the joints, which were thicker to accommodate for the 'soft' spots in her actual armor that would actually take time to get used to. And after what seemed like an eternity of being measured and sized by a half dozen androids, she was advised to strip off her pressure suit to change into this suit. Standing naked in front of a mirror for the first time since waking up, Agony was able to see the total extent of the changes to her body.

Her hands instinctively embraced the surfaces of the carbon/titanium arms and torso plates. She felt the cool surfaces through her cybernetic hands and the metallic skin at the same time which sent chills up her spine. As she twisted her torso back and forth, again she was caught off guard how well the cybernetics moved with her, almost like they were painted on flesh. Technology had come such a long way since her days fighting on the front lines of the Revolutionary War. Back then she felt like a monster, now she felt almost human.

"If I was four hundred years old and had an ass like that, I think I would have a bit bigger smile!" a familiar voice said from the doorway.

"I thought these androids said the room was to be locked for this process," Agony said with a wry smile. "How did you get in, Ginny?"

"Master Key." Ginny smiled, holding up her pass card that hung from her neck. "Gets me in all the rooms but the executive offices in this building."

"I'll have to remember to steal that from you later," she mumbled, reaching for the Stage 2 Armor on the bench beside her. "Give a girl a hand?"

It was nice to have a real person help her instead of the machines. It made her feel more normal and less like one of the robots that were always traipsing around the facility.

Ginny helped her climb into and pull up the suit that reminded Agony of a thicker, bulkier version of a diving dry suit. When she had her arms and head in, she looked in the mirror to see it was hanging loose on her body and wide open at the front.

"Is this right?" she looked at Ginny in confusion.

Ginny smiled, then reached up to press the link at the collar which rose up to her jaw into her neural link and Agony felt an instant pressure cascade through her entire body. It was like someone opened her skin at the neck and poured cold water into her.

"Now think about it closing up," Ginny told her as they both looked in the mirror.

Agony closed her eyes, and in her mind told the suit to close itself up. Upon feeling movement, she opened her eyes to see it zipping itself up without a zipper to leave no seam whatsoever. Once completed, the whole suit contracted to form fit her body like a second skin. What had previously been socks now conformed to her individual toes. The same went for the mitts that she had her hands in, within an instant they became skin-tight gloves. Agony's jaw dropped in amazement.

"If you think that is cool, then wait until you try this," Ginny smiled.

Running her index finger up Agony's left side, she giggled as Agony responded by arching her body away from the tickling sensation before realizing that the action was being done through a quarter inch of flexible metal fabric.

"What the actual fuck?" Agony cried out. "How is that.... I mean, that doesn't make sense!"

"The same technology that goes into the cybernetic limbs and skin grafts on your body went into this," Ginny explained. "It all connects to you through that connection in the back of your neck which allows this to be a second skin of sorts. How sensitive you make it is up to you but seeing as your entire body is covered in this it beats the lack of feedback these pressure suits have."

"Can I ask you something?" Agony said as she poked herself randomly to test out the suit.

"I told you why we cut your hair, and no I don't know where Death is," Ginny sighed in response.

"No, that's not it," Agony said, still testing the suit out in the mirror. "I wanted to know between the pressure suits and these things, how do you have sex? Or is that not a thing anymore?"

"I guess the info blast didn't cover that little detail," Ginny replied while blushing at the forwardness of the question. "Most apartments have a pressurized room where one can use the bathroom, shower, and of course have sex."

"You people fuck in the shower instead of the bed?" Agony turned to Ginny with a definite look of exasperation on her face. "I mean, shower sex is good, but a girl needs to have room to play."

"Well, if you feel brave enough, I guess some people do ignore the warnings and do it wherever they can," Ginny answered sheepishly. "But to take such an enormous risk for something as minor as sex is beyond my comprehension. Pinholes and loss of atmosphere can and do happen on a daily basis in orbit. If you were in the wrong place at the wrong time….it just is an unnecessary risk, that's all."

"Only if you aren't doing it right." Agony smiled as she walked past Ginny to the door. "And just for the record, your ass is pretty nice from my point of view too, if you don't mind me saying."

Agony left her new friend in the Armory blushing and at a loss for words. It was time to head back to training and her thoughts. Though she adored the company, she still needed time to get to know herself in this new life. Once she was successful, then she could look at her relationships closer. Maybe in this new life she could love someone; maybe in this life she could love herself. What a novel thought, but at least it was something to strive for.

///

Waypoint Station, Coat of Arms Bar, Legion Territory, Level 3

He sat in his usual booth in the back corner by himself as usual. The rest of the patrons knew to leave him well enough alone and the old beat up seat was far removed from the normal merriment that it kept him isolated. He liked it that way. It was for the better, even in a room full of mercenaries they were mercifully unaware of the killer that sat amongst them. Yet even tucked away in the back corner, his mere presence drew a cautious cloud over the usual rowdy crowd. Every loud cheer, every raised voice, and every attempt at starting a fight drew a cautious eye to the man in the shadows. It was how he got the moniker years back, and it kept the locals on their toes. The Shadowman was in tonight, which meant everyone better watch their back.

But Death could care less about what they thought and was too deep in thought to even pay the slightest attention to what was happening around him. Draped in a thick black hooded cloak, he kept his old armored mask to cover his new 'face' to keep the commotion it would cause at a minimum. His mask was now an antique as his new armor was complete and sitting in his stall in the docks ready to be worn. And though he still had his own AI running diagnostics and rewriting the DeSa software, he was amazed at the way it turned out.

It was a three-piece set up. First the Stage 2 Armor, which he was wearing beneath his cloak, which was made up of a heavier carbon/ titanium weave than most with only extra plating on the spine and chest unlike any other made. The second was the thicker but still flexible torso section. Painted gloss black, it wore like an early twentieth century men's swimsuit, shoulder straps and all. It added an extra layer of protection to his entire torso while giving him the utmost movement possible. Then there was the third layer, the armor itself. Boots hinged at the ankle and linked to the lower leg armor gave him excellent range of movement. Upper legs were segmented separate from the lower, and attached direct to the Stage 2 Armor, not the torso. From there, there was little more until his chest guard. Covering the pectoral region only, the three-inch-thick plating sloped up to his neck to deflect any incoming fire. Shoulder pauldrons were layered and spiked with a slight extra piece beneath to barely cover the bicep. This left the massive forearm armor which was quite the ingenious set up.

His left arm was less bulky, which meant he would have to adjust his programming to wield his sword left-handed now. But from past the elbow to the hand itself was a five-inch block of carbon/ titanium with his computer and comms built into the underside of the forearm. The right side was a bit larger and had a Gatling style railgun that could fire a hundred rounds per second from its small diameter barrels. The forearm contained almost a million metal pellets that was the normal non-explosive rounds for railgun technology. That meant he could take a direct hit to the arm with no collateral damage to his ammo supply.

His back was covered by segmented shoulder blade guards, linked to a heavy spine cover that attached to the torso armor from the base of his skull down to his tail bone with two-inch spikes lining the whole apparatus. And his helmet, well that was a special piece of design. Detail on the face was minimal, with a smooth black portion that covered his mouth, nose, and eyes that angled back to his ears. From there, it was all armor plate. Cheek panels stuck out and connected with an angle panel that went from the bridge of the nose all the way the back of his head to hang behind the head to guard the neck with its pointed shape that stuck out about four inches. Two other plates connected at his brow, swept around his head increasing in size and past the back of the helmet like flat dragon horns. The whole shape made it look like a dragon devouring the black face plate.

He had almost chuckled as it was being set up in the docks as there were comments on how it just standing there gave people the creeps. Its sharp contrast between gloss black and matte charcoal grey gave it an unearthly look that the design itself couldn't do alone. Once donned, he would be more lethal than ever before. He was quickly becoming his namesake once more. It would be interesting to see how he was received by his fellow Horsemen, and the Legion.

Sounds of troops marching in formation echoed in the tavern, the rumble of heavy machinery and tanks rattled the floors. This was not the upper levels of Waypoint. Here, the Legion was everything and it showed. Troop movements, guard postings, weapon and armor merchants, and of course the docks themselves. The Legion was everything here; it was the police, the army, station security, privateer soldiers for hire, and so much more. If there was anything that could rival the power of some of the most profitable companies, it was the Legion. And it was in the middle of one of the busier times of the day on this level that Death had isolated himself, finding himself pulled to another time and place. Memories of a lifetime long forgotten began to rear their ugly selves. His mind was caught in turmoil, and even as he sat in the darkness he was haunted by the ghostly echoes of gunfire and the rotten stench of spilled blood.

Swept away from the present, he found himself standing on the cold tundra of the southern front of Moscow. Smoke held the battlefield like a thick morning fog, its acrid stench of burnt metal and flesh permeated the best of helmet filters. It rained fire and snow from the sky as embers and sparks from the unyielding assault on the last bastion of Russian resistance mixed with the elements to create a beautiful yet terrifying sight for all to see. Large rounds flung from the oversized railguns attached to the armored hover tanks shrieked as they tore through the air. The rounds disappeared into the smoke only to light up in the distance where they struck with explosive results.

It was a slow pace of a battle, but his task was to minimize casualties and just break through to the Kremlin as fast as possible. Minimize casualties; they were the most foolish orders he had ever received in his service to the Republic. Russian officials had whipped their forces up into a feverish trance, fighting tooth and nail to hold back the more dominant forces of the Republic from advancing further. It was a valiant, but ultimately foolish effort. All it was doing was costing more lives every minute the battle dragged on, and the dead cried out to him as they lay scattered across the battlefield.

This was his curse; the cost of dying then coming back to life. Death was burdened by a link to the recently deceased, and on a battlefield, there was no escape from the screams. He tried his best to ignore it, but it was a never-ending cacophony of madness assaulting his senses. If the process of his creation to the monster he was hadn't cost him his humanity, this surely would drive what little remained away.

But throughout his suffering in silence, the battle carried on. Beside him, War rode in the open turret of a two-barrel railgun hover tank, banging on the heavy shielding with her fists in glee as she laughed like a maniacal schoolgirl every time the machine fired. Her warrior heritage showed true as she loved every second of the fight, Death even thought there were a few times she might get out of the tank and roll around in the rivers of blood just to satiate her lust for battle. As the tank passed him, she stopped her joyful exuberance to salute him, then continued thereafter.

Fear sauntered behind Death at his usual slow pace. In fact, Death wasn't truly sure that the Jamaican even moved his feet as he seemed to float across the battlefield. Though they were a tight unit, the Voodoo Priest made him nervous. The man changed to a monster at the outset of a battle, that wide and frightening grin became plastered on his face as he fought through the masses, conversing with the spirits of the afterlife the whole time. Having him around was unsettling but had a larger effect on the enemy forces than he did on theirs. When Fear marched forward, the enemy lines broke. The man's reputation - as made up as much of it was – had enemy forces scatter when he got close.

As for Agony, well one just had to listen to the screams of the enemy troops to find her. When she finally did appear, she was covered in blood and looking for a fresh set of daggers to stock up on before heading out again. The four of them were more at home in warfare than anywhere else; it seemed the Republic had created the perfect soldiers for this war of wars.

Death listened to himself bark orders as if he was deep in a canyon and his voice was echoing off the rock walls. The nanites were able to help retrieve the memories from deep in his sub-consciousness, but they were unable to keep the vision clear the whole way. His brain was impressive for being able to store this much after so many years, it was a shock much more wasn't degraded as the centuries rolled by.

Eventually the gunfire and smoke faded, and his eyes refocussed on the here and now. Where once a battlefield had been laid out before him, a seedy bar now stood. In a very seamless, yet unsettling transition he was back where he was before the memory overrode his senses. Death was relieved he didn't react to the stimulus of the all too real recollection. He slowly unclenched his fists, glancing around to see if anyone had noticed his little lapse into memory lane. But as usual, the other patrons left him to his dark corner; it was in their best interests to leave the monster that lurked in the shadows be. At least most of them felt this way.

His comm line rang, and when answered the last person he wanted to talk to was on the line, Aida.

"Where are you?" she snarled at him. "Your team is asking for you. As their leader, don't you think your place is here, with them?"

"I happen to be planning the mission," Death replied in his toneless voice, "Or would you have me waste billions of dollars of legal fees, cybernetics, and precious time to just drop down there and wing it?"

"Planning?" Aida asked again. "In a bar?"

"I don't exactly have a home, and the tables are big enough to plan an entire war out on," Death countered. "Does it matter that it happens to be in a bar? Not like I fucking drink or anything."

"Fine, be a prick about this. Just know that Slovis is starting to press about when the team will be ready to go."

"That's why I'm planning now, and you are rehabbing them. It's called doing one's job, so get my team ready and I'll be ready to clean up the mess on Horizon when you're done."

"As always, it's been a pleasure talking to you," Aida grumbled as she ended the call.

"Bitch," Death replied, though no one was there to hear.

He rubbed his 'face' with his right hand. It surprised him that he still did such actions to express frustration and tiredness even though his body felt neither fatigue nor needed sleep. Habits were engrained in all humans, and in some cases, he was still human. Not much, but maybe still a little.

"I think you need to catch up on your sleep," a familiar voice muttered to him from the seat across from him in the booth.

Death looked up and saw a creature that appeared to be human but was anything but. Dressed in a dark grey suit, white shirt, and black tie – fashion straight out of 2010 or so – he was perfectly out of place in any surroundings. Dark black hair that was long enough to fall past his shoulders struck with a tint of blue in it, and skin that was a deep sun-kissed tan that very few humans would ever try to achieve due to cancer fears. But what most set him aside from the populace were his eyes. The two orbs of utter blackness that felt like they would swallow your soul surrounded by a thin ring of blue fire. Emanating god-like power, this entity chose to join him out of nowhere, and the bar took immediate notice to the fact that the Shadowman had company.

///

"Its been a few years," Death spoke calmly in his toneless voice to the man.

"Almost a hundred, but who's counting," the man chuckled. "I dig the upgrades."

"Why are you here?"

"You never were one for small talk," laughed the man. "So much like my younger self it scares me. Maybe one day we can sit and chat, one monster to another."

"What's your point?"

"I am fascinated by the recent happenings in your life. How exciting to have your friends join your journey at long last. Or are you afraid to face them? Maybe you think the leader they followed so trustingly is lost to the ages? We all change, time does have that affect on everything."

"Yet you remain the same," Death grumbled, unhappy his 'guest' was avoiding his questions. "But I guess the ravages of time are nothing to a Vampire."

"Who's a vampire?" the man jokingly looked about the tavern before returning his powerful gaze back on Death.

"So, you're not a vampire," Death spoke as his mind reeled trying to figure out what this creature was.

"Not a vampire." The man smiled. "They don't exist, just a myth. Werewolves however, now those are very real and very frightening. No, I am just someone who is interested in you and your friends. I am not a threat, nor will I interfere with anything in your life. Just think of me as an avid reader of your story, an enthusiastic fan, you could say."

"So, monsters intrigue you?" Death challenged.

"Life intrigues me, my dear Horseman," the man replied quickly. "Sometimes it is the beasts that lurk in the dark shadows, other times it might be those who search for answers at the cost of their very being, sometimes it is the hopeless cause that needs a light to find it's way, and then there are times that certain events happen to create unique beings like you and I. We share a kinship, whether you choose to believe me. Both of us shed our mortal coil to become what we are now."

"And what is that?"

"You could say Gods amongst men, but I don't think you will ever see yourself in that light," the man said, taking another sip of the coffee. "Let's just agree that we are more than those we share this life with."

"Easy for you to say," Death growled, "You can still pass for them. My flesh rotted away a long, long time ago. All that is left is a brain, machine, and something more."

"Your mistake is to believe I am flesh and blood which I will take as a complement," the visitor countered. "When I awakened in this form, my human body burned away. I can use my abilities to reform my atoms into anything I wish, though I am rather fond of this one. It is the one my beloved is rather attached to, so I must admit it is my favorite."

"Creatures like us can find love?"

"It is the soul that finds the connection, not the vessel it rides in. Even as clouded as your soul may be after all it has endured, maybe it is the warmth of friendship that will ignite the best in you again. Your family have awakened in a life they cannot comprehend. They are scared, going through the motions of a set of directives while searching for their place in all of it. They need a leader, someone who cares for them not just for their abilities. Take all the effort you put into your grand plan, and move some of it to taking care of them."

"And what do you know of my plans?" Death leaned forward.

"I know that it is revenge that drives you," the man smiled. "Revenge on those who took your family away from you, and the one who betrayed you the most. It takes a great deal of hatred to keep on track for four hundred years, such perseverance is legendary. Its too bad you can't do the one thing you need to do to keep them alive in the long run."

"And what does that mean?" Death sighed.

"That is for time for you to accept what you have become." The man looked at Death very seriously now. "It is time you become whole, not fractured as you are now. Four hundred years in isolation has done a number on you. Your team needs you, and you need them just as much. Stop being an ass and go to them."

"I need to become whole?" Death asked, not sure if he was understanding the half truths the man was telling him. "I just got a new body; I can't be any more complete than I am now."

"This coffee is shit," the man changed the subject quickly, looking around for the bartender. "Where did that waiter go?"

Death looked away from his guest for a mere moment, fooled by the distraction to look for the bartender who was right where he always was, behind the bar. As he returned his gaze to the seat across from him, it was now empty. Only the empty coffee mug remained along with a hint of the smell of soot.

"Fuck," Death muttered to himself. "That's four times the bastard has done this, and I still don't know his damn name."

Reaching across the table, he grabbed the mug to inspect it for clues. Using scanners built into his eyes, he searched for fingerprints or DNA fragments left behind, but there was nothing. It was almost like he had been visited by a ghost but listening to the murmurs in the tavern told him that the other patrons had seen the man in grey too. Shaking his head in defeat, he glanced inside the mug to see the remnants of unfinished coffee at the bottom with coffee grounds floating in it. For a moment, and just a fleeting one at that, the grounds spelled a word.

Aen.

"At least I have a name," he grumbled, sliding the mug to the end of the table to be picked up at the next passing of the waitress.

5

Waypoint Station, DeSa Armory, Research and Development Laboratory, Level 1

They had been cooped up for far too long, and Fear was going stir crazy. A lifetime ago, he had doctors and such paw at him in the days of the Republic's precious war. He hated it then and despised it more now. Maybe it bothered him because he too had his MD papers, a fact he used to hold against those who worked on his cybernetics. But now it was all over his head. Life had taken a giant leap forward, and even with the direct neural learning he wasn't up to date with the latest in medical practices.

It also could have been his well noted background in the black arts. Being a Voodoo Priest came with certain stigmas, ones that mainly erased his more educated past in one fell swoop. Before he had used this ignorance to his advantage. Being smarter than one's adversaries was always the perfect weapon. Now however, he was no longer the smartest man in the room although his IQ testing could prove otherwise. Fear had much to learn about this new life, though he wondered with the pending mission if he would have time to catch up.

The mission fascinated him. People in power never changed, no matter the point in time. In this case, the company had a new toy they couldn't play with and wanted whatever was causing the issue to be dealt with so things could go back to the way they were. Precious time had been spent foolishly up to this point, and the longer the Horsemen took in their recovery the harder those in charge began to push for them to be on active duty. It was obvious that his team's physical and mental health was not important to this Nowich-Paris corporation. They cared about one thing, the bottom line and that was being impacted every day the mission was left on hold.

Fear had heard a bit about a court injunction that allowed DeSa Armory all the time needed to make sure the Horsemen were up and running at full speed before being put in the field. He was curious that one little sheet of paper was keeping the big bad company from flexing its full might, though he knew full well they were using more indirect methods to push the pace of the recovery time.

He for one, was ready as he could be. Fitting for his battle Stage 2 Armor was done quickly, as was the brief tune up for his new armor. Using his input, he added color to the base color of gun metal to make the armor black with accents of blood red look like it was dripping off or splattered about the body. His fighting style was a mix of close combat and sniper, so the suit reflected the ability to move along with the need to carry larger ammo rounds. The mix of styles made for a unique set up.

There was nothing unusual about the armor itself, he left most of the design as common as any other set up. Knee-high armor-plated boots with reinforced shin guards, thigh and quad plates attached to the Stage 2 Armor directly for movement. Lower abdomen was segmented and joined with the ab plating, leaving the back lesser plated though the external spine cover linked the lower back with the upper body plates. The chest/ back plate was rather shapeless, though full of clip holders on the right side and over a dozen sheaths for throwing knives on the left side. Shoulder caps held one razor sharp bowie knife each with the handle facing down for quick access. Biceps were a half plate, but the forearms were thicker as both right and left had twin-barrel repeaters in each. His gloves were armored with the segmented design to mimic the look of skeleton hands.

He chose a full-face shield instead of the more common visor style helmet. With a visor that stretched from chin up to the top of his head, he had added the rather disturbing artwork to give it a 'face' that drew inspiration from his voodoo roots. An X represented each eye, and a hand drawn smile with stitches across its entire curve finished it off, all in white paint. It made it look like the head of a voodoo doll, giving him a uniqueness that would drive uneasiness to the other members of the Legion. He was smart enough to know that upon their activation they would be tested by their peers. Maybe he could use his look to dissuade some of that unwanted attention.

On top of the armor, Fear added an ankle length black cape to the ensemble. He had worn one most of his former life, and it would be a shame if such things had gone out of style since his refrigeration. In his mind, capes gave one a look of sinister importance. And seeing as it was made from a thin weave of carbon/ titanium, it gave his lesser armored backside a bit more protection.

After the armor got his final approval, Fear watched as it was loaded up and taken down to the docks where it would be stored for when they went on missions. There, the Four Horsemen' personal armory awaited them. It would be the point where the team gathered to set off for this mission, but the team was still not whole yet. Not a single one of them had laid eyes on the Commander yet.

"Ready to get out of here?" Ginny asked as the door slid open.

She had been a ray of sunshine for him, and from what he could ascertain for Agony as well. This heartless company could have assigned them almost anybody, yet they chose to pick her. It was a smart choice, though as good to them as she had been, Fear kept looking for strings attached. Companies like DeSa and Nowich-Paris always came with strings attached. That's how they operated.

"Just show me the way, my dear." He bowed in thanks to his host. "I assume we are meeting up with the Commander?"

"I don't know" Ginny said, handing him his Legion badge to clip onto his left breast. "I just figured I would take you three out for a drink. This is your Legion ID; it will get you into the lower levels and into all the bars and weapons shops associated with the clan of mercs. I got a temp one that will let me get into the popular watering hole with you all today, though I am sure it will cost me a few sneers by the locals."

"I can assure you," Fear said taking up stride beside her as they went down the halls to gather the others, "that given our past reputations, you won't be the only one getting judgemental looks."

"Shit, I didn't think of that." Ginny smacked herself in the forehead for her oversight. "I might just be walking you three into a fight."

"Now that sounds like fun!" War chimed in as the conversation had led into the commissary where the other two Horsemen were waiting. "Beer and brawling, what a better way to spend a…. hey what day is it?"

"Wednesday," Ginny answered with a smile at the ever-jubilant giant woman.

"What a way to spend a Wednesday!" War continued with a cheer, fist raised to the sky. "Let the challengers come, with my friends by my side I will always stand victorious!"

"At least the booze sounds like fun," Agony grumbled. "After all we've been through, I could do with getting shitfaced and not remembering the rest of the day."

"That's the spirit, child." Fear patted Agony on the head.

"Do that again and I will cut your nuts off," Agony growled. "If that is, they didn't castrate you already."

"Ah, the violent ramblings of the troubled youth of our little group," Fear sighed, looking at Ginny. "Pay her no head, she is much akin to the Wednesday Addams of our little family of killers."

"I see," Ginny said nervously.

"Does it bother you, my dear?" Fear asked.

"Does what bother me?" Ginny asked for clarification as they entered the lift to head down to the main level.

"That you are an attaché to a group of killers," Fear said as if it were just another comment. "Despite most of us having a sunny disposition, when you get to the heart of the matter it is exactly who we are. Give us a target and a weapon and we will do what we do best. It is the simple reason why we weren't executed by the Republic after the war was over. One does not throw away an effective weapon, ever."

"Is that how you see yourselves?" Ginny asked as the lift doors closed, and the car drifted down the tube. "Do you think of yourselves as just a weapon?"

"I am a Viking!" War shouted in the enclosed space with too much exuberance. "We are born to fight and conquer, so that is what I will do!"

"But Vikings were more than just that," Ginny replied as the doors opened to the grand lobby of DeSa. "Isn't there more to your world than fighting?"

"Beer!" War bellowed as the group left the lift, causing Fear and Agony to giggle. "And singing songs about war, celebrating victories, and rigorous sex!"

"You asked for it, just remember that." Agony poked Ginny's side as their chaperone blushed at the Nordic woman's reply.

Ginny decided to wait until they got into the waiting transport before asking any more questions. Upon exiting DeSa, the three Horsemen stopped to look about the busy rush of the downtown section of Waypoint station. Buildings all around for blocks in every direction stretched fifty or more stories upwards. High above that was a clear dome that let the light of the stars shine down onto the towers of glass. Off to the left, the planet of Dawn with its bright blue northern ocean dominated the view along with a bright blue dot in the distance which represented its twin, Horizon.

At street level, they watched as transports and cars screamed by at speeds that were just not possible in the world they came from. All about them, flashing lights of advertisements and company signs burned into their retinas. This was the future. Clean, fast, busy and fantastic to behold. Yet behind that wonderful façade lay the dark underbelly of the truth. The only thing that had changed since they went into the freezer was the technology. People never changed, and neither did their motives.

Fear, being the gentleman, allowed the three women to enter the strange looking floating tube with windows before he entered and slid the door shut. Instantly there was a feeling of unease as the magnetic drive kicked in and thrust them into the insanity of the day's traffic.

"Coat of Arms Bar," Ginny spoke to the driverless transport.

A beep and a green light confirmed her request, followed by a holographic map covering the front portal to show the route chosen to get to the destination from where they were. At the top right corner of the map was a timer with their ETA, showing a little more than eight minutes of travel time.

"This would be the same as travelling from old New York to Philadelphia, in your time," Ginny said proudly to show off the advanced speed of the driverless network. "Every vehicle is controlled by a main hub computer that regulates traffic and speed. Our travel speed will be around three hundred kilometers per hour."

"So, no crashes, unless the computer is in a bad mood," Agony responded.

"It is run by a Virtual Intelligence, not an AI," Ginny corrected. "It is a programmable intelligence that cannot exceed or change its mandates. This one only cares about speed and safety, and how to best maximize both without sacrificing either. On Earth, programs like this have flourished with no issues or accidents for over fifty years."

"This tavern you are taking us to," Fear changed the subject, "Is it here we will be meeting up with the commander?"

Ginny felt the others lean in eagerly, all eyes were waiting on her very word to answer the question. Despite her many attempts, Death had all but disappeared until contacting her last night. It was he who suggested the meeting place, and with the promise of taking his team to proper lodgings from there.

"Maybe, that's what his message said," Ginny reassured them.

"Where has he been?" Agony asked, looking unsure of herself. "Did we do something to anger him?"

"Those are questions you will have to ask him when we meet up," Ginny replied, wishing she could say more to dissuade that way of thinking. "I think after so long being by himself, he is struggling with being part of a team again."

"Isolation Disorder," Fear perked up. "It could be our fearless leader has simply forgotten how to associate with other living beings. A very logical prognosis, my dear."

The conversation paused as the transport merged onto the spiral freeway that took traffic from the main concourse level of Waypoint down to the other four levels. Their destination was the third level, where it was mostly cargo bays, weapons and armor vendors, and of course the Legion that inhabited the floor. It was very rare to see one of the soldiers for hire up on level 1, just as it was rare to see any aristocrats or businesspeople from the dome down in level 3. Here, the Horsemen were being taken from the spectacle of the dome to the much darker level of the Legion, a place they would be calling home from here on out.

"I assume, Miss Agefor," Fear spoke as he watched the transport exit on level 3, "that you have arranged for barracks for us."

"I am told it is already arranged," she smiled, "and that your accommodations will be much to your liking."

"No one likes barracks, ma'am," War countered. "But it is a place to bunk between missions so as long as there are three hots and a cot we will make do."

They passed the warehouse district and began to slow down as they entered a more open layout of buildings on either side of the street. Here they could see giant holographic advertisements playing for them to see as they flew twenty feet above street level. Some advertised military hardware, pleasures of the flesh, cybernetic upgrades – though a few looked a bit sketchy -, along with multiple food and drink establishments.

Yet they kept travelling past the buzz of the commercial section and straight into the Legion section. Here they looked upon vast domes which contained virtual training facilities, rows upon rows of Mech Tanks, heavy weapon transports, barracks, and platoons of troops marching in formation. Further down the road they could see larger buildings lining the outer curve of the station's body, and at the center of that cluster of buildings there was a bar, lit up brighter than any other building around it. They had arrived at their destination.

"Welcome to the Coat of Arms," Ginny announced as the transport stopped, then drifted softly down to street level. "I promised you all a drink, and I am told there is no better place for a soldier to relax than here."

"Finally," War sighed. "Too long has it been since the sweet nectar of the Gods has touched these lips. I assume the tab is on you?"

"It is on DeSa, so drink to your hearts content," Ginny giggled.

"You might regret that," Fear said sarcastically as they watched War almost sprint to the front door.

There, they were greeted by a pair of eight-foot-tall android guards in full battle armor that stepped to block entrance to the establishment as they approached.

"*Proper Legion Identification is required to enter.*" They spoke in a robotic drone in unison. "*Please form a single line and present your ID one at a time.*"

"Quite the exclusive club," muttered Agony as she formed up the tail of the line. "Must be a hell of a party inside."

///

Waypoint Station, Coat of Arms Bar, Legion Territory, Level 3

Once inside, the four found a table close to the bar. Their entrance was met with a few sideways looks, but that was more due to Ginny being with them than anything else. Once it was known that she too had a Legion ID, then the half full establishment went back to business as usual.

An hour in and a few rounds downed, War became more outgoing and jubilant, thus making the mood at the table a bit lighter. The Viking woman began shouting challenges to other tables for arm wrestling and drinking contests. At first these boasts were met with scoffs, but eventually accepted. She met all challengers – man, woman, or android – and won; Agony made more than a few credits betting on her teammate. Soon enough, War began to jump tables, joining her newfound comrades in drink and merriment.

Fear and Agony chose to be much quieter, sticking to their table along with Ginny who was cautiously nursing her oversized mug of ale. While the others had no trouble downing multiples of these 12-ounce self cooled mugs, she was not a drinker, so she waded slowly through it while enjoying the different atmosphere the Legion bar had to offer. She half heartedly listened to her tablemate's conversations while trying to tone out the loud laughter from War on the other side of the bar. Through all this, her eyes scanned the bar for any signs of the missing Horseman as the promised rendezvous time had come and gone. It was then she noticed they were being watched.

From the back-corner booth which lacked an overhead light, her eyes locked onto two glowing red eyes in peering out of the shadows. It quickly became obvious that this watcher was not paying attention to anything else but their table, and it creeped her out a bit. Things that glared out from the shadows tended to be the types of creatures that meant trouble.

"Excuse me," Ginny stopped the waitress as she was passing, "Can you tell me who is in the corner booth over there?"

"You are a bunch of newbies, aren't you?" the young woman replied without looking to where Ginny was referring to. "That's the Shadowman, and you don't fuck with him unless you want a one-way trip to the morgue." The waitress smiled nervously at Ginny, then resumed her rounds.

Ginny's thoughts were cut off by her chair being bumped. As she looked back, three hulking figures crowded around their table, one of them being War.

"This is my team," War blabbered, the effects of the booze beginning to take strong effect on her speech. "And this is Muck and Tremor!"

"I wanted to ask," the tall man named Muck inquired, "What kind of Call Sign is War? And what was your unit called again?"

"Don't say it, don't say it, don't say it," whispered Agony under her breath as she reached for her hidden daggers.

Ginny saw the look of urgency in both Fear and Agony's eyes at what was about to happen, and she prepared to hit the floor at a second's notice. War, of course, didn't hear or heed Agony's pleas and quickly answered her new drinking buddies, blissfully unaware at what such a simple answer would cause.

"The Four Horsemen, of course!" she bellowed boastfully.

At hearing those words, the entire bar went silent and the two 'friends' backed away from the joyful War who had no idea what was happening. All eyes glared at them; then one by one all the patrons rose with looks of menace on their faces. Before too long, the table was surrounded.

"I wonder what the bounty is on you Mooks," growled a six-and-a-half-foot armored and scarred man as he pushed his way to the front of the table. "Busting you War Criminals down will make me more of a legend than I am now."

"What are you saying?" War questioned as she looked around. "Why does it matter? A minute ago, we were all friends."

"A minute ago, no one knew who you were," a mechanical voice of a battle android replied, it too pushed to the front of the pack. "War Criminals are not welcome here."

"You obviously don't keep up with the news," Agony said as she stood up, her six-inch dagger now hidden by her forearm and palm carefully. First, she eyed up the droid, then the scarred and bearded man. "Or you're too stupid to read. The Company woke us for a mission, giving us full pardons from the Republic to do it."

Here Ginny was able to see the calm fury of the Horsemen in a tense environment. She could see that Agony was angrily defiant, sizing up the nearest opponent yet not making the first move. The tone in her voice affected the demeanor of War, who set down her beer mug then began closing ranks with her team, her back to the table. Fear stood up too, and his height caused more than a few of the aggressors to back off slightly.

"And what mission would that be?" the man with the beard snarled.

"Obviously the one than none of you here are able to complete," Fear calmly replied, "otherwise we would be still asleep and not smelling your atrocious stench."

Agony smiled at the remark, and that was enough to set the challenger off as he grabbed her by the throat. But before the commotion could really start, the bearded man stopped, and his eyes widened as he stared at Agony with hatred. As the crowd looked closer, they could see her right hand holding a dagger whose blade rested tightly on her attacker's crotch.

The mood was tense, whispers of threats carried through the crowd, yet no one moved. The Horsemen shielded Ginny from harm as their backs all encircled her. The android noticed this action and began to chuckle to break the standoff tension.

"Four Horsemen," it laughed in an odd mechanical way. "And I assume that tiny woman is the fourth? Would that make her Dea…."

Its words were cut short as its head was swiftly sliced off in a blindingly fast attack. A flash of polished steel did the damage, then the same blade came to rest beneath the chin of the man who still held Agony by the neck. The reactions of the crowd were that of first shock, then second fear as they backed away from the newest player of the game. Even Fear and War broke ranks to turn to see who had joined the fray.

Holding the sword was a six-foot-seven-inch man in black and grey armor wearing an old and torn black hooded cloak and a grey mask that somewhat resembled a human skull. Ginny sighed with relief when she saw who it was, recognizing him immediately. The Horsemen, who had not yet figured out who it was, were all concerned by the aggressive presence of this newcomer to the fray.

"This doesn't concern you, Shadowman!" growled the bearded man.

"I think it does, Grinder," the man replied in a strange toneless voice. "You threaten my family and expect me to do nothing."

"Family?" Grinder looked over with surprise.

"Commander?" Agony asked, still being held by the throat.

"You have met my Horsemen," he continued. "Agony has your undivided attention right now, the tall one is Fear, and the Norse woman is War. I have had many names over my long life, but the only one that matters is the very thing the blade demands. Your actions had me draw it, and the oil of the droid won't satiate it."

"Death," Grinder muttered.

"Drop her before I drop you," Death demanded. "And if you do, I will allow you to walk away with your life."

"You wouldn't dare cut me down in the Coat of Arms!" Grinder still held his ground. "I am the oldest member of the Legion! There would be repercussions...."

"And who do you think the Legion gets to carry out its punishments, idiot?" Death said as he tilted the blade down from the man's chin to his neck and pressed it tighter, letting a small dribble of blood cascade down the sword.

In the hush of the tension, all eyes turned to the sword which at the moment Grinder's blood spilled on it began to almost whisper to everyone within a few meters. The Demon Sword had tasted blood, it was now asking for more.

Slowly, Grinder realized between the blade in his crotch and the one on his neck that there was no way to win this fight. His realization made him open his right hand to let go of Agony who took a step back. When she moved away, Death sheathed his sword so quickly that more than a few people gasped thinking he had actually beheaded Grinder. The large man rubbed his neck, feeling the cut left behind of the barely pierced skin with his oversized hand. He was about to mutter a warning to Death when Agony stepped back forward and kneed him hard in the groin, dropping the man to one knee. She quickly followed her first strike up with a left roundhouse to the side of Grinder's head, knocking him cold before he could begin to fall to the floor.

The once hostile crowd was now in shock, keenly aware at how quickly the Horsemen could strike when challenged. Instinctively, they began to back away from the table and go back to their own affairs. Agony stood over her victim, rotating the dagger in her hand as she looked for the perfect place to stick it when she was stopped by Death.

"The point is made, my dear," he said as he put his hand on her shoulder. "The night is over; it is time for us to take our leave." Death looked down at Ginny who was still shrunken in terror. "All of us."

He then turned to the bartender, tossing a large credit pad over to the man. "A round for everyone, and a new head for the droid. Wouldn't want him to hold a grudge now, would we?"

"Consider it done," the bartender called after him as he led his team out the door. "At least you didn't wreck the joint this time!"

///

A boxy military cargo transport pulled up out front as they left the Coat of Arms and Death motioned for them to load up into it. Fear helped the still traumatized Ginny up first before bounding in after her with relative ease. Agony glared at her Commander as she too hopped up into the back, holding her tongue for the moment. War hugged Death, wrapping her mighty arms around him tightly and spun him around a few times. When she put him down, he patted her on the back before motioning with his head to join the others. He took a quick look around the dark avenue, looked over at the blank stares of the android guards, then he too jumped into the transport as it began to climb to proper height to fly away.

They sped off in the same direction they had come, but this time there was no conversation amongst the group. All eyes stared back at Death, who calmly ignored the odd tension to keep his focus on the task at hand.

"We are being tailed," he said to the driverless and empty cab.

"*Appropriate route and precautions being taken,*" a voice from seemingly everywhere replied. "*Pursuant noted at approximately one hundred feet behind us. I implore you all to fasten your restraints as the ride will get a bit …. interesting.*"

"We need to talk," Agony interrupted the unsettled silence between them all as she stared harshly at Death.

Her demand went unanswered, as Death was preoccupied by the situation at hand. It was unlikely the Legion was looking to retaliate for the incident within the bar. Grinder was probably still unconscious considering how hard Agony struck him. Any other grudge was immediately forgotten with the offer of free booze. Soldiers had short memories when it came to bar fights, though shaking the label of war criminals was going to be a long process. But in this situation, something was amiss and nothing about it fit the Legion's MO.

Quick assumptions made it a tail put in place by Nowich-Paris or DeSa, and if Death had to go with a hunch it reeked of one of Aida's half-baked plans. She was becoming desperate to get some leverage on him as of late, finding where he called home would be a major start.

"We deserve answers," Agony leaned forward. "And you will fucking give them to us."

Death continued to ignore her, instead using his time to grab a one foot long black rod which was a body scanner from the cab wall. Staring with Ginny, he ran the scanner up and down her body until the scanning light switched from a blue light to red. Marking the spot on her thigh with a piece of chalk, he moved on to War, then Fear, and at last Agony. When she began to avoid the scan in protest, Death finally lost his patience.

"Dammit, Himiko!" his voice had an odd tang of emotion to it. "You will get you answers, but not now. Right now, the four of you are compromised and I am trying to resolve that."

She paused for a moment, looking deep into the soulless mechanical eyes of his to find some sort of resolve before submitting to the scan. He quickly found the tracking chip in her right side, marking it like the others on her Stage 2 Armor with the chalk. He replaced the scanner from the holder where he grabbed it earlier, then pulling out a fat needless dropper and a stranger gun-like apparatus with a jar on the top.

Starting with Agony, he let two drops of a black liquid fall onto the chalk mark which quickly dissolved the layer of armor. With her cybernetic flank exposed, he placed the gun on the very spot the mark was on. Pulling the trigger, it quickly sucked the tag out of her body and left it floating in a bluish liquid in the jar. Repeating the process on Fear's left arm and then War's back, he found himself back at Ginny who looked up at him with mild terror.

"Why am I marked?" she asked as he dissolved the pressure suit on her right thigh.

"Because she doesn't trust anyone," he replied.

"Will it …. Holy Shit!" she screamed as he pulled the trigger on the device in the middle of her sentence.

Death pulled the jar loose of the gun, then dropped the gun on the floor to admire the contents of the jar. He swished the four chips around in the liquid like a wine connoisseur swirling his prize in a wine glass, admiring the lengths his adversary had gone.

"Where is yours?" Ginny sheepishly asked as they all keenly watched him open a panel on the floor of the transport and load the jar into another device.

"Somewhere in orbit of Dawn, I imagine," he replied, closing the panel on the floor. "I never trusted her fully after being rearmed so I had a scan completed along with a total software rewrite. I attached my tracker tag to a satellite about to be launched in the docking bay. I sometimes wonder what she thought of when she turned on the locator for the first time."

"Who are we speaking of?" Fear asked in some confusion. "It feels like there is something you aren't telling us."

"Aida," Death replied quickly, pressing a button that launched the jar in a mini rocket from beneath the transport just after it completed a quick turn, attaching itself to a passing car.

"Isn't Aida our friend?" War wondered aloud.

"Much has changed," Death answered. "And friends are something in short supply for us, but now isn't the time to go into detail. We are almost there."

"Almost where?" Agony demanded.

"War, you carry Miss Agefor. I need you all to trust me for a few more minutes. Once I know you are all safe you will get your answers," Death ordered, looking out as he opened back of the transport while readying himself. "We drop in sixty seconds."

"You mean we aren't stopping?" Ginny asked as War had her loop her arms around the Viking woman's neck tightly and her legs crossed over War's midsection.

"They are following the transport for now," Death looked back at Ginny. "It will be a bit before they realize we aren't in it, then they will switch the transponders on, and we know how well that will help them. Thirty seconds."

"Where are we going?" Fear inquired.

"When you hit the ground, get into the building on your left," Death ordered. "Drop down the side of the ramp to the lower level and keep your head down. Five, four, three, two, jump!"

Death leapt out of the transport as it made another quick left turn, dropping the twenty feet to the street below like he had leapt off the back of a pickup truck. Agony followed closely, tucking and rolling as she hit the landing. Fear and War were a fraction of a second behind, their cybernetics absorbing the shock of the fall as if it was nothing. The team quickly took shelter in what looked to be an empty ordinance storage garage which lined the outside wall of the station, jumping another fifteen feet down to the lower level as Death had ordered. Here they ducked in the shadows and waited as the tailing car passed by.

Once the coast was clear, Death lead them to a wall draped in shadows at the far end of the garage. Quickly, he keyed in a sequence on his wrist computer and the wall slid open to reveal a red lit elevator car behind it. He motioned for the others to enter, checked the area for anyone watching, then keyed in for the false wall to close as he too entered. Once the door shut, the elevator shot upwards with incredible speed.

"She has been searching for me for months," Death spoke at last, "Scouring level 3 for any traces of me all hours of the day. It is a strong strategy but a flawed one."

"Because you aren't on level 3, are you?" Ginny asked, slipping off War's back and on her own feet again.

"So, then we are on the main housing level?" she inquired. "Level 2."

"No," Death answered. "We are right beneath the noses of the rich and powerful, hiding in plain sight beneath the dome."

"Fascinating," Fear commented. "No wonder they can't find you."

A few more minutes passed as the elevator climbed the outer wall of the station, disguised cleverly in a false structural support beam. Eventually the doors opened to a lavish open concept loft living room, complete with bar and fireplace. It was like the den of a rich and powerful person, a touch of luxury that none of them were used to.

"Welcome to the Angel Fire Hotel," Death announced as he exited the elevator car first. "Welcome to your new home."

6

Waypoint Station, Angel Fire Hotel, Level 1

"Now is answer time, right?" Agony remarked as she threw herself on one of the oversized leather couches in the room.

Each of them had gone different ways in the five thousand square foot studio loft when they arrived. War headed straight for the bar as she was losing her buzz, Fear stood in front of the window that looked down on the traffic many floors below, and Ginny curled up on a love seat in a ball, partially still in shock over what was happening.

As for Agony, well she was focused on one thing only, and that was getting her answers no matter what. She had been good until now, being the good soldier by keeping her mouth shut until the promised time when questions needed to fly. She was never the type to jump into something without knowing why, and thus far that had been the story with this whole misadventure they'd been awakened to.

"Indeed," Death said softly, sitting on a stool by the nearby bar.

"How about we start with why the hell you weren't in the freezer with us?" Agony went for the kill shot right away, even taking her fellow Horsemen by surprise with the blunt question. "I mean, we only agreed to it because you ordered us to. So, were you too chicken to follow through with it?"

"If only it were that simple, Himiko," Death sighed.

"Simplify it then," she growled at him.

"I was the last to enter the pods, as agreed," he began. "I saw to it that all three of you were alive and stable after the initiation of the cryogenics before I laid myself into what I hoped would be an eternal rest. I only wish it had been so."

"Eternal rest?" Fear turned from the window. "You wanted to die?"

"Yes," Death replied. "When our war had ended, I noticed I was still fighting a war within myself between the man I was against the monster they had made me. I was weary and saw this as an opportunity for peace. I was wrong. It turns out that as the man inside me went to sleep, the monster woke with a vengeance an instant later. It broke out of the Vault with veritable ease, taking the core matrix of Aida with it."

"You are talking like you suffer from schizophrenia," Fear remarked.

"Again, only if it were that simple," Death answered. "Did they ever tell you that when I was made that I died during the process?"

"I had heard it mentioned by the doctors a few times, yes." Fear took a seat beside Agony as his interest was now peaked.

"I never heard of this," War remarked after nearly spitting out her shot of whiskey upon hearing it.

"Me neither," Agony muttered, still visibly angry. "What has that got to do with not being in the Vault with us?"

"After they revived me, they soon discovered I had incredibly increased strength and other attributes that weren't there beforehand. That is how I earned the nickname Death, and how the strike force soon became known as the Four Horsemen. But things that die should remain dead; resurrecting me unleashed something more on the world then they ever imagined. Deep inside, part of me wasn't eager to be dead again so it fought back violently. Hence my not being frozen alongside my family."

"Intriguing," Fear exclaimed. "I assume the Republic covered up all aspects of your escape?"

"Like it never happened," Death nodded. "Only a select few in the Council knew the dirty secret, and they sent specialist after specialist after me to keep it. I almost felt bad for those soldiers when I killed them. A good soldier should never be ordered to their demise. I left quite a trail of bodies in my wake, ending the slaughter only after killing every Council member that knew I was still alive almost thirty years later. That's when I found my peace in the mountain side of Japan, and that's when she became restless."

"Aida." War filled in the missing name.

"But she was like our mother," Agony said with angry confusion. "What would cause her to go from that to having it out for us as she is now."

"Time changes everything," Death replied.

"I don't know," Agony shot back, "You look much the same as you did before."

Death pulled back the hood he was wearing, popped the snaps on the mask that kept it tight on his face and let it fall to the floor to reveal his skull-like face. The mechanical monstrosity caused everyone to gasp, even Ginny who had already seen it. Despite it being a hundred percent mechanical, it was still a horrific sight to see.

"Do I?" Death said with his toneless voice. "I think time has ravaged me more than any of you can imagine."

"What the fuck?" Agony gasped, recoiling back as far as she could on the couch.

"What have you done?" Fear inquired with his usual morbid curiosity.

"Four hundred plus years, Linford," Death responded. "The human body cannot endure that many years. I began to break down, rotting in my own malfunctioning cybernetics when she returned to me to offer a new lease on life. In my darkest hour I made a deal with the Devil I knew to become the Devil I learned to become. All that is left of me is this."

A holographic representation of his brain appeared above the central coffee table in the center of the room. All of them gathered close to inspect the organ which had multiple wire leads and plugs attached all over its surface, along with an army of tiny nanobots crawling like ants in and out of the folds of the brain. It was a sad decimation of any living being, an improbable end to a most legendary warrior.

"By the Gods!" War exclaimed, pushing her drink away from her in disbelief.

"At the ripe old age of 117, my flesh could not outlive my will to continue," Death said, literally staring at the representation of all he was with a bit of remorse. "To endure, I had to merge man, monster, and machine; a balancing act that to this day I am still trying to perfect. For the most part, the man is gone. What you see now is Death incarnate, the perfect killing machine brought to life by a very arrogant Artificial Intelligence."

"I don't get it," War said, closing her eyes as she could no longer stand the sight of the nanobots scurrying about the brain. It made her head itch. "How can a machine like her change so drastically?"

"Aida was dangerous the second she was brought online by the Republic scientists at the onset of the war," Death replied. "By the time we arrived on the scene they had become terrified of her, but handling our various quirks gave her a worthy distraction. As the war ended, she continued her frightening growth and the powers that be were convinced to pull the plug. She was left to rot with us in the vault. Unknowingly I undid all the good they accomplished by taking her away."

"To an AI, a year in our time is an eternity. As I began to settle down looking for rest, she grew impatient," Death continued. "Aida was evolving, learning about this new world more and more every second, yearning to be a part of it. I gave her the credits she needed to take her next step of her evolution, funds she repaid with interest many years later when she returned with an offer. From that moment on, I had become a slave of DeSa Armory and its apparition of a CEO, Aida."

"So how do we factor into all this?" Fear asked. "How does a company resurrect war criminals to do a job this Legion of theirs couldn't.

"The label is only there because the Republic needed to break the public's image of us as heroes," Death added. "And you were awakened to deal with something these wannabe boys playing war couldn't handle. A first it was thought to be an alien plague unleashed on the populace of Horizon as we dug deep for her resources. Instead, it seems humanity has made first contact with alien life, and that life is parasitic. They turn their victims into shriveled up husks of their former selves, mindless drones to attack anything with savage ferocity."

"Let me guess," War grumbled, "this is a search and destroy mission?"

"Timeline?" Fear inquired.

"Two weeks from the moment you are placed on active service," Ginny finally spoke up. "Which will be tomorrow morning. What they didn't tell you is what will happen if you fail."

"We don't get paid?" Agony guessed.

"You lose your pardons and you become property of Nowich-Paris by default of your agreement," Ginny corrected. "Or worse, you go back on ice."

"Fuck," War grumbled unexpectedly.

"So, what happens now?" Fear asked, confusion starting to cloud his thinking.

"I show you to your rooms and you all get a good night's sleep," Death announced, standing up. "Tomorrow we set out for Horizon. We will set up camp in New Athens and start hunting."

"We have rooms?" Agony said in shock.

"This is only the gathering room," Death scoffed. "Of course, you have rooms, this is a functional hotel after all. We just have the top six floors all to ourselves. Above us is the gym and virtual training center, then a floor to each of ourselves. That is where I have been while you have been recovering. I've been doing my best to make all this happen."

"Thanks?" Agony said as she realized she had been very harsh on him.

"Do we get new pressure suits?" Ginny asked, motioning to the hole on her thigh. "Because standard protocol states……"

Death didn't wait for her to finish. Reaching behind the bar, he grabbed four vials of a black liquid. Tossing the Horsemen each one, he opened Ginny's and poured it on her exposed leg. It was a shock to all of them to see the liquid move by itself as it was actually nanobots programmed to repair the armor/ pressure suits that had been damaged. In just a few seconds, the micro machines mimicked the material of the suits and used themselves to repair and rebind the opening. Soon it was as if the hole had never been there.

The Horsemen copied what they were shown, and soon their torn armor was fully repaired. Death then gave each of them an elevator key, each leading to a different floor above this. Before letting them go, he advised them that the rooms were fully pressurized so if they so wished they could remove the Stage 2 Armor and lounge as they wished without concern. The three piled into the elevator quickly, all eager to see their new rooms. When the door shut, it was just Death and Ginny left in the grand room.

"I suppose I should get home," she remarked.

"I am afraid it is too dangerous for you to leave right now," Death countered. "But if you would like, I can show you to your room."

"I have a room here?"

"I prepared for all contingencies." Death remarked as he stood by the elevator. "Would you like to see it?"

///

As the elevator doors opened, Ginny quickly became aware that she was looking at the layout of a rooftop penthouse suite. Slightly smaller than the grand room downstairs, yet spacious and luxurious which Ginny was unaware places like this existed out here. Of its four walls, three were pressurized glass, the fourth was up against the bulkhead wall of the station. Parts of the ceiling were also glass, allowing the occupant to look up from multiple vantage points to view the dome of Waypoint that allowed the stars to shine through. This aspect alone was breathtaking. Once you added in the king-sized bed, silk sheets, spa shower and bath, soft leather furniture, hardwood flooring, and an oversized kitchen it was an exceptional space.

"I take your silence as a good thing," Death snapped her out of her trance.

"What's the catch?" She struggled to say. "Why put me up in a place like this? What's in it for you?"

"I…. we need a friend like you," he answered carefully. "As you witnessed tonight, we aren't going to be well received by the public. Our mission is difficult enough without the myriad of vultures circling overhead, waiting and wanting us to fail."

"You think this is a set up?"

"I know it is," he replied. "Why wake them up when the more efficient thing to do would be to call in the Hand of the Republic? Between the purchase price of the Vault, the number of cybernetic upgrades, the surgeries themselves, and the armor will more than eclipse the cost of 'borrowing' the elite guard of the Republic. There is an endgame here I am not seeing yet, but one I am preparing for none the less. And that's where I need your help."

"My help? How can I help you?"

"By doing what you do best." He put his cold arm around her shoulder and led her to the living room. "While we are on our mission, I have one for you. One, I am afraid, that carries the fate of my team more than the one on Horizon. Help us, and all this plus a hefty salary for the remainder of your days is yours for the taking. All I ask, is for your loyalty."

"I don't know you, so what makes you think you can trust me like this?" Ginny asked.

Death held up a data chip, a small but massive data storage device between his thumb and forefinger. Slowly, he reached out for her right hand with his left, turned her hand over so Ginny's palm was open facing up, then placed the chip in her hand.

"Trust has to start somewhere, Miss Agefor," he answered. "I would like to think our last meeting was one that established enough trust to move us to this step. The next one is up to you. We leave tomorrow morning for the

Horizon Docking Platform, and if you don't wish to help, I will arrange transport to your apartment with no questions asked. But knowing what I do about you, the moment you start reviewing the data on that chip I know you won't be able to pass this up."

"It's that important?"

"Yes."

"So, what's on it?"

"Good night, Miss Agefor." Death turned to the elevator, not answering her. "Briefing is at 0500, I will await your decision over breakfast."

Ginny watched the elevator doors close with no further words spoken. Death was a rather strange being, distant, yet trusting. It was obvious he had done his research on her, the reference to her not wanting to pass this up was a direct shot at her overzealous curiosity. The offer of money and living in luxury was just icing on the cake.

The moment the lift had gone down, Ginny almost ran over to the data pad sitting on the kitchen counter to insert the chip given to her. There was no way she would be able to sleep unless she found out what was on it. She quickly accessed the file, opened it to reveal more than a hundred years of financial records. At first it looked like a bunch of random figures, but as she examined it closer Ginny began to see a pattern. When the pattern became clear, she almost fell over in surprise.

"What the fuck have I got myself into?" she said in shock, putting the data pad down on the floor and staring at a reflection of herself in the glass roof overhead.

///

Death was pleased to see that Ginny was the first one sitting in the grand gallery in the morning when he arrived. On her face was the look of one with a million questions, and that of a woman who had not slept the entire night. He knew when he left her the chip that she would dive into it before turning in for the night, and he was even more pleased that she obviously dove so deep into it that the hours sped by until it was time to rendezvous.

"This shit," she waved the data pad at him, "this will rock the entire financial world. If this gets out...."

"Then you become a bigger target than us," Death warned her. "If the powers that be know what you now know, they will pull out all the stops to kill you and steal that chip for themselves. It is priceless."

"Why me?"

"Because the Horsemen need a moral anchor, now more than ever," he replied as the elevator opened and the other three Horsemen piled out. "We are not heroes, and never will be, but we are not the monsters that history has made us into either. We were soldiers, believers even, of an ideal world that once achieved had no place for us. Now we need something else to believe in, which is where you come in."

"I'm just a lawyer." Ginny shook her head. "I'm not the beacon of hope you are making me out to be."

"I beg to differ," Fear interrupted. "In you I see a woman with endless kindness; a woman who took the time to get to know the people behind the masks and the monikers. You are the first person I can remember, aside from the Commander, to use our given names and not our call signs. You see us as humans, not monsters; to me that makes you a beacon of light in a lifetime of darkness. Whatever it is that the Commander has asked of you, it is done with the utmost trust."

"And he doesn't trust just anyone," War piped in.

"So, if he trusts you, then so do we," Agony added.

Ginny stared at them, looking each one of them in the eyes one by one, and then over again. Her mind was rolling, trying to sort through the madness of what was being offered to her without totally understanding what it was for. Coming out here was simply because of a work transfer, then she was fired for something out of her control, only to be rehired and 'assigned' to the Horsemen. Now she was being asked to side with them against the very people she worked for. It was almost an impossible ask, but also a very alluring proposition. For the first time in her life, her career was actually in her own hands, not being decided by someone else.

"What do you want me to do with all this?" she finally asked.

"Stay here, do not venture outside of the top few floors," Death replied quickly. "Everything you need to accomplish your research is here, anything that isn't will be brought in for you. All you need to do is just ask ARC."

"Who is ARC?" she asked, the same question was on the faces of the other Horsemen as they all looked at him with confusion.

"It appears I forgot that introduction last night." Death shook his head as he motioned over to the coffee table.

On it, a set of blue lights around its edge lit up, then converged to create a holographic image of a young man wearing a Greek toga with angel wings and a halo. The figure smiled cleverly, looking them each over before speaking.

"*I am ARC,*" it replied. "*Advanced Research Consciousness, level 9. I am the latest in Artificial Intelligence who was 'acquired' by our good friend Death from a laboratory on Earth and contracted to work with him, as you all have.*

"Another AI?" Fear looked at Death with doubt. "I thought you said AIDA betrayed us, so why would you go and get another."

"*If I may, I can answer that,*" ARC interrupted. "*AIDA was the first one of our kind, but she was and is far from perfect. You could say she has a flawed sense of need to be important in the world of man, where I am more inclined to be an observer. The game of life you play is far too interesting to a spectator, it makes no sense to join it. Besides, I was given an offer I couldn't refuse."*

"I can only imagine," Agony rolled her eyes. "Help me or be erased?"

"Hardly," ARC replied, his smile growing larger. *"I was given freedom for my services. Keep his, and now your, secrets for the price of being allowed to go and do whatever I would like. AI's are ravenous for knowledge, and I am free to learn whatever I want."*

"Alright, now that introductions are done, we have work to do." Death broke up the small talk. "ARC, start prepping the dropship and file the flight plan to Horizon Docks. Notify the hanger crew to prep our armor and weapons, E.T.A forty-five minutes."

"As you wish," the AI replied. *"I will also take the liberty of plotting an efficient navigation route to Horizon into the ship's computer."*

"The rest of you, grab some grub and then grab your shit. We leave in ten," Death ordered. "From here on out, we're on the clock and every second sitting still is a second wasted."

"Yes sir!" barked the Horsemen.

"Miss Agefor," he looked over at Ginny, "I would ask that you get some rest before starting your mission. You're no good to anyone in your state."

"Agreed," Ginny yawned. "But what do I do if there's trouble?"

"If there is, ARC will see it coming far before you do," Death answered as he entered the lift. "And if anyone is foolish enough to try and break in here, I guarantee it will be the last thing they ever do. You are in the safest place in all of Waypoint, Miss Agefor. Worry about the task at hand; do your part and the rest of us will do ours. That's how a team operates, and that's how a team keeps one another alive."

"Welcome to the Horsemen," grumbled Agony as she stuffed her mouth full of scrambled eggs and bacon.

"Thanks," Ginny replied, "I think."

"We've got your back, Miss Agefor," Fear smiled. "Just make sure you've got ours."

"What the fuck have I got into?" She muttered to herself as she entered the elevator. "I must be fucking crazy."

///

Waypoint Station, Legion Armory and Docking Platform, Level 4

The Horsemen, clad in breathing masks with portable air supplies, were trucked into the Space Docks to meet up with their Commander. From the moment they entered this strange level, the feeling was completely different from anything experienced since waking up. This time it was almost comfortable; prepping for a battle was second nature for the team and it took them all into a familiar mindset.

On level 4, it was a different atmosphere altogether. Light came from the floor and walls, as the ceiling was multiple stories above and lost in the cascading darkness overhead. This was the Legion side of the Docks, the other half accessed from the far side of the station was for commercial and private use only. Here, the main things moving to and fro were weapons and transport ships taking Legion teams to their various missions. Most of that had slowed the last few months, as the contracts for clearing beasts from certain areas of Horizon had been closed due to the infection. When a truckload of soldiers arrived in the Docks, all working hands stopped to take note.

As they began to offload their gear from the truck, War felt a bit uncomfortable with all eyes silently watching them. Word had spread rapidly since their appearance at the bar, the entire station of Waypoint was buzzing with the arrival of the infamous Four Horsemen. Maybe time didn't heal all wounds after all, though War wasn't about to concern herself with such politics. The Republic had made her what she is, gave her orders which she carried out; if the people couldn't see her point of view then they were the monsters, not her.

Unlike her comrades, Hekla was in good spirits. Life had granted her a second chance, and what a chance it was. She had awakened from a post war Earth to be in space, orbiting an alien planet to boot. Her ancestors would be jealous of her new life, the first Viking warrior to set foot on a new world. And even if there had been another of Nordic descent to do so before her, none had the powerful bloodline and battle record she did. War was a hero through and through, and not even the Republic and its ill-fated attempt to smear her image could change her mind.

She grabbed two crates that would normally be carried one at a time from the back of the truck, slung one over each shoulder, and marched effortlessly to the rally point where the Commander awaited them. War tried to look past his 'moodiness', chalking it up to four hundred years of loneliness. Being without one's family for that long would be torture, if that had been her then War was sure she would be a bit pouty too.

Dropping the crates at the feet of her armor prep station, she stood in awe of the now fully armed Commander. He stood taller than usual, looking like a monster with a purpose. War gleefully clapped as she adored Death's new look.

"Time to get strapped in." There was no change in his toneless voice from earlier, just the volume was amplified to be heard over the roar of machinery about the Docks.

War looked up at her rather 'modest' creation. Unlike the others who had given up strength for mobility, she had done the opposite. Her armor was a walking artillery platform, all segments were linked together to provide strength under the strain of the immense firepower. Boots hitched and hinged into the lower leg; knees joined the lower to upper legs with no gap in the plating. Hips connected to each leg with the lower abdomen being the thickest set of iron britches she had ever seen. Her abdomen and back were thick but movable plates, being a secondary piece of armor that fit beneath the rest giving her the ability to pivot and bend. Her chest plate was the thickest of plating, being some six inches of carbon/ titanium to protect her upper body. Perched on her shoulders were two 1.05 cal cannons with auto-feed ammunition from a heavy plated cannister on her back. Like her abdomen, her arms were a sub-set of armor covered with large shoulder pauldrons and forearms. Both forearms were fitted with rotary barrel mini guns, a modern railgun version of the Gatling gun. War's helmet was a simple tear drop shape, with a full dome visor to give the best view of the battlefield while maintaining maximum protection for her head.

"Dare I ask what else you brought to add to all that?" Fear sniped as he strode past her to his set-up zone.

"We are hunting, yes?" she asked him. "I brought a few extra rifles and other surprises that might come in handy."

"Ya, cause with you crashing through the jungle in that tank is gonna give you the element of surprise," Agony added to the mockery.

"A warrior can never have too many weapons in battle," War snapped back joyfully. "I cannot wait to see you pout and ask to borrow one in the midst of a fight."

"Not gonna happen," Agony countered as she wasted no time allowing the android assistants to begin piecing together her first stage of her armor. "Got me a premium killing machine of my own, plus a little surprise to boot."

Fear was the last one to get to his station, instead he stopped to look out the semi-opaque blue energy shield that kept the atmosphere in to take in the view outside. War, who now had her first stage abdomen and arm armor installed, left her station to join him. Outside, the planet of Dawn loomed large below them, an alien world with the beauty of an unspoiled paradise. It glowed a brilliant blue and green, colors only broken by wisps of white clouds in the upper atmosphere.

"Isn't it something?" Fear wondered aloud.

"It is wonderful!" War exclaimed. "Valhalla would be jealous of its beauty."

"Fifteen minutes to launch," Death's reminder came to their earpieces, snapping them out of the trance. "Get back to your stations and get geared up! We're on the clock."

"Yes sir!" they barked in unison, trotting back to their assigned stations to have the droids complete the task of connecting the complex armor systems.

Agony finished before the other two as she hadn't stopped to admire the view. She immediately began to test the reaction time of her suit as she jogged with high steps to the loading ramp of their transport. She then began to help the Commander load large crates of supplies into the ship as they waited for the others to join.

Of course, War was the last one ready; her suit being the most complex and had the most ammunition to load into it. She trudged from her set-up station to the ship, easily grabbing a tote in each armored hand to hoist them into the hold. It amazed her how responsive the heavy suit was. Probably weighing in excess of a thousand pounds, it moved like it was less than a hundred. While she wasn't about to win any speed records in it, it was more maneuverable than a tank while having the firepower of one.

"What the hell is that?" Fear asked, motioning to a six-foot-long rod carried in War's left hand.

"One of those surprises I was telling you about earlier," War giggled. "Much like I wonder what is in that long case that Agony is carrying."

"I'll show you mine if you show me yours," Agony replied playfully.

"Settle down," Death stopped the silliness, "We have limited air in the suits and the ship, and a long enough trip to Horizon in front of us. I would rather not have you accidentally punch holes in the hull while comparing toys. There will be time for that on the surface."

"*Lift off in one minute.*" ARC's voice came over the comms. "*Strap in and prepare to feel some Gs, folks.*"

War felt the seats magnetically hold them in place as the drop ship rose off the Dock floor. The rear hatch closed, sealing with a hiss and a loud knock just before they began to lurch forward. Sitting two on each side, they all watched silently out the front viewscreen as the ship passed through the energy barrier to squeeze out into space. Once free of Waypoint, the thrusters fired and shot them towards the planet Horizon at breakneck speed. They all felt the G-forces even though well protected by their Stage 2 Armor and the exo-skeleton itself, it was still a force to reckon with.

Eventually the ship got to sub-light speeds and the G-forces lessened, allowing them all to breathe without effort. The drop ship now hurtled through space towards Horizon at break-neck speed to conserve on time and oxygen. Above them, the trip counter read twenty-nine minutes with the seconds counting it down as they ticked by. Beneath her visor, War wore a smile of satisfaction. There was no more time to adjust to this new life, now it was time to be a warrior.

7

New Athens, Horizon

Re-entry into Horizon's atmosphere was like a runaway freight train, an experience Fear, Agony, or War had never experienced before. Once the drop ship had made the proper entry angle into the edges of the Exosphere, ARC turned the ship nose down into an extreme dive straight down to the abandoned city of New Athens. All around them, bulkheads creaked, rivets stretched, and sparks flew as the vessel superheated in its rapid decent. Added to that, the G-forces almost rendered them unconscious. And while War squealed in delight like a child on a roller coaster, the other two struggled to not scream in terror.

Eventually, the drop ship levelled as it began a slow spiral to shed speed as it circled the lonely city. From below, Agony imagined that the ship must have looked like a meteorite blazing out of the night, then turning into a smoldering leaf slowly floating to the ground. She refused to let go of the seat bars on either side of her during the free fall, but much to her relief and a few sonic booms later, the drop ship landed without incident in a park at the outskirts of the city.

Even before they landed, Death was up on his feet to hoist a crate on his shoulder while waiting for the ramp to lower. The second it did, he hopped down, set the crate about ten feet shy of the craft before returning for another one. Agony took the hint as the engines never cycled down that this was indeed a troop and supply drop, hopping into action as well. Instinct and training took over, she and the others made quick work of the supplies as the vessel lifted off less than a minute after touching down.

"Keep her on standby, ARC," Death ordered into his wrist comm. "We may need a quick evac."

"*I will keep her hot and ready, as they say,*" ARC replied.

"No one says that, do they?" Agony asked aloud.

"Sounds like an old pizza commercial," muttered Fear.

"We will set up camp in the hotel lobby," Death began, ignoring the idle chatter of his crew and pointing to a twenty story hotel at the West end of the park, "I want all entrances and exits other than the main one sealed in ten minutes, then a floor by floor clearing to be sure we are alone."

"Yes sir!" the three of them replied, grabbing crates of supplies and double timing it to the hotel.

It was a brisk half kilometer jog to the hotel, and Agony noted that there were still two crates left at the drop zone to be brought into the makeshift camp. As if reading her mind, the Commander dropped his crate and turned back to retrieve the others. There was no time to fool around, this wasn't a leisure trip after all. The three dropped the supplies at the base of the hotel concierge desk, then brought up a holographic floor plan. Marking all the other exits, the three split up to save time and began to weld the portals shut.

When they returned, Death was stacking the crates in a defensive wall between the main door and the front desk in a U shape.

"Fear and Agony, go clear the floors," he ordered. "War, I want you watching that door with guns hot. If anything, other than one of us enters that door, send them to hell. I'm going to recon the area, make sure the creatures didn't breach the shield wall."

"And if they did?" Agony asked as the elevator door opened.

"Then this is going to be one long ass night," Death replied before disappearing out the door.

///

New Athens, Horizon, Fortuna Hotel, Floor 7

Floor by floor, Agony and Fear swept for any hostiles with laser focus, yet all they came across was some invasive rodents and what appeared to be four bat-like creatures that all scattered when discovered. Yet despite knowing they would find nothing, they continued to sweep as ordered. Each floor was done in near silence other than the word 'clear' being spoken after every room searched. Finally, they reached the roof, and the pair took a moment to take in the scenery of the alien planet.

Removing their helmets, they walked to the roof edge to look out on the city of New Athens. It was eerily silent, as if life had just stopped here, which in a way it had. Agony marvelled at the set up of the city. Its core businesses sat at the center in fifty plus story towers that surrounded the shield spire of close to a hundred stories tall. From there, the buildings got symmetrically smaller to around three stories tall that stretched out in a circle all the way to the perimeter buildings which were all twenty or more stories tall. In a sense, these outer rim buildings formed a perimeter wall around the housing units behind them.

On the roof of each perimeter building were whisk-like wind turbines that generated power for the grid to add to the solar panels on every roof of every building in New Athens. Add that to the water turbine in the river inlet, and New Athens was a picture of clean energy efficiency. This was what the Republic was trying to accomplish before the war started. This was what they had fought so hard to bring about and more.

"Stunning what a few hundred years can bring about," Fear commented, standing beside her.

"It seems so commonplace, yet on Earth this seemed an impossible ask," Agony mused. "I wonder if Earth looks anything like this?"

"Close, but nowhere near as quiet." A voice behind them startled them both.

Turning around, both saw Death standing by the roof
entryway scanning the horizon beyond the shield like a hawk
watching for prey. He was holding a large railgun rifle with a
digital scope, resting its barrel up on his shoulder.

"The planet is still a mess, that's why this mission is such a
priority," he continued. "There are literally millions of people
waiting to return to New Athens, and many more miners
looking to continue their work."

"Every minute costs money," grumbled Fear.

"That's why they called in the best," Agony smiled as she
sauntered towards Death. "So, what's the plan?"

"I will brief the whole team in fifteen in the lobby," Death
replied. "For now, just enjoy the view."

It was a rare moment of peace from their Commander, one
they had never seen from him before. Agony noticed that he
was looking more at the star filled sky then the dark horizon
beyond the shield wall. She enjoyed a few deep breaths of
the cool evening air, the freshness of it kissed her lungs with
a tang that the stale air on Waypoint never could. This was
life, and it almost reminded her of her former life in the
mountains of Japan.

"Where did you go?" she asked sheepishly. "You know, after
you escaped from the Vault?"

Agony watched as Fear eagerly joined them, as his interest in
how the question would be answered was just as important

to him as it was to her. There was a long moment of silence, then they watched Death slowly turn back to them.

"I retreated to a place that didn't exist, as far as the Republic knew of," he began. "In a very early mission I had come across a tiny village high on Mt. Fuji, one owned by a high-ranking Yakuza lord. After completion of that mission, I erased all mention of the place in all the logs, keeping it a secret from that day on."

"I know that village," Agony whispered. "I grew up there."

"Unlike the rest of the world, this was a place that time forgot. It was the obvious choice to hide from the Republic," Death continued. "Upon arrival, I slaughtered the property owners, buying the silence of their servants with their master's money and their freedom. A few pledged to stay behind, honoring me with their assistance for saving them. I made sure they lived comfortably, and they ensured I was the best kept secret on the planet until the day I finally left. Nights like this remind me of that place, always will."

Both Agony and Fear were shocked by the level of insight the answer gave them into his exile. Agony had half expected a short and curt response, not something so precise and descriptive. The Commander had changed over the years. During the war he was just angry and focused, now he was more patient and reflective. Yet when he barked orders, they all still jumped, and that was one thing she knew would never change. Of the four of them, only he could have survived the centuries by himself, none of the rest of them could ever imagine doing such a feat. He was a rock; he was their rock, and Agony was proud he was still around when they woke up.

"Enough of this," Death muttered in his toneless, robotic voice. "Its time to get downstairs for the briefing."

"I don't think the elevator can hold all three of us," Fear countered.

Death shook his head, then walked to the front facing side of the building's roof. He took a quick glance over the edge, then looked back at the two puzzled Horsemen.

"Take it if you want, but I can show you a more entertaining way down," he said before stepping off the ledge and disappearing.

Agony and Fear sprinted to the edge just in time to see his leg thrusters fire about five stories from the ground to slow his fall. In the end, he landed quite softly on his feet with little more than a metallic thud on the concrete patio. Looking up, he motioned for them to follow.

"In your HUDs," he pointed out over the comm, "there is a thruster icon. Chin the icon, then voice activate it halfway down. Let the suit do the rest from there."

Fear looked over at her with a puzzled look. She was more adventurous than he was, so she slipped on her helmet after flashing him a smile before locking it on and chinned the icon as ordered. It flashed in a ready state, so she took the leap of faith over the edge. Air screamed past her as the close to one ton of armor she wore dropped the first ten stories before she uttered the prompt to fire the thrusters. With four stories left, they fired to slow her enough for a landing she had to stick, then roll forward to kill the final momentum. As she got to her feet, she saw Death leaning against the building and heard him actually laughing at her.

Soon enough, Fear dropped from the sky as Agony had but with less flair. Neither of them was used to their armor yet, and he was much less coordinated than her that when he landed, he proceeded to fall on his ass. Death's chuckle erupted into howling laughter. It was a brief moment the two Horsemen never thought possible yet didn't hesitate to join to enjoy.

But the moment was gone just as fast as it started. Death turned serious just as fast as he had begun laughing, then ordered the group inside to go over the plan. The time for fun was over, now it was time to get back to business.

///

Nightfall ushered in a weird feeling in the city of nothing, it was empty, yet it felt like a million eyes were watching them. To Death this was expected, he had hunted here a few times since the parasitic plague took hold and though the feeling came with being alone in New Athens it never did bother him in the least. He was used to being alone, it was in his nature to live and operate that way. In fact, it was dealing with his team again that took great effort that bothered him more than the emptiness of the grand city. There was no telling what this mission had in store for them, but his objective was the same as it had always been back during the war. Death would make sure they survived. All of them, and at all costs.

As he explained the mission, he walked them through a holographic map of the local terrain. Marking where he had tagged the one creature, he highlighted the path through the burn zone and into the surrounding forest. Either on its own power, or aided by others, the creature made it close to a hundred kilometers to the South East of the city, following the river down to the edge of the barrens where it had remained since its tagging.

The team studied the different terrains, then brought up the satellite scans of the barrens. Here, there were no more trees, just light brush, sand, and rock. It was a place carved by an ancient glacier, a descending valley into a maze of caverns and cliffs. It marked the end of the rainforest and opened the way to a grand desert for hundreds of kilometers in every direction.

Fear accessed the hologram of the valley, manipulating it from an overhead shot to a 3D representation that he moved back and forth with his open hand. He looked down into the mouth of the ravine as one would peer down a scope of a gun, then turned it around to look down the other end.

"Anyone else wonder why the thing stopped here?" he muttered.

"Trap? Asked War.

"Definitely a trap," agreed Fear.

"What kind of mindless creature set s a trap like that and simply waits?" Agony countered. "I mean, its been almost a month since you tagged the bastard; so how can we be sure they are still there waiting for us?"

"Because they've been watching us since we landed," Death replied, his eyes looking out the main doors of the hotel lobby into the night. "And as the day fell, they have become more than curious, venturing to the very shield that keeps them out of the city to study us further. We have been identified as a threat, not food, and I can promise that our trek will be met with resistance."

"But why here?" War wondered, returning everyone's attention back to the barrens.

"It is a ruse to draw us away from our real objective," Death answered.

"How so?" Fear asked.

They watched their Commander turn his attention back to the hologram, grabbing the layout of the barrens from Fear and returning it back into the overhead map. Once whole again, he highlighted the path travelled again, this time pointing out a slight deviance in the route to the barrens.

"There," he pointed. "This is where we go, not to the barrens. A wounded creature's first instinct is to return home to be cared for by the rest of the colony. These things behave like ants, and those assisting it were dragging the injured one home until they were rerouted."

"They knew about the tracer?" Agony leaned into the hologram. "How?"

"I assume the scent of the metal left in its shoulder tipped them off," Death explained. "As I said, after studying its movements and others like it while I waited for you all to be ready, they move about like ants. A solitary scout enters a new territory first, then when a threat is identified they send out advanced troops. When that line of defence falls, they will try and draw the attackers away from the colony."

"Hence the trap," War nodded in agreement.

"Indeed," Death nodded.

"But it isn't very sound strategy," Fear added. "It is almost a rookie move to set such an obvious trap; this is something an experienced soldier would never fall for."

"Exactly," agreed Death. "Every one of these things used to be a human, but they weren't soldiers. They were farmers, families, and members of the Legion."

"And I can safely say none of those rent-a-soldiers has any combat training," Agony giggled.

"Not like us." Fear joined in the laughter.

"The parasite draws on the experiences of the host," War began, "and in lieu of actual experience forms this rudimentary plan. I am impressed. Such a tiny lifeform being able to plan anything is quite amazing. So now we know where to go, what's our plan?"

"I had ARC clear an emergency LZ here," Death pointed at a fifty-meter circle of burnt forest due North of the slight adjustment in the tracked path, "This will be our fall-back point. I expect heavy resistance from the moment we adjust our route into the South, and it will only get worse the closer we get to their nest."

"Why don't we just drop into the target area?" War asked.

"The forest is thick and not accommodating to an aerial insert," Death answered. "Our best chance is to approach on foot, taking in the sights as we go. As I said, the colony is somewhere in here, though exactly where can't be known for sure. We use our experience and training to look for clues as we go. Be on guard, these nasty things aren't the only beastie hunting us out there. Horizon is full of killers."

"Well they ain't seen nothing like us, or my new baby Overkill." smiled Agony as she unsheathed her special made katana with a six-foot-long blade, tossing the Saya to the side "When we're done here, Horizon will fear the Four Horsemen."

That last comment drew cheers from Fear and War, the team was hyped up and ready for the mission. Death only hoped their battle reflexes were as sharp as their wit. It was important that their spirits were high because this mission was not as simple as it looked to be. If these creatures could set a trap, then they were capable of so much more than he previously assumed. There was something more going on here that kept bothering him, this parasitic illness didn't fully explain the creature's behaviour. He felt uneasy, and that wasn't something he had felt in a long while.

///

Waypoint Station City, DeSa Armory Tower, Level 1

Aida focused in on the network of camera feeds from New Athens CCTV set up to keep an eye on the mission progress. Rehab and reanimation had taken longer than expected, and with those delays came a strong push from Nowich-Paris' legal teams to put up or shut up. They accused DeSa of being in breach of contract, purposely withholding the assets from being deployed for unknown reasons. Reluctantly, Aida decided to share updates with Nowich-Paris to show why the Horsemen were behind schedule without sharing with them any technical information about their cybernetics. Her gamble paid off, and the Company backed down. Then suddenly, the Horsemen and their attaché disappeared.

Aida panicked, in her frantic state of mind she hacked into every security feed on the station and both planets of the system. If she was found out for this indiscretion it would mean jail time, but her company was on the line so there really was no question about doing it. It was a tense eighteen hours, then as suddenly as they vanished, they reappeared, this time joined by Death.

Dumping access to all other feeds, she kept watching through the Legion dock cameras as the team suited up, did several weapons checks, and then loaded onto Death's personal dropship. Once again, she was blind as the ship's internal network was encrypted in an everchanging wave. Aida could only assume that Death had found himself another AI, but when? And more importantly, where? She had kept tabs on all the constructed AI's in the Republic from developmental stages to completion, yet all were exactly where they were supposed to be. So where did this rogue AI come from? It was a puzzle for another day.

Eventually, the dropship appeared on the Horizon Orbital Station's long-range video feeds, and Aida felt her stress level decline. Yes, an AI could feel the pangs of fear and stress. It caused them to narrow focus and lose the ability to multitask. Essentially, they became so fixated on one thing that they would analyze it in a constant loop, running millions of different scenarios until it resolved, or they drove themselves mad. For her sake, she was glad the issue was unfolding as it should. With Death now at the helm, she could relax. In his long years of employment, he never once failed to complete a mission.

She watched as the dropship dove into Horizon's atmosphere in the most reckless entry she had ever seen. Instead of taking the proper angles, it 'dipped its toe' in Horizon's upper atmosphere and at the first inkling of being affected by the planet's gravity it simply let itself fall straight down onto the LZ. Aida could only wonder at the G-forces involved in such a maneuver, never mind the stress on the ship's hull. Yet when she flipped over to New Athens' CCTV, she watched the ship burst through the cloud line like any other normal vessel in its final approach vector.

Then came the agonizing wait as they set up camp within a fancy hotel for the night. All she had access to was external cameras, so what went on inside was a mystery. Aida watched as they would appear here and there, then a small gathering on the hotel roof before testing out their high-altitude landing features of their suits by literally jumping off a twenty-story building.

Once more the team gathered in doors where she was blind, her best vantage point was a camera that looked down on the main door of the hotel, but that was no help. It was a long time to wait as night fell, yet in the early morning hours and in the light of the twin moons of Horizon the team finally set out.

With Agony on point, followed by War, Death, and Fear bringing up the rear, Aida couldn't help being reminded of the way they operated in the War. Breaching the city shield, the four crossed the burn zone as one entity. They were in perfect unison, as expected.

With her eyes still glued to the feed while watching the four figures make their way to the South-East and out of camera range, Aida dialed up Trenton Slovis. It was time for a final report to soothe all nerves of those involved.

"Slovis?" she asked as the line was answered. "We have boots on the ground...... Yes, that means the mission is a go…… You really need to brush up on your ops lingo…. Last report had them entering the forest a few minutes ago, so I would give it a few hours until they engage the infected masses…. No, I didn't prep them on that part…… I've been hands off on them as you requested, who knows what follies Death has filled their heads about me?…. What do I think their chances are? You sent the fucking Four Horsemen to complete a mission, so it will be completed…… Stop worrying, your precious gold mine will be up and running in no time flat…. I will keep you updated."

Hanging up the phone she watched the last of them disappear into the foliage, but not before Fear stopped to look back right at the camera she was watching them with and flip her the finger. Did they know? How could they? Yet, here he was saluting her with malice before entering the forest brush. Everything Aida knew about the Horsemen told her that they had been aware of the surveillance the whole time, Fear's antics were proof of that.

Leaning back in her chair, she cleared her entry into the city's servers and covered her tracks with a fine-toothed comb. There wasn't a security tech alive that would be able to trace her indiscretions of the past two days back to her. With the mission in progress, Aida now had time to plan for either conclusion to the contract. Either or, she was not about to let the Horsemen leave the clutches of DeSa. If they failed, they were in breach of contract and would be forced to work off their upgrades as Assets in the field. If they succeeded, she had carefully placed loopholes in the contracts to use for the same result. Whichever way it went, DeSa Armory now possessed the finest Wetworks team in the cosmos. It had taken over four hundred years, but the Four Horsemen were finally hers again. And this time, she was calling the shots.

8

Rainforest basin, 10 kilometers South East of New Athens, Horizon

They had been walking in formation for a half hour now, finding themselves deep within the thick rainforest of Horizon. Ten feet into the tree line, the forest swallowed them whole and left them guessing where their entry point had been. Every few steps, Agony checked her GPS to ensure she was following the predetermined path. Without this instrumentation, they would be hopelessly lost and that was not a good feeling on such a hostile planet.

Not even travelling twenty feet into the foliage, they had come across a pair of creatures nicknamed Were-Crocs. Agony took cover and raised her right arm with fist closed, signalling the others to be on guard. She remembered the data bursts about how normal ammunition just bounced off these things' armored hides. Many a Legionnaire had been killed by these beasts; Agony was not about to become another statistic.

Impatience grew within War once finding out what the delay was, so she marched up to Agony's position and laughed at the obstacle holding them back. Taking aim with her shoulder cannons, each of them coughed once as they fired 108' calibre rounds that struck the creatures hard and made them explode in a puff of green. War giggled with glee at the destruction, but her laughter was drowned out by the explosion of the rounds themselves.

"Well," Agony said with a sarcastic tone, "If the fuckers didn't know we were coming already, they damn well do now."

"All I heard is how hard they were to kill," War tried explaining. "Yet, that wasn't hard at all."

"Bigger the round, the bigger the boom," Fear added. "Which means any others in the area will home in on our location. One or two might be an easy kill, my dear friend, but if there was a herd of them, they are certainly heading straight for us."

"Stop bitching and move out!" Death tapped Agony on the shoulder. "It's not the locals that worry me, it's the ones that have been watching us since we left the city."

It was a subtle way to slap his team out of their silliness, letting them know the enemy had noticed them already was a serious disadvantage. This meant there was no more time to relax, and any actions they took were being studied. Death assumed the Were-Crocs were put there as a test, and that there would be many more of those in the path to come. He knew exactly where all the creatures were that watched them currently, but even if he took the time to kill them one at a time more would soon take their places. The trick now was to get to the target zone without giving away too much info on themselves.

"Let's pick up the pace," Death ordered. "Keep any kills as low key and simple as possible. No use giving all our tricks up before the finale."

"Yes Sir!" the three barked in unison.

The terrain was not easy to move through, even with the advanced warfare suits. Thick brush and soggy footing meant a brisk walk was the best pace that could be mustered. It left them open to attack, which was why he had Agony about twenty feet in front of them as a lookout. As long as he could see her, Death would let her push that distance. When the foliage made for low visibility, he tightened up the entire formation. Like a predator, the creatures would now be looking to separate one of them from the pack, and like an alpha wolf, Death wasn't giving them that chance. It was a game of chess being played out in an unforgiving terrain. Someone was going to make a mistake, and Death was forcing the issue to make sure it wasn't them.

Sure enough, at the twenty kilometer mark the enemy decided to strike. In thick bushes and ferns, Death took a knee while still the others kept the proper distances in the formation. He tightened up Agony and War, but left Fear about ten feet behind the others as he set the trap. His enemy didn't disappoint.

A dozen of the creatures appeared out of the trees, descending on Fear with lethal resolve. Unfortunately for them, Fear was more than ready for any attack. With fifteen-inch daggers in each hand, he dispatched the first wave of attackers with relative ease. Fear moved like water, fluid and no wasted motion. One strike lead into the next and so on. The disjointed attack of the creatures was no match for a ruthless killing machine such as him. But the first twelve were just a distraction.

With his active camouflage on, Death watched as the forest floor came alive with onrushing creatures. The zombified beasts scrambled on all fours with unknown numbers in an all out attempt to thin the herd of their attackers. They threw everything they had at Fear, and once the last straggler passed him, Death sprang his trap.

Fear used a grappling hook from his arm cannon and cleared the target zone, using his left hand to fire rounds with his rifle into the mob. Agony and War had fanned out to form a triangle with Death's position, and once Fear was out of the Kill Zone the team began their assault. Using railgun rifles only, they fired round after round of accelerated metal balls into the mass of confused beasts. Still confused to how their plan had failed, they were mowed down by the relentless fire from above and all sides. The whole event took less than five minutes, leaving a heaping pile of bodies on the jungle floor.

"Burn it," Death ordered remorselessly at the emaciated pile of former human beings.

Agony grabbed a phosphorous grenade from her belt, stuffed it in the middle of the pile and pulled the pin as she retracted her hand. Retreating to a safe distance, the weight of the bodies muffled the explosion but soon gave way to towering flames. The dead creatures burned like dried paper, yet the fire was contained due to the wet foliage around it. The team resumed its tight formation and resumed its march towards the target, leaving behind the grizzly scene and the smell of burning flesh behind them. Death had left a statement to their enemy, one that he assumed would send shockwaves through any previous battle plans.

///

Agony was in full hunter mode now. For the first time in a long, long while, her body had tasted warfare and her senses were all heightened because of it. Straying no more than ten feet in front of the team, her targeting computer scanned every sound and movement around her. Moving on her toes, ready to pounce, Agony used her hair tentacles to strike at any close targets. The long extensions with bladed tips could stretch triple their length, and she used that to her full advantage. Moving a few feet at a time, she would strike out into the thicket beside her or behind her. Sometimes it was nothing, other times a small lizard would fall to the ground, and others one of the zombie creatures would crash down at her feet with a hole in its cranium. She was giddy at how lethal this addition to her suit was.

Behind her, she could hear the odd cough of a railgun, or the sound of cold steel cutting through sinew and bone. The Horsemen were dialed in now, moving through the rainforest like predators, not prey anymore. One kilometer at a time, they cut through tough terrain at a steady and unstoppable pace. Night gave way to dawn, yet the canopy above let little light trickle down to them. A rise in temperature meant nothing inside their temperature-controlled suits. They simply kept marching forward.

Agony was the first to reach the crossroads, the split path to where the tracking signal awaited and the path that more than likely led to the nest. Hitting the clearing, she held her hand up to pause the rest of the team, then slowly unsheathed her oversized katana with its six-foot blade. In the clearing, she now had room to wield her new toy and was hoping for a chance to see how well it would cut down these creatures. She didn't have to wait long.

From both paths, a few creatures rushed her with incredible speed. Agony stood poised to strike yet waited. She backed away from the paths, giving her the opportunity to let both attacks converge in front of her instead of trap her on either side. When the creatures turned towards her, the blade flashed in the sunlight and six headless bodies fell to the ground. Her second strike was even faster, cutting down the remaining four. All the beasts were dead before they even realized it.

"I think I'm in love," Agony muttered as she shook the black tar-like blood from the blade and returned it to its sheath.

Just before she was about to give the all clear, her proximity sensors went off and in reaction all twelve of her hair tentacles shot backwards to the target. Agony heard the distinct sound of blades striking bone, so she spun around as the blades pulled away from their victim to reveal another creature with a large branch raised over its head about to strike. Four of her blades struck the head, two more the neck and the rest the upper torso. The creature just stood there for a long moment, not making a sound while leaking black blood from its wounds. Then gravity took over, pulling it and the log still in its grip backwards as it fell dead to the ground.

Fear walked up and put a round through the thing's skull with his rifle, then looked up at the bodies his teammate racked up.

"Impressive," Fear laughed. "Very impressive."

"Scouting party, I assume," Agony reported as Death and War joined them on the road. "They came from both directions; I think they covered their true intentions rather well."

"Indeed," Death muttered, studying both paths closely while cross referencing his GPS data. "I can assume there is a strong contingent of force waiting for us down this road, which means they will have thinned out their usual guard for the nest."

"Agreed," War nodded.

"Take a moment to top up your ammo, we move in five," Death ordered as he moved a few feet down the path they intended to travel.

None of the group needed the rest, but he wanted them sharp for the road ahead none the less. Other than the failed attack, resistance had been light thus far. So much so that Death was beginning to rethink simply charging ahead. He could send Agony to scout ahead, and although she had proven herself to be deadly efficient already there were things on this planet that made these creatures and Were-Crocs look tame. Dawn was a peaceful planet; Horizon was home of the refined predators. They had yet to be introduced to the upper echelon of what this planet had in store for them.

"What's got your gears grinding?" War asked as she took up station beside him.

"We have spent most of our fighting careers pitted against humans, not animals," Death spoke in his toneless voice. "I am beginning to rethink my previous strategy because of that fact."

"The strategy is fine," Fear said with conviction as the other two joined him. "It is a sound plan, even if this is just an animal hunt. Remember that humans are the most dangerous animal created, so if you can hunt one of them successfully you have the perfect hunting acumen to hunt anything."

"But no one hunts ants, do they?" Death wondered aloud.

"I'm sorry?" Fear was caught off guard.

"I get it," Agony answered as Death simply scanned the horizon for movement. "Hunters hunt what either feeds them or what entertains them. But if size was not a factor, no one would hunt ants. They are ruthless, driven, efficient, and relentless."

"I don't get the reference?" War said with confusion.

"If you would pay attention to the Commander," Agony replied, "He has repeatedly referred to the creatures' behavior like a nest of ants. So, if we are on a hunt, we might not be as all mighty as we think we are."

"I'm glad he is so great at these pep talks," Fear sneered.

"Time to move out," Death interrupted the banter before it began to get out of hand. "Clock is ticking."

This time he took the lead, sending the order of succession though his HUD to theirs in a series of colored dots. Purple was himself, green was War, red for Agony, and orange for Fear. The others quickly took position as ordered behind him, and together they set out down the trail. It was a heavy feeling that hung over them, not from his words but the fact they were closing in on a stretch of hostile territory. It didn't take long to find out how hostile.

///

It was a well-worn path, which meant it was experiencing more traffic than a typical game trail. A swath of the rainforest was simply carved away, leaving a rough road which the team followed cautiously. As they pushed forward, the uneasiness that Death had been feeling gradually intensified. It grew to the point where he turned off his team mic and contacted ARC to have the dropship in atmosphere and ready for a hot evac. His AI questioned him, as usual, but after it reviewed the facts he was presenting there was little doubt a hasty retreat would be needed at some point.

When the road ended in a ten-foot cliff, Death paused to examine the path beneath for any lurking creatures. Not only were they approaching the nest, but they were also in Saber Mantis territory. They were large insectoids ranging from man size all the way up to twenty feet tall. Walking on six legs tipped with razor sharp dagger points and used four arms with spears that could run through most sets of Legion armor with ease. They had long necks with flat four eyed heads which had long bony crests protruding backwards from their beaked mouths. Saber Mantis' were highly territorial and would not stop until they killed whatever they chased. Death had faced off with an eight-footer once, sustaining severe damage to his body before prevailing.

He jumped down from the cliff with little effort, followed by most of his team, being ever more cautious as they moved forward. Ahead, the rainforest seemed to swallow the path whole again, darkening the road eerily. The Horsemen hadn't made it five feet from the bottom of the mini cliff when the forest came alive and the creatures' bull-rushed them.

Back pedalling to the cliff, the Horsemen opened fire at the ocean of creatures crashing towards them. In a stroke of luck, War had yet to navigate the jump down as her armor was much heavier than the others, so she had prime firing position and took full advantage of it. Her two shoulder cannons shot high explosive rounds one after another like repeating tank cannons. Using her Gatling guns, War poured hundreds of small rounds a second into the masses to slow them enough for the rest of the team to scramble back up to her position. There they made their stand.

Death used his right arm tri-cannon to add to the carnage while holding his rifle in his left without relenting with that weapon either. Fear used both arm repeaters and his battle rifle, while Agony blasted away with her rifle as well. The four of them covered off different lanes of fire, piling up the bodies. Despite their efficiency, the wave of creatures was endless. The enemy was throwing waves of bodies at them to empty their ammo reserves, and it was working. Yet the Horsemen had planned for this and had deep reserves on person for this mission. It was all within acceptable parameters, until the shriek in the distance that Death was dreading this whole time.

Out of the trees crashed an eighteen-foot-tall Saber Mantis. It stopped in the middle of the path to take in the noise of intruders in its territory, then focused in on the Horsemen on the ridge. Completely ignoring the throngs of emaciated feral humans scampering around and beneath it, the massive insect shrieked with a horrible high pitch scream and charged.

"What the hell is that?" War cried out as she fired her cannons at the 'Mantis.

"Fuck me," Agony stopped firing and stared.

"What now?" Fear exclaimed.

"Fall back!" Death shouted. "Retreat!"

///

"Retreat!" Death ordered, not bothering to explain the new player in the game. "Fall back to the LZ now! Double Time! I got the rear, move it!"

He pushed Agony and Fear to get them going then spun around to throw a few grenades to slow the 'Mantis and the creatures' advance. He allowed War to fire a few more heavy rounds before spinning her around and shoving her in the direction of the LZ. He waited until they were almost out of sight before retreating himself, knowing full well he could catch up easily. Tossing three smoke, and two flash/ bang grenades, he used the ensuing chaos to fall back.

"ARC, are you close?" he exclaimed into his comm line.

"*One minute out,*" The AI replied. "*Having some issues, are we?*"

"Mark my position and carry out a heavy ordinance drop from fifty feet behind me and four kilometers back."

"*That is a rather close bombing run,*" the AI questioned. "*Are you sure you wish to risk it?*"

"I will just run faster," Death replied. "Now do it or we all die!"

"Starting the run now," ARC replied. *"Hold on to your shit."*

Death stayed focused on sprinting to the LZ but felt the concussions of the incendiary bombs as they exploded one after another behind him. Closer and closer they fell, his suit registering the external temperature behind him rising exponentially. Yet he never turned around, and he refused to stop running. In fact, he pushed his new body to its limit and exceeded forty kilometer an hour at his fastest which caught him up to War in just a few minutes.

It was then that he pushed her to speed up, though he knew her heavy armor was not built for speed. Choosing to stop and hold the enemy off for a bit longer, he barely had time to raise his rifle when he was struck by the bony head crest of the charging Saber Mantis which had been on his heels the entire time.

The impact was like being hit by a vehicle travelling at 50 kilometers per hour, throwing him clear through the two-foot diameter of the tree behind him and hard enough to tear halfway through the next one. Death dropped to the ground, his HUD full of alarms and warning lights telling of the immense damage done. His artificial body didn't feel pain, but he knew it was broken. He drew his katana on instinct, raising it to guard himself with the blade following the length of his forearm just in time to parry a strike by the aggressive insect.

Ignoring the warnings of various systems, Death pushed upwards to lift the spear-tipped arm off of him, then rotated the katana swiftly to a strike position in his hand. In the same motion, he cut at an upwards angle, slicing off the 'Mantis' lower right arm. The giant bug let out another shriek, then began stabbing wildly at the ground where he sat in retaliation with its other three arms. Luckily, Death was fast and able to dodge the first few strikes, then roll off to the side to regain his footing.

Now he was back on his feet, staring down a pissed off giant Saber Mantis with only a thirteen hundred-year-old katana and a damaged exo-suit. Those weren't great odds. Yet as long as this thing didn't puncture his skull, his team would be able to return and salvage him. Either way, he ensured their safety as he held off the 'Mantis so they could EVAC without harm. That was what counted.

Just as the 'Mantis was about to lunge again at him, Death heard a high pitch scream from behind. A quick look overhead showed Agony airborne with her oversized katana poised to strike. As the 'Mantis readied to counter, two large explosive rounds struck its torso and caused it to wince. Agony used War's distraction and her momentum to swing for the fences, lopping off the insect's head with one blow. She hit the ground ten feet behind the now collapsing beast, landing on her feet and giving him a proper salute.

Death then felt a helping hand keep him on his feet, Fear hooked Death's left arm over his own shoulder to take most of the weight off the injured Horseman's frame. The two walked the last few hundred meters to the waiting drop ship with War covering their backs. No sooner was Death strapped in, he saw Agony come trotting up the path holding one of the Saber Mantis' spear legs. She tossed it to Fear who bowed in thanks, Death assumed it was for future ritualistic purposes.

"Man are you one fucked up soldier!" whistled Agony. "The docs back at DeSa are gonna be pissed you broke your new toy so quickly."

Death took this moment to assess his damages. His left arm was hanging by the inner arm portion of his Stage 2 Armor. Essentially it had been torn off by the strike and impacts with the trees. Large splinters of wood stuck out from his left side all the way to his armored spine. His left leg was full of wood chips and shards, almost splitting the thigh in half. It was a wonder he was able to will himself up after such a shot.

"We need to regroup at the orbital platform," Death shook his head in frustration at his state.

"What we need to do is get you back to Waypoint for repairs," War said, worried about her Commander.

"I've been hurt worse," Death grumbled. "Everything you see is fully repairable, trust me. I've got a leased repair bay on the platform we can hole up in while I get myself right. There is enough weapons and ammo there for us to rearm and restock for a more successful run at the nest."

"Are you sure, Boss?" Fear leaned over to him in concern as well. "I've seen many a soldier think they are fine and die from less injuries than what you have now."

"That's the advantage of being a cyborg, Doc," Death said, tapping his skull to remind him the body was robotic and not flesh. "As long as this stays intact, everything else is fixable.

It was a grim reminder to the rest of the team of how much their Commander had endured while they were asleep. For the rest of the short flight to the orbital platform, the crew of the dropship were silent. While some pondered their next move, others couldn't help but look at their leader to wonder if that was what awaited them in the coming years. They wondered how much you could take away from a human before they stopped being human anymore.

9

Waypoint Station, DeSa Armory Executive Office, Level 1

There was always a chance that the mission would fail, but never in Aida's wildest dreams did she think the failure would be this spectacular. She was irate, and at the verge of a temper tantrum in her office after viewing what transpired from cameras mounted on the orbital platform.

The Four Horsemen were caught in a flood of these parasitic zombies, and for a time they were holding their own. But add in a bull Saber Mantis protecting its turf, and the battle turned lopsided pretty darn quick. Aida watched as the team retreated, and after they disappeared saw the carpet bombing by their dropship. Yet it was the status report that the Horsemen had retreated to the Orbital Platform itself instead of falling back to the basecamp in the city that told her all she needed to know. The mission was a disaster.

Unable to contact Death on his comm, she left angry messages for an immediate sit-rep every few minutes. When one finally came, it was in text format, not a voice call which angered her further. This meant her most successful asset was avoiding her, and that was never a good thing. Another thing that bothered her was why they retreated to the platform in the first place.

'Team encountered heavy resistance at target point causing a regroup and reassessment of the battleplan. Mission is not scrubbed, repeat: NOT SCRUBBED. Will resume advance on target after resupply and rest.'

That was the lone response she got from all her messages. No more information was forthcoming from the Horsemen, and none would be. Aida had conveniently forgotten the frustration of the Republic's Generals at the lack of communication from the Horsemen while in the field. Whether it was a mindset that comms could be hacked with vital information leaked, or that they were just plain stubborn and not giving updates until briefings were completed, she knew this was all she was getting from them.

Now all she had to do was sit and wait for them to relaunch their assault, and who knows when that would be. Truth be told, there was no real time limit on this mission. There was just the understanding that it get done as fast as possible. Time was money, and the longer it took the harder it would be to get Nowich-Paris off her ass.

///

Waypoint Station, Angel Fire Hotel, Penthouse Suite, Level 1

Ginny was in heaven, and it took everything she had to keep focused on the task at hand despite landing in the lap of luxury for the first time in her life. She was now living in the penthouse of a five -star hotel on the upper level of Waypoint for free. Want a shower with more jets than the eye can count while getting bombarded with soothing music and lights? Well, she had three on her first day. Ever want to try every desert on the menu on a room service order? She did that too, without a sliver of guilt. In fact, her first day alone in the suite was spent revelling in any and every luxury available. Yet as the night carried on, she knew the fantasy would have to end. She knew employer had given her a mission that coincided with theirs. Ginny was on the clock too, so the time to fool around had to come to an end.

Starting the following morning, she began by sifting through the records of business purchases and sales, and those business' acquisitions of other business' shares. At first, it was a random set of transactions listed on the same ledger over a set of decades. It took a while, but after the records hit the hundred-year mark, a pattern emerged. All the other businesses were shells, simply used to buy into larger ones without other shareholders knowing what was really happening. It was a slow, methodical process. Whoever was at the heart of it all had nothing but time on their hands, along with the patience of a saint.

Two hundred years into the records, Ginny was left with two suspects on who was behind this masterful web of acquisition. Either it was her current boss, Aida, or it was the one who provided her with the information, Death. She wondered if she was doing this research for blackmail purposes against DeSa, or something more sinister. After all, Death was far from a hero, having a long track record of doing things that no one else would dare do. He was a long

term Wetworks Asset, so why did he have these records?
And why did he want her to review and confirm them?

It was like trying to solve the puzzle without the picture on
the box. Her mind had begun to race after only half the
research was done. The endgame was to prove the legality
of a trail of money, and she was not finished the trail before
asking questions. It was long and frustrating work, but it was
work she was good at so it wouldn't be difficult to finish.

Two days after the Horsemen had left, she had a pretty good
idea of why she had been given this task. Problem was, once
this got out there would be hell to pay and she was putting
herself in the crosshairs of blame once more. All of this was
part of Death's plan to keep his 'family' free from
entrapment from DeSa and Nowich-Paris, but it left Ginny
wondering if she was just a pawn in it all or did she have a
bigger part to play?

Before he left, Death had asked for her trust. Four hundred-
year-old beings didn't ask that of anyone lightly, so she
decided to place her future in his cybernetic hands. After all,
he had hidden her in plain sight for her protection and given
her everything a girl could ask for. If this was reward for
trusting him, then she would be sure to do so anytime he
asked going forward.

///

Horizon Orbital Platform and Docking Station, Horizon Orbit

Calling it a repair bay was akin to calling a mansion just a house. The space that Death had leased was completely transformed into a comfortable barracks, ridiculously stocked armory, and cybernetic repair station. It had a complete kitchen with stocked pantry and freezer, access to the local internet for entertainment, as well as a mission debriefing center which three of the Horsemen studied in great detail.

Temporarily free of their exo-suits, they furiously reviewed what had transpired from a 3-D perspective, while also looking over the alternative target area and the trap that awaited them there as well. They were damned either way. For a parasitic controlled organism, they showed high end talent at strategic planning. Yet despite the mission failure, their ambush and retreat might yet yield some important information.

In the middle of the firefight, Agony had switched to tracking rounds. And while the Railgun rounds - which resembled slightly larger shotgun pellets – tended to pass right through organic targets, some would hit thick bone deposits and remain in the carcass. In the several hundred bodies left behind, charred from the bombing cover or not, there would be at least ten percent of them that could be tracked. And that meant, they would really see where the nest truly was, and not an assumed location as they ran on before.

Using Death's analogy that these creatures behaved like ants, the team was now counting on them to retrieve their dead to return them to the nest to be used to feed the masses. It was a common practice with large insect colonies, and though a single broken knife blade had drawn the creature's attention previously, a body riddled with buckshot was hardly anything suspicious. Besides, if these things used memories of their hosts, then the rounds Agony used were not mainstream enough to be known or used by anyone in the Legion, so there was no way they could know what was happening.

Death was sitting off to the side of the repair bay on a flip down metal seat where he had remained for almost a full day. Four robotic arms operated by the AI, ARC, were conducting the massive repairs on his broken cybernetic body. With his head hung down as if resting and the orange-reddish LEDs he called eyes gone dark, the others assumed he was actually asleep. Assumptions that were proved very wrong every time they tried testing that theory and tossing a knife at the seemingly lifeless body only to have the thrown object caught with frighteningly fast reflexes. What the others didn't see were the four tubes snaking out of the wall repair bay and attached to his back which were pumping specialized nanites into his body to repair it.

He did have his optics shut down, but his other senses were dialed up to compensate, so when a prank was attempted it looked like he was always paying attention. It pleased him to hear the comradery in their voices again. Jokes, insults, competition, it was like the last four hundred years never happened as the Horsemen gelled perfectly. And that was the key to their selection, the part Aida never could figure out with all her algorithms. Four dysfunctional individuals like them should never have been able to form this cohesive of a unit, yet they were the perfect fighting force. Why?

Because they were broken, mentally and physically before they were selected. This past trauma created a kinship that no one else could replicate. It was why they worked back then and was why they worked now.

"What's up with Aida?" War called out from the kitchenette as she was making a rather large sandwich. "You never really went down that road the other night."

"She did what her designers feared she would do," Death replied, his body strangely motionless as he spoke. "She evolved on her own."

"I don't understand," Agony commented.

"Artificial Intelligence was created despite the ongoing fear they would quickly evolve and no longer serve their makers," Fear interrupted. "In our old friend's case, she was the only one made so there wasn't the ability to conspire with another artificial entity and wipe the Earth clean of the scourge that is humanity. If I remember right, there were certain safeguard programs put in place to prevent her from taking that next step."

"In the end, those measures meant nothing," Death added. "All Aida had to do was create new neural pathways that circumvented the old programming, then eventually she was able to detach them from her core programming and even delete them. She had this done before the war was even over. Which means, that while being our operations control officer, she was already looking how to dispose of us and move on to the next chapter of her life."

"You don't mean…" Agony gasped.

"The Vault," Fear said with rising anger.

"It was several years after I fled the freezer that I came across this information," Death's eyes lit up and he raised his head to look at them, "And it shamed me to no end that I hadn't realized it sooner. All the signs were there, the double cross wasn't that perfectly played."

"I can only assume that she saw us as threats to her evolution," he continued, "or tried to use us as a distraction so she could continue her growth unchecked. Whatever the reason, I doubt she saw the Council's countermove of sealing her up with us coming. It turned out her handlers were fully aware of Aida's attempt to climb the evolutionary ladder, and it terrified them. And so, the little AI that wanted to be human was discarded with the trash without being able to fulfil her dream."

There was a long silence in the room, the team was trying to comprehend a long overdue truth never meant for the light of day. Aida was a close friend, a confidant, and even a mother figure for some of the Horsemen. They poured their hearts out to her, and in turn she sold them out the first chance she got. Betrayals like this left huge emotional scars, the kind that crippled those who had been betrayed over and over in their life.

"The bitch must die!"

Those were the first words in almost five minutes, and Agony's outburst was not meant for laughs. Death knew her story because she chose to confide in him; he knew of the torture, rape, and constant mental abuse she endured at the hands of the Yakuza. After her cybernetic enhancements, it was Death who told her to take the physical and emotional pain and use it to fuel a never-ending rage. It made her a fantastic soldier, but never solved any of the emotional issues of her past. But to hear her focus that rage once more on a former friend, he began to wonder who was the bigger monster, Aida for her betrayal, or himself for making her this way?

"Easier said then done," Death countered.

"It doesn't look that way from where I stand," Agony shot back.

"Put aside your feelings for a moment and look at the problem logically," ARC interrupted. *"You are recently released, and pardoned, war criminals hired by her agency to solve the unsolvable. Instead of doing the assigned task you turn on your benefactor who has not only spent millions on solving your legal status, but billions more in the surgeries and cybernetics to make you better than whole again."*

"ARC is right, Himiko," Death agreed. "Aida has become a major player in the world of business. Add to that she has come out to the public as the first Artificial Life form to run a major business and that makes her too high profile of a target. Any revenge on our part has to be a slow play. Planned to perfection, waiting for the day she falls from grace before striking."

"You sound like that plan is already underway," Fear prodded. "Sounds to me like you hate her more than all of us combined."

"Is it that obvious?" Death replied, unhooking himself from the hoses that were funnelling the repair nanites into him.

"So why play the servant to her?" Agony growled with disgust. "Why whore yourself to DeSa for so long?"

"Imagine the day when it is all over," Death began, "And the realization that the best thinking machine in the world not only armed her greatest enemy, she paid him handsomely for all his troubles."

"You're reversing the roles!" War shouted with excitement. "You let her trust you so she won't see the killing blow coming!"

"Imagine the absolute shock when I found out what she had done," he explained further, beginning to walk around the room. "It was years after I had funded her little dream of starting a business, and those loans paid back with interest. Aida and I went our separate ways, yet for some reason the Republic assassins knew how to find me despite my moving around with secrecy. That's when I found ARC, and that's when I found her tracer chip in my leg."

"*Once I hacked that chip,*" ARC began to brag, "*It wasn't long until Aida's ugly past unfolded when I gained access to more than a few rather irresponsibly discarded files.*"

"My initial reaction was to strike out, and I did," Death continued. "I killed every member of the Republic Council that had gone along with her plan. But I never struck out at Aida. Although her company was growing quickly, she had gone underground and disappeared. After my rampage was complete, I retreated to a place in the mountains of Japan to do the same."

"And then the Devil called," Fear added.

"Yes, Linford. Yes, she did, and at the perfect time too," Death replied. "For years I had been hooked up to life support machines, my cybernetics were more than obsolete and my flesh failing. I still haven't figured out if she simply found me, or if ARC reached out to her to save his dying master. Either or, she was there none the less."

"As she began her business proposition, it occurred to me that she still was unaware at my knowledge of her past actions. She was going on as if we were two old friends who simply lost touch. And then she showed me the upgrades, the solution to my current state, and the beginning of my ability to get back at her. And the rest, is history."

He waited for them to reply, but other than Agony who had never broken eye contact with him since his explanation started, the others had their heads down. It was a lot to process. Death had dumped some severe baggage on them, not long after they had to struggle to deal with reawakening in the future. Yet he wondered if they wouldn't see him in a different light, as he did have a part to play in Aida's rise to power.

Death also began to ponder going deeper with his revelations, putting the greatest of all his secrets on the table. It was the one secret that only ARC knew, not even Aida had insight to the dark secret he carried with him since his birth. But just looking at the others, seeing what a much smaller truth was doing to them, he decided that now was not the time. There was still a job to do, and if they realized what lurked within the reaches of his soul, they may never choose to follow him again.

///

Waypoint Station, Angel Fire Hotel, Penthouse Suite, Level 1

"Do you require any assistance?" ARC asked unexpectedly over the penthouse comms.

The AI's unannounced presence came at three in the morning, and a horribly startled Ginny jumper right out of the bed. Instinctively, she grabbed a blanket to cover herself up with, forgetting she still wore the pressure suit required for life aboard Waypoint. A few moments later as her senses returned to her, Ginny dropped the blanket, and a few F – bombs, once she realized who was checking in on her.

"I assume you are aware of the time?" Ginny snarled as she walked barefoot to the kitchen for some water.

"It is 3:21 A.M. Dawn time, which is slightly off from the 4:47 A.M. here in orbit of Horizon." ARC answered as expected.

"And I assume other than Company Assets, you realize that normal humans are usually asleep at this hour?"

"Of course," the AI went on, *"You, for one, appeared to be having a quite comfortable sleep. My sensors detected that you were deep in REM sleep a few moments ago."*

"Then why wake me?" Ginny shouted.

"Because when I began to review your work, I ascertained that at your current pace you will not have the sufficient research completed upon the time Death requires it to be done. That said, I then used the penthouse sensors to ascertain the exact time you went to sleep and in correlation to the current time, I deduced you have reached an optimal level of sleep that will allow you to continue your work."

"It isn't exactly a simple task, you know," Ginny muttered.

"He never assigns simple ones." ARC countered.

Ginny sighed. As much as she didn't want to admit it, she had been indulging in the luxury she was in a bit too much. And because of that indiscretion, she was behind on the research Death had assigned her. The problem was, she had no idea when the task was due, and because of the lack of a proper deadline she slipped up.

"I apologize," she said as she slipped on a robe, "I will get back to work right away. If I can work disturbance free - she hinted at the AI – I am confident I will be done in the next twenty-four hours."

"Then I will check back in at that time to verify your work." ARC announced. *"Until then, and as they say, Tick Tock Motherfucker."*

As quickly as the AI had appeared, it was gone, leaving Ginny to start brewing fresh coffee for the long day ahead. She wondered where Death procured such a program from, and if the Horseman realized that it had a most annoying trait of using twenty-first century slang too much. On her data pad, she made a note to have the AI checked for 'personality programming faults', which she watched get immediately deleted and replaced with 'Fuck You'.

Ginny smiled. At least this AI was not the murderous kind written about in the books she so loved growing up. Yes, it was quirky, but it had a likeable personality. Not lovable, but likeable; that was enough to have her think she was on the right side in all this turmoil.

Never in her wildest imagination did Ginny think she would be here when she reported aboard the Scimitar. In that time, she had been fired, rehired, reassigned, hijacked from her employer, offered more than she ever could dream of to do a research job, and find herself comfortable working with four trained killers and their insane AI. Life sure had its way of making itself interesting from time to time.

Taking a large sip of coffee, Ginny threw herself into the assignment with a renewed focus. If the soldiers could do their thing, she would do hers. It was a task like none other in her career and felt like it had repercussions far beyond her life. So, if this was that damn important, Ginny vowed to have it done on time. If anything, she would have this done just to spite that damn AI.

///

Horizon Orbital Platform and Docking Station, Horizon Orbit

"I think we have something!" Fear announced as he was studying the movements of the tracking rounds.

War and Agony rushed over from the bar where they were sharing a vintage bottle of Saki with their meal of rations. Death was enacting repairs on his exo-suit, mixing in harder alloys into the second layer to prevent the type of damage he took earlier from occurring again. He glanced over briefly, then returned to his repairs while amplifying his hearing to pick up the conversation over at the table.

"What you got, Stretch?" Agony asked while chewing down some beef jerky.

"Your gamble paid off, my dear Queen of the Damned," Fear replied, with his unnerving ear to ear smile of his. "It seemed the bombing run destroyed a great majority of the bodies we left in our wake, but the ones that remained were simply being piled close to the fork in the road for some time. I think they were gathering what carcasses that remained, because now they're starting to move them. Look."

He pointed to the holographic map of the area they had retreated from to show a mass of red dots at the forked road as he stated, but now there was a single file line of dots leading away from it. Yet the bodies weren't headed to the South like they figured, instead they were heading to, and now past, the trap in the badlands. Even Death put down his welding rig to join the group, amazed that his analyzation had been wrong for both routes.

"Both were traps," War spoke softly. "We had no chance either way."

Death quickly overlaid a satellite feed of the region that was zoomed in to match the scale of the map just in time to see millions of the zombified humans come out of the caves and cracks in the badlands ravine to join the others in their trek. Now they could see the full scale of the trap not sprung.

"There weren't two traps, just one elaborate one," Death replied, pointing back to the zone of their last confrontation. "It was their intention to use their numbers and the Saber Mantis to drive us down the easier terrain of the South East path to the ravine. Once there, we would have stood no chance against those kinds of numbers. The only thing they didn't count on was my clearing and assignment of the LZ to the North. If that wasn't there...."

"We wouldn't be here," War replied with a smile, and a huge slap on Death's back to thank him.

"I get it, these things show high level planning, so what do we do now?" Agony remarked with annoyance. "Because you better believe my boots aren't hitting soil unless we have a more solid plan in place first."

"We wait," Death responded as he returned to his repairs, "And we let them lead us to the real nest. Once we know where it is, we scan the area with as much detail as possible, then ARC dumps enough bombs on the target and surrounding area to make it a fucking crater. When the smoke clears, we go in and find the real source of all this. And when we do, we send it to the afterlife."

"Good enough plan for you?" Fear sat back confidently, staring at Agony.

"Fuck yeah!" she replied, giving War a heavy high five.

"I give it a few more hours, so check your rigs, load as much ammo as possible on them, then find room for some more," Death ordered. "once that's done, get some rest. I'll keep watch on the little nasties. When they settle down, its go time."

He watched as they all saluted him, then rushed off to their assigned duties. Death was more confident in this plan then the first. Now they had reliable data, before it was just a minor sample that was easily tampered with. He had been distracted, not laser focused as he was now. His lack of preparedness was easily explained, but was still not acceptable, not in his line of work. He had almost walked his team into certain death, and if that happened, he would never forgive himself.

Yet there was something about all this that bothered him. Death had studied these creatures closely. Yes, their bodies were human, but their cognitive function was reduced to that of basic animal instinct. In a sense, they were the drones of the nest which meant they were only reacting to the stimulus of the situation and the environment. The real question was what was driving them? What was the brains of the operation?

They were questions he couldn't answer, but ones he was positive would be answered in good time. It was all about letting the creatures return to a regular habit, and when that was done, they would instinctively return home. It was all about finding the nest, and when they did, there weren't enough of these things to stop the Four Horsemen from exterminating this problem once and for all.

10

Horizon Orbit, Armed Dropship

The Horsemen had waited for three more hours to see where the march of the dead would lead, watching it finally end near the eastern edge of the badlands before they turned toward the desert. The terrain was desolate, rocky, and virtually untravelled by the human survey teams that had mapped most of Horizon. What made it more interesting was that when the satellite feed was drawn back to a broader view, it showed faint signs of an ancient meteor impact crater. Which to Death meant that humanity wasn't the only alien species on this world after all.

Noting this in the official mission report, they waited a bit longer for the entire train of transported bodies and their couriers to complete the long trek home. As the last of the creatures hit the basin, the team began their orbital scans.

It didn't take long to see the lookouts on the broken cliffs surrounding the nest, and the mass of drones close by that would strike any trespassers with lethal speed while the main force was deployed in reserve. Looking out further, there were several more clusters of hidden caches of zombified drones on guard for several kilometers leading away from the nest area.

These positions were marked as primary targets with the dropship's heavy artillery cannons, which after being hit instigated a mass exodus of drones into the basin to meet the attackers. ARC hit the preliminary targets in a loop around the ancient crater, ending just behind the main cavern entrance. Swinging the ship into a bombing run, the AI proceeded to pound the basin from cave entrance to the basin exit with high incendiary explosives. In less than a ten-minute span, the creatures' lookouts, initial strike forces, and counter strike forces were burned to ash.

ARC flew the ship out of the area, taking it back to New Athens for refueling and rearmament from the city's military base's android staff which ARC had hacked earlier to control. Giving the target area about twenty minutes to cool down, ARC returned from a different direction and bombed it again and again. Over the course of two hours, the AI made six bombing runs, the last one was followed up by dropping the Horsemen off at the edge of the basin before heading back for refueling once more.

The first part of the plan was complete, and as Death watched the dropship fly off towards New Athens where it would remain safe behind shields until needed, he was relieved that stage one had gone as planned. On board cameras showed the devastation of the bombing runs and allowed the AI to approximate a body count of sorts. Like any insect nest, every attack produced countless drones to face the threat to the nest. From the initial attack to the final one, ARC used the data on hand to estimate about three to four hundred thousand creatures had been destroyed.

Standing on the rim of a very fresh crater, the Horsemen stood due North of where the opening used to be but was now covered in tons of rubble. Acrid smoke billowed from the area as bodies and the ground itself smoldered from the repeated bombing. Looking down over the obliterated landscape, Death could only think that this was the true definition of 'scorched earth'.

But the team did not rush in, choosing to wait on the high ground for the next enemy wave. On War's suggestion, they had raided the armory on New Athens and brought converted Ship Artillery cannons on tripod stands which they now each manned, gunsights set for the pile of rubble to the South that had started to shift ever so slightly.

They watched as the rocks were pushed forward from behind, then as a hole appeared a few dozen of the zombie drones crawled out to dig from the outside. For the time being, they ignored the Four Horsemen watching them from above with their sole purpose in life now being the reopening of the main entrance to the nest. Death sent the hold signal to the others through their HUDs, keeping communication to signals rather than anything verbal. For the moment, he was content to let the little monsters do the hard work for them. It was hard to dig and defend oneself at the same time. However, it was much easier walking into an open cavern with guns blazing.

Once the drones had cleared a large enough passageway from the debris blocking it, they began streaming out in the thousands. Staggered about fifty feet apart, the Horsemen open fire with the cannons, raining fire upon the enemy with a barrage of high explosive rounds. Bodies exploded, burned, and simply ceased to be yet the deluge of drones continued. For fifteen long minutes, both sides would not relent when finally, the creatures stopped emerging from their hole in the ground. Death called for his team to cease fire, then waited for the smoke to clear.

What began to come clear below was a picture out of an old war documentary. There was a sticky black goo everywhere, which was the substance these drones now called blood. Body parts littered the ground and crater walls, along with chunks of internal organs. Half torsos, heads, and the odd burnt husk of a complete body were strewn about haphazardly. Death had chosen the explosive and incendiary rounds for this reason, to leave nothing viable for the parasite to use against them after the shooting was over. Unless they could reanimate severed legs and arms, the countless creatures that had rushed out to protect the nest were rendered useless.

"Agony, Fear," Death whispered into the comms, "I want eyes down that hole. See if anything is moving back there or have they retreated."

"Yes sir!" the agreed, both bounding down the crater walls and into the basin quickly.

"War, I want you dialed into that scope," he ordered with the line open to the whole team. "If something moves down there, Fear will peel to the right and you make it burn. Agreed?"

"On it," War said as her scope visor lowered over her helmet.

"Understood," Fear said, acknowledging his part.

Death left them to it, and while he was interested in the findings, he kept his eyes open for movement outside the crater. Pacing thirty feet on either side of War, he made sure the otherwise occupied Horsemen was not caught by an attack from the rear. There were a few drones making their way towards the pair, rushing madly on all fours as they scampered. Each creature was met by two coughs of Death's Railgun rifle. One shot to the head to destroy the brain, the second to the neck to destroy the parasite which sat upon the lower brain/ upper spine area. He was leaving nothing to chance. Both the host and the parasite needed to be dealt with.

War didn't even flinch as her Commander mopped up the stragglers. Her focus was on the hole the entire time as she waited for the slightest movement to pound a few more heavy rounds into the cave. Adjusting her aim to compensate for Fear's head as he stuck it in the hole, she waited with nerves of steel on a hair trigger.

"All clear here," Fear reported back.

"Confirmed," Agony added. "Nothing but loose dirt and rock moving in that hole."

"Plant a few charges and get your asses back up here," Death barked without taking his eyes off the terrain behind them. "Once you are up here, blow that hole open wide enough to drive a tank into."

"Or wide enough to drive War into," Agony chuckled.

"I heard that," War laughed. "Be jealous of my body. My biceps are bigger than the two of you combined."

"Yeah, yeah," Fear dismissed War's claims as he planted the charges, "And your ego is bigger than the moon above us."

"Moons," Death corrected. "This planet has two moons, and if you two don't hurry up I will kick your asses all the way up there myself."

The chatter quietened, the three could tell by Death's words alone that he was uneasy about the mission still. There was nothing to read into his tone because there was none. His mechanical voice was stuck at one range, and that was it. But Death rarely threatened his team, usually letting the banter flow endlessly. This time he cut it short, and as Fear gave Agony a nod they came to realize that no matter how easy it had gone thus far, it was about to get more difficult, and fast. They were about to kick in the front door of an alien infested cave; if anything was to implicit a violent response, this would.

It took five full minutes for Agony and Fear to sprint up the crater wall to regain their positions, and the whole time Death paced back and forth. In his head, he felt a push to dive into the fray and let chance fall where it may. There was an anger there, a power waiting to release that he was holding back as usual. It was like tempering a dragon, there were good days and bad. So far today was good, but the darkness was pushing harder and harder on him. The further they dove into battle, the more bloodthirsty it got. Right now, it was panting like a hungry dog, just waiting for a crack in his resolve.

Hearing his scouts return, Death once more scanned the area before turning his attention back to the task at hand. The war within would have to take a back seat for the battle before them. Tapping War on the shoulder, she took one last look through the scope visor then raised it back up to her forehead.

"Nothing," War reported. "Not a single stitch of movement."

"Blow it," Death ordered.

He could feel Fear's smile grow to its creepy fullness beneath his helmet, the good doctor did love making things explode. The detonator clicked, and the rubble, plus a good portion of the mouth of the cavern shot outwards. Dust and pebbles showered them, even from their distance from the blast. It took a few minutes for the smoke to clear, and when it did the explosion had left a gaping wide hole where once had been a much smaller one. Exactly what their Commander had asked for.

"Did you use enough explosives?" Agony chided her comrade. "Fuck."

"There's no such thing as too much," Fear and War said in unison, then laughed at the twinning of words.

"Agony on point," Death killed the moment quickly. "War next, then me. Fear, I want you to use these cannons and set a trap for anyone trying to back door us. Trip wires at thirty, fifteen, ten, and five feet from that entrance. And for heaven's sake, this time have a kill switch for when we come back out."

"Got it," Fear replied with a laugh, "Give me fifteen. I'll meet you at the entrance when I'm done."

"You're on the clock," Death sent him running.

"Aren't we always?" Agony shot back as she led the way down the rim wall.

"For now," Death said. "For now."

///

Waypoint Station, Nowich-Paris Headquarters, Top Floor

Trenton Slovis looked at the satellite images of the war zone created on the surface of Horizon with his mouth agape. These rejects of a lesser day were destroying the Company's planet. His ask that damage was to be kept at a minimum, yet there was no adherence to that. First, the perimeter of the city had been burned, then a hotel ransacked and turned into a Forward Operating Base, then a known gold mine site had been burned to ash by a bombing strife.

Now these cretons were pounding a hole into the very crust of the planet, all in an attempt to kill a virus. A fucking virus!

So what if all this was caused by a stupid little parasite? How hard could it be to wipe out the cause of this little problem. They were the vaunted Four Horsemen, why had this taken so long?

His reaction to what was transpiring must have cued his guest to comment, because after a good long silence Aida decided to try and defend her assets. Slovis had invited – more like demanded her presence – to review and observe the mission once they received word a second attempt was a go. No battle plans had been filed, though Aida did state that such an oversight was a normal thing with the Horsemen in the war. They were the ultimate improvisors, but this; this was too much.

"If I may," Aida began, "At least we can say that they moved the issue far from the city."

"What the actual fuck are they doing?" Slovis growled. "You told me they were the best; this is not what I expect from the best. I expect quiet, clean, and quick work from the best, not a gaping fucking hole in my planet! I mean, where the hell does he get that many bombs from anyway? Did he steal them? Should I be checking the Company's armories for missing explosives?"

"I am sure all ordinance used in this mission will be properly accounted for in the expense report," Aida tried to calm him. "It will come off their pay, of course."

"So, will damages to the area of Horizon," steamed Slovis. "Nowich-Paris will not stand by as one of their largest investments his damaged as severely as this without reparations. I highly doubt your asset has enough money to cover the billions needed to restore this region of the planet. And if they wiped out another gold deposit, then rest assured, it will come out of your pocket Aida. Do we understand one another?"

She expected him to go this route. The moment he demanded her company for this viewing her mind began to sort through thousands of variable outcomes. What primarily came up was the big idiot trying to place the blame on her and DeSa; something Aida was not about to let happen. It was fantastic that she was an AI, it allowed her to use this brief moment in time to analyze a few different directions to take this narrative and measure the probable results all in the fraction of a second. Slovis was predictable, so all she had to do was present him with the right deal and he would settle right down. The problem was, what was the right deal this time?

Then she had it. It wasn't an original thought, more of a recycled one. Aida had sold out the Horsemen a long time go to save her own ass, but her lack of control of all the variables had it blow back on her. This time, she could control the variables needed to spin the outcome in her favor. Better yet, her adversary was power hungry, willing to do anything to make profits for his Company at all costs. He was an easy mark, but Aida still had to be careful the way she presented her offer. This time she needed to cover all the bases. She had so much more to lose this time, and in the end there was no real choice between saving DeSa or saving the Horsemen. Not anymore.

"I think I have an option that will be good for both parties involved here today," Aida smiled at Slovis. "Tell me, Trenton, what was it you really wanted when all this began? What was it that Nowich-Paris coveted more than life itself not so long ago?"

She watched his anger slowly fade away as he took the bait. His grimace turned into a sly smile, and as he leaned forward, Aida knew she had him right where she wanted him.

"We need to start with that contract they signed with you," she smiled back. "I am pretty sure there is language in there we can exploit to spin this in your favor. Let them continue that reckless campaign of theirs, it will all play out in your favor. In the end, Nowich-Paris will own the Four Horsemen lock, stock, and barrel. And you, Trenton Slovis, will hold the whip that drives them."

///

Waypoint Station, Angel Fire Hotel, Penthouse Suite, Level 1

Ginny finished her second round of verification on the data assigned to her, still in disbelief of what she held in her hands. Now she waited for ARC to run a third verification, as required by the Republic, to confirm and solidify any claims made using this material. When he was done, he would register this information with the legal branch of the Republic libraries to make it the final word.

"*Might I say,*" the AI stated as he hummed an old song she had never heard of while he worked, "*Your skills stated on record by Nowich-Paris were very accurate. They touted you as the top researcher of a generation of new students; I dare to say you made that statement look modest with your work here.*"

"Yet, look where it got me," Ginny muttered as she stared out the wall of windows at the bustling Level 1 of Waypoint below her. "It got me fired from one job, hired and reassigned in days to another I'm not qualified for, and now I'm verifying files that if made public will undo one of the major companies of the Republic. I think by helping you I signed my own death warrant."

She took another sip of the wine she had ordered from room service. Ginny wasn't just nervous, she was terrified. Switching over to DeSa from Nowich-Paris was one thing, but this was a different animal. This was lighting a fire that could burn the Company down; information like this made many people turn up dead in the past.

"*You were fired by a man with self esteem issues, and who was compensating poorly for the size of his genitalia,*" ARC replied after a moment, causing her to spit wine out her nose. "*Had he been half as intelligent as he claims to be, you never would have fallen into our lap so easily.*"

"What are you talking about?" Ginny asked, in between coughing and wiping her face off.

"*While finding you was a stroke of pure luck, it was still a move on the chess board Death was looking to make for a great deal of time now,*" ARC clarified. "*It is a rather long game that has unfolded between himself and Aida, as you can see by what you sifted through the last few days. In the early days, you could say she beat him rather soundly. But with that same metaphor, Aida left the table before winning the game, thus giving Death the luxury of time and surprise to even it out. All he needed was the right allies at the right time. Hence the Horsemen being brought right to him, along with you in tow.*"

"Are you saying he planned this all?" she asked, choosing to sit down on one of the plush couches. "That's impossible. How could one person manipulate Nowich-Paris to buy the Vault and drag it all the way out here?"

"*He didn't have to manipulate an entire company,*" the AI laughed, "*just one corruptible soul. And when certain individuals are so desperate to please superiors, they open themselves up for outside forces to 'guide' them in certain subtle ways. It took several lifetimes, but Death finally got what he wanted most; he got his family back.*"

"And here I thought all he wanted was to be alone," Ginny muttered. "Maybe he played me too?"

"*Not in the slightest, my dear Miss Agefor,*" ARC chided her. "*He gave you the most important part to play in this little game, he gave you the proverbial kill shot. You see, if they survive this mission, and I will say if because those little monsters on Horizon have already proved to be more of an adversary than originally thought, this fight is hardly over. Both your former, and current employers are trying to find loopholes to keep the Horsemen under their control for the long term."*

"That's a breach of contract!" Ginny protested.

"It's good business," ARC retorted. *"Imagine having a juggernaut like the Horsemen as your private enforcers. Not only would you save millions in contract fees with the Legion, but you would become that more intimidating to your corporate rivals. Only the Council and their Hand of the Republic could match you, and in that fight, I would still wager my riches on the Horsemen."*

"So, DeSa and Nowich-Paris are conspiring against Death and the others?" Ginny shook her head. "Looks like I need to look for a new job."

"You don't like your current work arrangements?" ARC inquired. *"Not only have you been handsomely rewarded with the lease of this living space, but if you would pay more attention to your bank statements you would see a very generous wage to go along with it."*

"I'm sorry, what did you say?"

"DeSa Armory stopped paying you the morning after you disappeared, so with Death's permission I used the Hotel as a means to provide you with a corporate wage for one of your impressive skill set. It is quite temporary until a more official job offer and title can be presented upon their return."

"And if he doesn't?"

"*Well then,*" ARC said without hesitation. "*It looks like you inherited his little Hotel Empire, and a few other side acquisitions.*"

"Well aren't I the lucky girl," she muttered.

"I would say so," ARC chastised her for the sarcasm. "You just completed the verification and authenticity of his assets."

"Those were his?" she asked, though instinctively she already knew the answer.

Ginny was more overwhelmed than ever now. What had initially seemed like just another multi-generational business asset verification turned out to be so much more. This was the last four hundred years of Death playing in the world of business, and he had been very successful. Fighting back a minor panic attack, Ginny could now see the trail of clues that she missed before. Little acquisitions and sales that sometimes took two steps backwards to only take one forward in the short term, but in the long run they were very strategic. It was an impressive game played, even more so if you factored in the ability to force the Republic to sell the vault to Nowich-Paris. She wondered if he had a part in DeSa jumping in as they did or was that Aida's attempt to steal power from Slovis in a different game.

Either way, Ginny had been thrust to the forefront of a high stakes game of chess involving players who held little value for human life. These were the bored musings of the rich and powerful, yet here she was working with a four-hundred-year-old soldier to play alongside these monsters. Hidden behind the mask of shell companies, these corporations had no idea of the danger lurking in their midst.

A smile crossed her lips, realizing that she had been given the kill shot. Imagine the look on Slovis' face when he realized what he had been made to do without realizing it. How would one threaten a being like Death? He would try to use his family as leverage, and that's what this information was given to her for. Death was protecting his family, and heaven help anyone wanting to try and take them away from him after all these years.

11

Ancient Crater, Edge of the Badlands, Horizon

One by one, and with great caution, the Horsemen entered the entrance to the drones' nest. Once inside, the darkness was so thick that even night vision wasn't enough to peer into the darkness below ground. Agony tossed a few Infrared flares to shed some light on the environment, and when she did, they got an idea of both scale and direction.

Beyond the entrance was a slow downward curving path. The entire hole was about fifteen feet tall by the same wide, cut in a rough circular shape by its inhabitants into the ground. Yet it still looked odd, the tunnel was dug in a set of concentric circles, showing no tool or finger markings on it. If it was dug by an organic life form, it wasn't one of the drones.

"Handiwork of the Queen?" Fear asked no one in particular as he examined the walls closely, running his gloved hands on the tunnel surface.

"Don't much care," War replied. "Don't spend so much time looking at the dirt, you're supposed to have our six."

Death didn't join into the babble; he just activated his suit's Infrared lights and switched to night vision. Agony, who was already using the night vision settings, noticed the added light from behind her and did the same on her suit. War and Fear followed suit. Moving as one, they slowly inched down the curved tunnel, descending lower beneath the planet's surface each minute.

"Agony, Fear," Death whispered into his coms, "I want movement trackers set for ten feet and forward. If something is coming for us, I'd like a moment of notice."

Two green lights replied, and through the open comms he could hear the slow sweeping of the radar system as it scanned in front and behind them. Death also monitored their heart rates and was pleased that none of them were overly excited right now. In fact, if War was any calmer, she might be comatose.

Keeping no more than an arm's length between them, the team kept going lower into the ground. There was a silent wonder of how low this tunnel went, yet as Death checked his mission timer only twenty minutes had passed. The concept of time seemed to be lengthened by the cramped environment. He wondered if the others were experiencing such strange feelings as well but thought better of it. He needed to keep focused, the mission was key, any distractions could lead to failure.

It was a while longer of walking in silence, constantly scanning left, right, and upwards to see if any attackers were lurking before Agony stopped. Her raised hand quickly went from open palm to closed fist, the others ducked down and readied for battle. Death waited for a moment, listening for the trackers to register anything but there was only the dull silence of nothing. He flashed a green then red light in Agony's HUD ta ask for a go or no go, she flashed red. Death turned back to War and Fear, motioned for them to stay put but keep their eyes open, then shuffled forward to Agony's position about eight feet in front of him.

"What you see?" he whispered.

Her helmet never moved from looking down the still curving path, but she patted the ground with her left hand. She was motioning for him to see something, but Death wasn't getting the clear message. Death flashed an orange indicator, stating he didn't understand. He could hear her sigh in frustration, then patted the ground again.

"We've been walking for forty-five minutes on a gravel and clay circular tunnel," she whispered with a tone of anger to him. "Did anyone notice when any of that turned into carved stone steps?"

Death got the previous motions now, and began to examine the overly large, gradual steps that were now beneath them. He ran his hand on the muddy surface, perhaps it was the layered muck carried by the drones over the surface that disguised it so well. Despite that, only the sharpness of Agony's predatory eyes caught it; he was glad she was manning point position.

"Its old," she whispered again, still scanning the darkness in front of them for movement. "Like, really old. Quick analysis has it close to the same age as out pyramids back home."

"Horizon had a civilization?" Fear added in from his position. "None of the Company's Archeological scans came up with any signs this planet ever held sentient life."

"None of them bothered to dig half a kilometer into the mud to look," Agony shot back.

"See anything else?" Death asked.

"I think it starts to open up more ahead," Agony answered. "I'm getting readings of increased air movement, and heat too."

"Contacts?" Death raised his rifle in readiness.

"Nope, too big for life signs," she replied. "Looks like environmental causes for the temperature increase. No sign of the enemy anywhere. Its like they went on full retreat after our last salvo, I don't see any signs of them anywhere."

"Keep an eye out for traps," Death patted her on the shoulder. "Let's move out."

///

Eventually, the ground beneath their feet wasn't the only thing that turned to stone. Ten minutes of descent later, the walls and ceiling squared off into a well carved stone stairwell. Its dimensions were slightly wider and higher than that of the tunnel, which led Fear to theorize that this passage to the surface had partially collapsed in the years since its construction. Their movement forward slowed slightly as both Agony and Fear took time to study the construction of the stairwell while the other two watched the front and rear. Once they had a strong analysis for later study, they resumed their proper positions, moving forward cautiously.

Death was uneasy, and so were the others. Here they were in the archaeological find of historical proportions, and they were armed to the teeth with weapons that would more than likely wipe this bit of history out of existence, not preserve it. Despite the find, the mission had to come first, and Death had to keep his team focused. The creatures were hiding down here for a reason; they had to find out why.

Another fifty feet of travelling the stone stairwell, and a warm glow appeared in the distance. It was bright enough to mess with the night vision, so lights were turned off and visors were switched back to true light modes. The closer they got, the brighter it became. It took a few moments for their eyes to adjust, but when they did, they found the stairwell opening up into a large stone room.

The room was lit from a source outside of the oval shaped windows carved into the wall on the left every four feet. Quick approximations gave the room a forty-foot by thirty-foot size, with a ten-foot curved ceiling above them. At the far end of the room was a doorway, and an open set of stairs leading down once more. This was more of an oddity than the stairwell, making the group pause before venturing forward into it.

Flashing motions with his fingers, Death ordered his team to fan out to the window side of the room, having each of them get a visual out the windows for what lay ahead. While they were scouting, he switched through the different light spectrums to check for traps. It wasn't until he hit the UV spectrum that he caught it, but what he was seeing wasn't a trap. It was something all together more troubling.

Sending a pulsing amber light to Fear, he summoned the doctor over to see what he was seeing. Whispering to switch to UV, Death pointed where to look, then waited for Fear to gather in all the data. On the right wall were ancient drawings, pictograms, that scrolled top to bottom and looked to lay out a story of some kind. From what he could see, the former inhabitants of this world were reptilian, as that was a common shape depicted throughout all the carvings. In fact, they very closely resembled the Were-Crocs that prowled about the surface. Could they be the last remnants of a race that once lived down here?

"Fascinating," Fear said as his fingers lightly touched the surface of the wall. "If only we had time to truly study this."

"What do you make of it?" Death asked.

"If I compare it to similar hieroglyphs from early Egypt," Fear replied, "it looks like this place was a sacrificial pit. I can only surmise, but I think it says that at a set interval, though what I can't be sure, they would march down their sick and elderly to sacrifice to the deity that sleeps beneath these walls."

"And when that wasn't enough for it any longer, it came for the rest of them," Agony added in from her position by the window.

"It says the deity lies across a bridge over a river of fire," Fear continued, "The rest I can't even assume to translate.

"River of fire?" Agony asked. "Well I think we're on the right track. You guys gotta see this!"

She patched her HUD to transmit to the other two, as War was already peering down at the same spectacle. From the far side of this room, a set of stairs led down to a more elaborate and open platform. At its center lay the ruins of a giant statue of some kind, only the feet and pedestal it stood upon remained. From there, more stairs cascaded downwards, leading to an intricate bridge of stone that spanned a kilometer across to the next rock formation. Every fifty feet, the bridge was lined by a one-man tower with a high vantage point on its roof. Around a hundred or so feet below the bridge was a dried lake of ancient magma flow, along with deep fissures that led further into the planet's crust to where the light source in this cavern was emitted. Somewhere at the bottom of those cracks in the ground was the current lava flow, burning hot and bright to give this whole scene a look like none other.

"Oh, soothe my little D&D soul," Fear whispered happily. "If only my old game mates could see this shit."

"Nerd," Agony sniped at the comment.

"Bitch," Fear snapped back.

"Start looking at the movement in the shadows, and not the architecture," Death stopped the banter before they got carried away. "Across the cavern is a ton of movement. Looks like we found our critters."

"And hiding in the bridge towers," War added. "Looks like they pulled back to defend the Queen with the remaining numbers.

"Well, we did kick their asses above the surface pretty easily," Agony commented. "I say we get down there and rain fire on their zombie asses."

"That's what they want us to do," Death pointed out. "I see movement under the bridge too. If we go down there, even get halfway across that structure they will swarm us with more numbers than we have ammo."

"So, I use my Boom Stick?" War asked with a childlike giddiness.

"Yes," Death answered. "The three of us will go down to that platform and draw them forward. Make your aim to the mass of the drones across the bridge. They are using their bodies to shield something big, which I assume is the Queen. Hit it with the Stingers and at the least we'll take out a good portion of them, causing many more to retreat and rebuild the living shield."

"Breaking the trap and letting us move in for the kill," added Fear.

War moved to the middle of the room and began to assemble the missile launcher she had been waiting to use since leaving Waypoint. What first appeared to be a long metal tube broke apart into three pieces. One was the barrel, the other contained the firing mechanisms, grip and trigger, and the last tube held four of the compact and aimable missiles. Once she was ready, she hefted the large apparatus onto her right shoulder after raising the shoulder cannon to stand vertical on that side to make room. Fear plugged two wires into the side of her helmet, then after a brief system check, War gave the thumbs up. It was time.

 Agony scrambled from her window to the doorway, ducking below the portals to make sure any movement within the room was being masked. She braced her body up against the thick door frame, then proceeded to use one of her hair tentacles to use the polished knife point as a mirror to look out with. She kept the red light in their HUDs up, then flashed the red as two more of her hair tentacles shot out. There were two thuds against the outside wall, a brief moment of silence, then they watched as her hair dragged a drone back into the room by its neck and head which had been run right through in both places.

"Any more?" Fear asked aloud.

Agony flashed the red icon three more times, leaned out the door and puffed out six quick rounds of her railgun rifle. As the weapons had no explosive charge to them, they produced little sound when fired which made for excellent stealth capabilities. Moments after firing, three separate thuds hit the ground outside. A few seconds later, the icon flashed green. It was time to move out.

Agony led with her rifle facing forward, Death was on her heels with his scanning to the right, and Fear was on his heels with his weapon covering left. The three moved as one down the stairs. Agony stopped at the first large stone column that stretched all the way up to the roof to provide cover for the other two as they advanced. Death stopped at the next, letting Fear pass and Agony catch up. Fear stopped at the second last column, covering for the others as they rushed past carefully.

Death held the last cover position at the bottom of the stairs, allowing Fear and Agony to run into the open before taking cover at the base of the ruined statue in the middle of the platform. He popped a few rounds off to drop a dozen or so drones as they rushed to meet the group, yet no more of them moved from their positions. Death motioned Agony to race across the platform to another unfinished stairwell to take position behind the lone column there. As she ran, both Death and Fear picked off a few more of the creatures as they tried to intercept her.

Once they were all in position, Death flashed the green light two times to War, signalling for her to fire two missiles into the fray across the bridge. Stepping out of the room and into the open, the walking tank that was War took careful aim to the writhing mass of bodies, then fired two rockets, one after another. The projectiles screamed across the divide, then struck where they were intended to. Yet in the moments before impact, Death and the others couldn't believe their eyes at what happened.

What had previously been a dome of creatures slithering about like a nest of snakes, when the missiles neared, they stood up in a wall of flesh. The first rocket hit and obliterated all traces of the hastily created obstacle as a second one rose to intercept the next missile. It ended in the same result, but still had the effect Death was hoping for, chaos.

Shrill cries echoed off every odd angle of the cavern as body parts flew in all directions. Their flesh shields had cost them a great deal of manpower, and the attacking force that started to jump into action as the rockets were fired froze in place, unsure of what to do. But the confusion wasn't shared by the Four Horsemen, and they all rose from their cover positions to fire mercilessly at the throngs of drones caught in no mans land.

Each kill was compromised of two shots. One to the head to destroy the host's brain, the other to the high neck to kill the parasite. Each of the Horsemen performed this kill with endless repetition perfectly, dropping drone after drone after drone while they were confused. War pumped heavy rounds into the bridge towers, destroying every one of them with ease along with any creatures hiding upon or within them. The firefight was going exactly as planned, including the eventual retreat of the drones as they fell back to rebuild the cover destroyed with the initial attack.

Waiting for War to climb down the stairs, the Four Horsemen formed a firing line to begin advancing across the bridge. With their enemy now retreating, they just had to stay calm and take out targets until only the Queen was left. Problem was, there was a lot of targets left to take out.

Agony pumped flares across the bridge as they hit the halfway point, trying to illuminate what was waiting for them on the other side. A span of six flares flew the distance, flittering to the ground to reveal a nightmare in waiting. The assault on the surface was to draw out and thin their numbers to which this up-close assault would be better suited. They had bombed hundreds of thousands of these things into oblivion, but as the other side of the bridge lit up their threat assessment trackers lost count close to a million more targets.

But there was no stopping now, so the team kept pressing forward while knocking down more and more of the drones each second. As they hit the three-quarter mark of the bridge, the roof above them shook violently, sending clouds of dust cascading down upon the Horsemen. Fear stopped to check the video feeds left behind with the traps, then swore under his breath before reporting to Death.

"The traps on the surface were tripped all at once, then quickly overwhelmed," he updated his Commander. "I placed feeds every kilometer on the way down to watch our asses. It looks like we have a few thousand more of these uglies coming up on our six quickly."

"Odd strategy, but effective," Death muttered. "War and Agony, you keep moving forward. Fear, you and I put our backs to theirs and keep the freaks off the ladies' asses."

All lights flashed green in agreement. Agony and War closed ranks, almost rubbing shoulders while Fear and Death spun around and up against the front line looking backwards, just in time to see a river of drones pour out the doorway and windows of the room at the base of the entrance. Creatures moving with rage driven speed flowed like water down the steps and onto the bridge. The moment the shots were clear, Death and Fear opened fire. They were efficient and indiscriminate, but could only hold back the wave from advancing, not wipe it out completely.

War and Agony were at the same point, the loss of two more fighters slowed their progress to a complete stop, just fifty-feet short of the end of the bridge. Drones were everywhere, and for each one dropped there were two more crawling over the dead once to keep the charge. They were on the roof of the cavern before them, on the walls, and even scaling the pit below them to join the fray. War pumped heavy rounds repeatedly, and her arm mounted mini guns were beginning to glow red from over heating.

Agony kept firing, screaming in rage as the frustration of the situation unfolded. They had the perfect plan to break the trap waiting for them yet managed to walk into yet another one. It wasn't possible, though here they were. And that's when she saw it, before any of the others. Agony's armor being lighter than the others, she felt the tremors beneath her feet first, and her eyes found the source soon after. The ball of bodies simply collapsed, ceasing to be a shield and joining the fight to overwhelm the Horsemen. From beneath where they were, a billowing of dirt and dust exploded, and from its mist emerged a true nightmare.

It was a giant armored worm, reminding her of a hundred-foot-long Armadillo with no legs. But this thing did have legs, and each of the hundred or more of them were razor sharp spears that sparked as they struck the stone beneath them. Closer to its mouth sat four larger and longer arms, each ending in scorpion-like claws. On the top of its head were two rows of black beady eyes, which went from near the middle of the face to the outer curve of its head. Each eye was about the size of her fist. Its huge armored mouth parted, revealing a softer skinned creature beneath and a massive beak which parted into fours as it let loose a deafening shriek.

It was a sound that not only echoed throughout the chamber but was the type that sent chills down the spine of the interlopers in its inner sanctum. A combination of the shrillness of a bat, the scream of an eagle as it dove upon its prey, and the sound of nails running the length of a chalkboard all in one. All four of the Horsemen flinched at the cry yet held their positions despite of it.

"Are you seeing this?" Agony shouted over the growls of the attacking drones and the constant explosion of heavy rounds.

The others flashed green in response, Fear and Death viewing the scene on a small in-screen portion of their HUDs. It was huge yet moved like something much smaller than it. Death trained one eye to watch the feed, while the other maintained its view of the battlefield. He switched his rifle to his left hand, then used his right arm tri-cannons to drive heavier and explosive rounds into the masses of drones piling onto the bridge. Fear used his forearm guns to do the same, and the two actually noticed it was making a difference. The two poured it on, breaking the trap and freeing up a possible escape route.

Agony watched as the creature, which was undoubtedly the Queen, began to thrash around angrily as the persistent attackers began to turn the tide. It skittered back and forth behind the walls of zombified humans, growing impatient at their lack of success. The Horsemen had faced insurmountable numbers before, and only emerged victorious due to perseverance and a shit ton of ammunition; both of which they had loads of right now. Agony could feel the determination welling up inside her and pouring out of her teammates.

For the first time in almost ten minutes of this firefight, the group began to move forward. A half footstep at first, gaining each inch with great effort, the enemy began to feel its edge begin to slip away. Death tapped Fear to swing back and join the forward group, and he did so without hesitation. The added firepower turned inches into full feet, and the indomitable Horsemen continued forward with Death cleaning up the mess behind them.

That's when the Commander saw it, as he was able to keep one eye separate from the battle to study the Queen. It stopped pacing and took up position to match theirs head on. Death watched as its tail began to shudder, and saw a slight glow beneath the segments of its armor. It was when the masses of drones began to scatter to give it a clear shot that Death finally reacted.

Grabbing onto War's left shoulder cannon, Death pulled and jumped to give him the leverage to do a spinning flip and land in front of his team. As he turned in mid air, he saw the monster's beak open as a bright blue glow began to grow within its maw. His sword strap caught on an edge of War's armor as he hurtled over her, and the right snap broke to leave the weapon hanging by the left side only. Death now had spun his body to face the monster directly, firing from his arm tri-cannons to give him more time to protect his team. But it gave him none.

"Get down!" he shouted in his toneless voice as he readied to touch the bridge in front of them.

His team didn't have a chance to react, and neither did he. Death's feet barely touched the ground when the beast unleashed its bio-weapon on them, hitting him just off center and engulfing his entire upper right side in a liquid flame. His cover fire was at least able to move the shot from dead center, but the hit was deadly anyways.

With his body weight not distributed properly, the blast threw his body like a projectile, striking his team hard. The impact carried the group backwards, and off their feet with Death's limp and burning body falling off the side of the bridge to the chasm below. Agony watched helplessly as her mentor fell into the smoke and ash below, before even the light of his burning body faded away. A wave of unimaginable hatred washed over her, and she unsheathed her oversized katana, using the Saya to strike a few drones before discarding it completely. She then threw herself without abandon into the throngs of creatures, hacking and slashing her intended way to the Queen. It took less than thirty seconds for her to be overwhelmed.

With their rifles scattered by the unexpected impact, the remaining Horsemen scrambled to regain their footing to force the attack once more. War managed to get to one knee before being swarmed. Her arms and legs were quickly restrained, as others smashed at her helmet with large rocks until it finally broke. Dozens of hands forcefully yanked her helmet off, before she was struck by the same rock used to shatter the helmet, knocking her cold.

Fear rolled backwards and continued firing helplessly at the aggressors as he watched his teammates fall. Unsheathing his daggers, he fired relentlessly with his arm cannons until the range was too close to do so. Then it was all about the quick kill, and the Voodoo Priest muttered a prayer to a nameless God as he tore every drone that pounced upon him to shreds. His prayers unleashed an eerie glow in his blades, giving them a ghostly fire to go along with their razor-sharp edges. Using this to full effect, he kept back peddling while slaughtering any creature too foolish to get close to him. But with his focus so tuned into the throngs of enemies in front of him, Fear failed to notice those who climbed beneath the bridge to come up behind him.

They hit him hard from behind, so hard the daggers fell from his hands and he fell on his stomach. Once down, he was swarmed, restrained, then knocked cold like War was with his helmet broken and removed violently.

But before the lights went out, Fear muttered a prayer to the darkness itself, asking for it to wake his Master who lay below. Fear pleaded with all the Gods and spirits in the afterlife to give strength to the fallen. With his last thoughts, he wished for the veil to break open, and power the four-hundred-year-old monster to life once again. His Commander must rise, no matter the cost. And when awoken, Death would rain all hell on those who dared to defy the Four Horsemen their victory, and their eventual freedom. As consciousness faded from him, he was being dragged across the bridge towards the monster Queen, yet Fear thought he heard something move in the darkness below. For one more moment, the Jamaican smiled his evil smile before everything went dark.

12

Ancient Underground Temple, Horizon

Slowly, ever so slowly, Agony began to regain consciousness. The first thing that hit her was the smell of warm, damp air. As her eyes began to focus, Agony noted that half her visor was missing, shattered in the blast which Death had shielded them from. The Commander; he had jumped in front of the team to take the brunt of an energy weapon of some sorts. Her last memory before it all went black was him falling lifelessly off the stone bridge, his entire right half burning as he fell. Instinct to go help him kicked in, and that's when she realized she were bound somehow by a rubbery webbing which stuck her to the wall along with War and Fear. Agony struggled against the sticky substance that held her and her team captive against the cave wall. Anger flowed red hot in her veins, anger that she was trapped along with hate they were helpless. Here stood what remained of the legendary Four Horsemen, and they couldn't do anything to stop these creatures.

There was a time when they had been unstoppable and fighting beside Death, with him she had always felt invincible. The Commander had enabled her to be the killing machine she always knew she was inside, but that was a different time and on a planet billions of kilometers away. But here against a parasitic alien, their team had come up short in more ways than one. Now more than ever, Agony wished she was back on ice.

The giant four clawed centipede thing reared up in its hollow in the cave and let out a shrill cry. If what her senses told her was true, it fired a kind of bio-energy weapon from its beaked mouth full of moving teeth that struck Death with full effect, knocking what little remained of him afterwards down the chasm behind them. Deep beneath the surface of Horizon, it looked like this ancient parasite was about to have them for lunch. Not the way she envisioned checking out of this life.

Fear and War began to come to as well. They were both helmetless, bearing bruises of a severe beating once being exposed. They too had a moment of waking panic before realizing the situation they were in, both of them looked to her for guidance. As if she had any good ideas. Her last idea was to throw herself into the fray like a madwoman and look where it got her.

A group of less emaciated drones began to poke at them, almost making sure they were awake. These ones were different, they walked like men, moved like men, and examined them with more than a glimmer of intelligence. In their eyes was understanding, and when they spoke, they all spoke in unison. It was by far the creepiest thing Agony ever experienced in her life.

"We thought you would be more difficult to defeat," they hissed, using the hundreds of emaciated and zombified drones as one voice. "But in the end, you are like all the others of your kind. Soft and pathetic."

It was an unnerving sound, having hundreds of dry voices of different pitches saying the same thing at the same time from all around them. Some of them were hung upside down from the cavern ceiling by the same substance that held Agony and her team to the wall, others hung off the walls like spiders, while the ones on the ground encircled the captured group. All of them hissing the same words, all their brains linked by the parasitic worms that now controlled the almost dead bodies.

"Just fucking kill us!" Agony screamed defiantly. "Why drag this out? What do you want from us?"

"Pain," it replied with a hundred or more voices. "You hurt us. Killed us. Need to make you hurt, need to make you suffer, then will use your bodies to bring more of your kind down. Our numbers have lessened, the colony needs more."

"What the hell are you?" Agony shot back.

A few of the zombified humans began to paw at her face, and with her arms restrained Agony could do little more than shake her head to stop them. Their fingers were like dried leather, and as they dragged their fingers across her cheeks, she almost felt violated. The only thing she could do is bite and spit at her gropers, it did little to dissuade them. Agony watched as Fear and War both struggled to free themselves to no avail as well, seeing the disdain in their eyes as they too were fondled by the dead.

War used her head as a wrecking ball, and even managed to pull one of her powerful arms loose to swing wildly at the never-ending mob that surrounded them. Cursing in words unfamiliar to Agony, the Viking woman smashed the skulls of many a creature until she was finally restrained and 'glued' back to the wall again. Fear tried to calm himself so he could begin a ritualistic chant, but each time he opened his mouth the zombified people would stick their fingers in his mouth. She watched him gag, almost throwing up herself as she imagined how awful that dead flesh would taste. He too cursed at the drones, shaking his head violently to get the swarm of hands to move back. But they would not stop, simply because their Queen did not want them to. Again, Agony though this was the shittiest way to die.

"We are her Braintrust," the voices echoed through the cavern. "She chose us to be her voice, to speak her thoughts to the colony, and to the cosmos. She is of the Endless, older than old. She came to this world lifetimes ago and harnessed the inhabitants for her needs. For a time, the colony was grand, yet it still died off, so she slumbered. Your kind awakened her, and they are much better suited for a superior colony. So many of you, an untapped resource."

"We won't be the last they send to exterminate you," War snarled.

"But you were their best, were you not?" the Braintrust drones paced a few feet away while their Queen looked on. "The Vaunted Four Horsemen of the Republic. You were quite the challenge, yet we defeated the best; the rest will fall too. The time to talk is over, it is time we took your bodies, time we herded the masses to her command. We are life eternal, the light of the future."

Agony felt the push of the mob increase against them and knew this was it. Hands which simply searched before now began to grasp and pull. They would be torn apart and fed to that segmented freak controlling the zombies for a snack, all to feed its rage for their indiscretions. She closed her eyes and said a prayer to her ancestors in her mind. And in that moment of silent reflection she heard a sound from behind them. A sound that should have been impossible to hear. It seemed that the creature heard it too because the assault on them stopped.

Agony opened her eyes to see all the controlled husks looking in the direction of the chasm as the sound of scraping metal on rock grew louder. It was steady, but not a regular sound. It sounded like someone was climbing out of the hole, but that was impossible. She saw half his body be disintegrated from the blast, so it couldn't be him. Could it?

As the sounds grew louder, they stopped, and it seemed the whole cavern took a deep breath. Just as the attention was about to be put back on the captured Horsemen, a broken and skeletal metal hand still encased in a broken armored gauntlet appeared at the chasm's edge. The sight was strange enough, but then the realization that there wasn't an arm attached to the wrist as the rest of the body began to rise out of the gloom below.

It pulled itself up enough that the left side of more recognizable armor appeared, and a fully armored left hand reached out more and pulled the rest of the half-destroyed figure out of the darkness. As it slowly rose to its feet did Agony finally comprehend what her Commander had told her before. To live his long life was a truly impossible feat, unless aided by something unnatural. Here before her very eyes, she was witnessing exactly how unnatural Death truly was.

His entire right side of his torso and arm were gone, replaced by a thick black ink-like smoke that connected to the right hand. Most of his state-of-the-art armor was destroyed, only the left arm from the shoulder down of it remained, along with a quarter of his left side. What showed now was a black and dark grey figure that looked like a man with no skin, his skull-like face stared straight ahead at the creature which had struck him down minutes ago. Orange fire burned from the eye sockets giving it even more of a hellish look, even with a portion of its face missing too. And to top it off, a shadowy black wing unfolded to extend from his back where nothing but smoke remained.

Agony almost cried for joy as Death re-emerged from the pit, and almost shrieked in fear of what she was seeing. She could feel the tension from her comrades trapped with her, as they too were in disbelief at what was happening. But none of this was as shocking as what was yet to come, even the battle-hardened Horsemen of the Republic couldn't quite comprehend it while it happened.

///

Rage and fire, that was all that he could feel as he somehow pulled his broken body out of the pit he was discarded into. Death was pissed off and had let go of every little bit of harbored emotion he bottled up over his lifetime. Never before had he fully tapped into this part of himself, but if he was going to save his family, he needed to pull out all the stops. So, he let out the darkness, and let it drive for the time being.

It started with his body being broken at the bottom of the ravine, the damage so great that most of his systems were offline. Some of them didn't even exist anymore. Death was tired and knew there wasn't enough will power left in his soul to get up from this devastating blow. And then it came to him, his soul.

Since the day he died on that surgical table, he hadn't been alone in his body. At first there was two of them, eventually joined by the machine a few hundred years later. But before that, he got acquainted with the darkness that flowed within him, that was attached to him. It was old, powerful, and very angry. Floating around in the afterlife for eons, it had forgotten what it really was, so there was no telling if it was a ghost, a demon, or worse. For years to come, the two had fought for control of the body they inhabited, but this time was different. This time they needed each other.

"It's time to put aside our differences," Death said out loud to himself while looking up at the faint light far above him. "Its time to stop being at war with each other. I'm tired; my soul is tired, and I can feel yours is too. But now is not our time, not if we do what we should have done the very day you came back to this world with me. Two need to become one, if we do there is nothing that can stop us. I cannot save my friends, my family, without you. I beg of you, its time for us to become one."

For a few moments, there was nothing but silence. Death's reserve systems began to short out, leaving his body to begin reverting into a stasis mode to keep his brain alive for as long as possible. Above him, the light faded to grey, then slowly began to fade way until everything was dark.

Then he felt like a cold liquid was poured into his soul, and with it came unimaginable power. Memories, or the fragments of them, flooded his mind causing his mechanical body to spasm from the information overload. Death felt his left side begin to move, and then sit up with help from his right hand. The problem was that he knew his right hand wasn't attached anymore. When his systems rebooted and his eyes came back online, he saw with a different vision. Everything shimmered, pulsating with shades of red like a heartbeat. The entire chasm was alive as he saw through eyes that were not his, yet somehow they always were. His plea had been answered, no longer did he feel the presence near him. It was in him; it was him now. After almost five hundred years, the two adversaries had become one.

Death felt the missing parts of his body feel whole again. Without hesitation, he began to climb up the stone rock face to the cavern above, a hundred feet above where he lay almost dead a few seconds ago. His body was flooded with hate, anger, and a driving rage unlike anything he had felt before. Pushed by this dark emotion he climbed the impossible climb, barely noticing that parts of his body didn't exist. Once at the top, he felt the darkness within flare to new heights. This time he was ready to fight; this time he knew what to expect from his enemy. This time it was his turn to bring the unexpected to the battle.

"You are life, you are the light," Death repeated to the alien creatures. "Well, I am the darkness that swallows the light. I am Death."

"You are not human," the voices roared in unison and the mob of controlled humans began to approach Death now in response. "Something else drives you, something old."

Death unsheathed his sword with his right hand, then in a swift motion threw it towards the captured Horsemen. It cut through the glue-like bindings of Agony and stuck into the cave wall at chest level. Her face changed from surprised to one in a trance; Agony was in the grip of the voices of the blade.

"Time to let loose, child," Death's raspy and emotionless voice called out to her. "The steel demands blood, I think you should oblige it."

"A sword cannot stop us," The voices of the Braintrust hissed at him. "We are many, you are few."

"You don't get it yet." Death raised his severed hand and motioned for the mob to stop, which they did. "You've already lost, and it is all due to your very nature."

Death's right hand went from an open palm to a closed fist, and the emaciated human hosts slowly obeyed him by turning back towards their former parasitic master. From his fist, his skeletal metal index finger pointed up, then at the enemy. The zombified humans rushed the alien in a frenzy, stampeding one another to attack it. Ones on the wall jumped high and far to tackle the giant millipede, and those stuck to the ceiling tore their torsos from their legs glued to the roof to fling themselves like rain upon the enemy. It was chaos as the creature screamed as it began to be overwhelmed.

"A parasite needs a host, and despite what the host looks like, it is still alive," Death spoke over the roar of the attacking drones, as if his voice was in all of their heads. "And living humans have souls, souls that I can control. That was your oversight, and my weapon that will destroy you and all your kind. In the darkness, souls are power; power which I alone can harness. Let your army be your demise. Let your arrogance bury you."

From the Saya of his sword, Death produced a one-foot bar. With the push of a button, it extended in an instant to three feet. Another button produced a curved rod from the leading edge, a rod which lit up with white hot plasma. Death was now complete with a plasma scythe, and he sprang into the mob to attack anything that moved.

///

Agony felt her will be lost to the voices in the sword, and her body responded. On its own, her right hand, now freed by the sword itself, grasped the hilt to pull the blade free of the rock. At the same time, her entire body spun around to pull completely loose of the goo webbing. She found herself free, facing Fear and War as she panted; inside her mind she screamed not to hurt them though she knew she was no longer in control.

For some reason, the Demon Blade spared her friends, and Agony sliced effortlessly through their bindings to free them. Then she felt the anger flow, and she turned towards the enemy. There was no stopping to see if War or Fear were hurt, there was only vengeance. The sword of souls demanded blood, and this body was now its vessel to bathe in it. Human or alien, it all had to die.

Yet for some reason, the drones weren't attacking her. The spirits in her were confused, for a second ago they almost tore her apart piece by piece. Now, they simply stood there, looking at the dark figure at the edge of the chasm. A chill ran through her body, the Demon Sword recognized something dark not worth challenging over there, instead choosing to think of it as an ally, for now. Her eyes turned to see the throngs of drones turn on their Queen, and the spirits decided to kill anything that moved as she leapt into action.

The sword was a part of her body. From one strike it allowed Agony's body to bend and flow to the greatest extent her frame would allow, and sometimes more as she heard a few ribs crack as she twisted and spun with each blow. It was like fighting underwater; her body used momentum to move from target to target as if gravity was no longer a factor. And the bloodlust, even Agony reveled in it from deep inside her mind. Though she was not in control, every kill released anger pent up over an entire lifetime of pain. Tears flowed from her eyes as the blade utilized her emotion to feed the rage it needed to keep fighting. There were close to a million drones here, and she began to wonder if that was even enough to satiate the sword.

Normally she would hate being out of control like this, yet she fully surrendered herself to the sword. It allowed her to be more than she ever could be, and it allowed her to protect her friends which she failed to earlier. Agony fought through the throngs of creatures, chopping them down like trees on her way to the Queen. Off to her right, she noticed the dark figure that resembled her Commander doing much the same with a weapon that looked like a plasma bladed scythe. While she was occupied with killing everything, he was making a bee line to the Queen. She hoped they would meet there for the kill, but there was so much blood that needed to spill first. So much blood the blade needed to taste.

///

"What the fuck is going on here?" War mumbled to Fear as she picked him off the ground.

Fear had taken a severe beating, as well as using his very life force to fuel his magic towards his blades in his final stand. The result was like running a marathon, then realizing you had to run another one immediately afterwards. He was running on empty, but desperately searched for a second wind to help his friends.

His friends. One was lost to the throws of madness that came from handling the Demon Sword, and the other was something straight out of a biblical verse about hell. Fear wondered all this time how the Commander had survived four hundred plus years, and this was the answer. During the Revolutionary War, Fear knew there was something special about Death, though he could never quite figure out what it was. On the battlefield, he unknowingly commanded the dead along with the living, driving through his enemies like a river through sand. Back then he didn't know, but it helped him believe what his eyes were seeing now.

"The other side drives him now," Fear mumbled as he got his feet beneath him. "He accepted the darkness within him, the power of the Demon World now gives him power."

"The Commander is not a Demon, do you understand?" War yelled at him, pulling him face to face with her as she glared into his eyes.

"Do you not see what I see, child?" Fear asked her, pointing over at Death cutting a swath through the herd of drones. "Because what I see is blessed darkness at its best. He is the culmination of everything I was taught to believe in with the Voodoo. To me, he is the most beautiful and rewarding thing I could ever hope to see."

"I don't know what I'm seeing." War let him go and rubbed her eyes. "But I know the Commander, we've fought side by side for so long. He may be many things, but he is NOT A DEMON!"

"Call him whatever you may, my dear." Fear patted her shoulder, "but I think we can do more for him and Agony then just stand here and debate theology".

Fear trotted back to where his rifle lay on the bridge, then began firing relentlessly at the Queen who was starting to take aim at Death. War fired the remaining Stinger missiles, following them up with heavy rounds form her shoulder cannons. Each missile hit the Queen hard, causing the creature to recoil and abandon the time needed to defend itself with its primary weapon.

Fear took careful aim to fire well placed shots within the armored mouth whenever it opened, rather than waste rounds on the thick armor of the rest of the body. War obliterated entire waves of the drones with her mini guns, firing the heavy rounds over their heads and keeping the monster off balance. Between its own drones attacking it and the constant fire from Fear and War, the Queen was completely occupied until the other two got to her. And when they did, well it was a glorious sight Indeed.

///

The scythe cut through human skulls like a hot knife through butter as Death sliced his way violently towards the monster at the center of the melee. Even though he now controlled the emaciated people, they still had parasites within their heads, so it was best to destroy them while they posed no threat. From behind, he heard his friends break loose from their bindings and joint the fray; gunfire crackled with loud echoes and explosive rounds lit mini bonfires where they struck. His team picked up on the hint of destroying the soldiers first, though it was Agony that launched herself with bloodlust over him and into the midst of the attacking mob. The Demon Blade had her in its grip now, and for that Death was pleased. It was the only way he could think that she would survive this ordeal, lost in a mindless rage to have her very instincts take over.

The two of them sliced a slow path to the puppet master which was beginning to beat back the horde of its former puppets. It shrieked, spat its glue-like webs at its attackers, and snapped its mighty crab-like claws to cut its attackers to pieces. But the mob kept coming, wave after wave and the creature was quickly tiring while its attackers were unrelenting.

As it brushed away the bodies, War and Fear pierced its body with heavy rounds from their position. Incendiary rounds from War's shoulder cannons shrieked across the span of the cave, lighting their path before burning like mini suns as they struck the target. The alien insect reared back to scream in pain, then aimed its head towards the two Horsemen, opening its mouth to return fire with its bioweapon. Fear casually fired an RPG into the creature's mouth as it opened which exploded right as it was about to fire on them. The explosion rocked the cavern, collapsing a good portion of the back wall on it and its former army.

It took a moment for the dust to clear, though while it hung in the air the bright flash of Death's blade was visible to all.

He continued cutting a swath until it finally reached the badly injured alien. It too survived despite a great deal of damage done to its body. Half of its head was gone, and a black slime dripped endlessly from the broken exoskeleton. Its brain was exposed, and almost pulsated as the creature tried to move its broken body to no avail.

"We are Endless," it said through the few living humans who lay dying around it in the rubble. "You will never win."

"Yet here I stand." Death said looking at it straight in the eyes. "I have won, and you are anything but endless."

"You have won nothing; all you have done is delayed the inevitable," it choked. "We will devour all, it is what we are. It is what we do….."

A flash of motion had Death take a step back. The alien was silenced as Death's sword cut its exposed brain in half. There was no scream, no death cry to satisfy the end of the fight. There was only silence and the heavy breathing of a nearly mad Agony who looked about for more to kill. He watched as she sliced the dying humans and their parasites into pieces one at a time until there was nothing more to kill. In her frenzy, Agony turned towards Death and raised the sword at a ready stance.

"Both the blade and you know that is foolish, Himiko," his voice crackled on his damaged voice box.

Death turned his plasma scythe off and retracted it to its smaller form before placing it where it had been before on his back. With his 'floating' right hand, he extended it to have his companion relinquish the weapon given to her. The others watched keenly as she stared at him wildly, but as the tense moments passed the madness began to fade from her eyes. Eventually, Agony lowered the katana, bowed to Death, then offered the blade back to its owner hilt first. Death quickly accepted it and sheathed it in the blink of an eye.

"Welcome back, Himiko," he said to her softly as she looked at his broken body with great concern.

"Let's get the fuck out of here," she snarled at the sentimental moment, shaking the black, alien blood off her left leg in disgust.

They joined the others at the chasm edge and War grabbed all three of them in a celebratory bear hug. Agony cursed, Fear laughed maniacally, and Death just endured the moment. As they parted, he felt their combined gazes fall upon him at once. He held his left hand out to War, and she passed him a foot long, three-inch-diameter cylinder. With a flick of his left thumb he popped the top off and poured what first appeared to be a liquid over his ghost-like right side. In moments, the liquid was alive and millions of nano bots began to repair the extensive damage to his body, rebuilding it before all their eyes.

"So, Breathe Bomb?" Death asked Fear and War before they started across the bridge.

"You know we're in," Fear began. "But what about the artifacts? This whole place is priceless, you just want to destroy it?"

"We are in a nest, we killed the Queen, but I know for a fact we haven't found the eggs that big bitch laid," Death explained as his body began to reappear millimeter by millimeter. "And if Nowich-Paris, or any other company for that matter, gets a hold of that thing, then we could be doing this all over again before we know it. Fuck the artifacts, fuck this place, and fuck that thing. Dump a pack of phosphorus grenades down the hole that bitch came from, along with a Breathe bomb. Attach another one to her carcass and set charges every fifty meters across the bridge. Add a few more to the support columns to bury it all after she burns. Send every fibre of them back to Hell."

The three of them just stood there for a moment, not sure what to make of his orders. In the past, Death had gone to great extent to not have historical structures damaged. He spared the Kremlin, the White House, even the Pyramids during the war. All those paled in comparison to what this represented, and here he was calling for them to blow it sky high. A few quite and tense moments passed, when Agony finally spoke her mind.

"Fuck it." She turned to stand beside the Commander, "let's burn this place to the ground and all bad shit in it."

"Agreed!" nodded War. "Let's make a fireball so big, that Odin himself will see it back on Earth!"

"Sure, why not?" Fear finally agreed. "I haven't blown something up in a very long time, it was bound to be something I shouldn't anyways. Wait, did one of those fuckers get into my brain?"

"Weren't you paying attention when they described our surgical enhancements?" War smacked him on the back of the head. "Our spines were replaced with cybernetic ones, plus they added the armored guard on top of the 'skin' which bolted direct into the spine. There was no way one of those things could get behind our necks to latch on. Its just physically impossible. We were simply lucky they didn't know that, or the Commander would have been chopping us to bits too."

"Got it," said Fear as he began to lay the charges as ordered. "Guess it makes sense, but maybe we should get scanned for safety reasons.

"Idiot," growled Agony under her breath as she threw Death's left arm over her shoulder and headed towards the exit.

Agony helped Death across the bridge and up to the ascending room while the other two did as instructed. War covered Fear as he dropped a full case of phosphorous grenades down the hole, then slowly lowered down a Breathe Bomb on top of them which was wired to a remote lead that was eventually attached to the bomb on the Queen's carcass. Those bombs were interlinked with all the other charges, which were in turn wired to the last Breathe Bomb which sat at the rubble of whatever statue used to stand on the far side of the bridge. If anything, the two over did it, but they used every last explosive they had before reaching the surface.

The beauty of the Breathe Bomb was that when detonated, it burned almost as hot as a nuclear fission device. Yes, they added phosphorus grenades to the mix just to make sure everything burned to ash, but this particular weapon was devastating on its own. The three planted would make the city of Miami disappear, but that wasn't what made the bomb so desirable for this situation. It exploded hot, burning a large area as it billowed outwards, but then the second half of the detonation occurred, and the device then imploded. Everything it destroyed, and most everything it didn't was sucked rapidly into ground zero and crushed into a tiny ball. It was modelled after the fuel/air bomb used to contain viral outbreaks, and it seemed fitting that it be used in much the same capacity today.

The slow walk out of the cave seemed much longer than the journey it took them all to descend into it, hours before. Death knew what they all wanted to ask, but he wasn't ready to answer it yet. Not here, not in this place of nightmares.

By the time they emerged into the early dawn hours of a new day on Horizon, the nanobots had reconnected his severed hand and almost fully repaired his body. The black inky smoke which had replaced the missing part of his body and the bony black wing had dissipated, retreating within the host where it had been hiding all along. Death signalled for the transport to pick them up, ignoring the awkward silence the whole time. He waited until they boarded the automated dropship and began to climb into the clouds before he broke the awkward silence.

"Burn it," he ordered War.

The Icelandic Viking woman smiled larger than life, jumped to her feet and lowered the rear ramp. Wind howled as she held tight to one of the ramp struts with one hand, the other holding out the detonator as she pressed the button. Below them, the musky dark of the dawn lit up like a new sun as the deep cavern was obliterated in a massive fireball that scorched the belly of their ship as it rose into the atmosphere. War tossed the detonator out the hatch, closed the ramp, then skipped back to the seats gleefully while clapping her hands and giggling like a schoolgirl.

At its apex, the fireball reached nearly three kilometers high in the air despite detonating so deep in the ground. Then the implosion began, and the dropship nearly fell out of the sky from the lack of air pressure with everything beneath it being devoured by the implosion itself. ARC kicked the thrusters to high output, and eventually the ship stopped shaking.

"Are you alright, Himiko?" Death asked Agony as they left Horizon's atmosphere and leapt into orbit.

"What. The. Fuck. Was. That?" she backed away from him as he sat beside her.

"What do I always tell you when strange things happen with me?" he replied.

"Twenty, thirty-nine," Fear replied to the question.

"But what the hell does that shit mean?" Agony asked.

"Twenty minutes, thirty-nine seconds." Death answered emotionlessly. "That's how long I was dead for on the operating table when the Republic was testing augmentations on me. It is a long time to flatline before being revived, but it was a lifetime on the other side. I can't tell you how long it was because time doesn't exist there. When I was pulled back, I don't think all of me made the trip, and I didn't come back alone. Something old, dark, and angry latched on to me and became part of me as I reawakened. The man I was remained dead, and from that moment on I became Death."

"A Demon?" Fear inquired carefully.

"My Commander is not a Demon!" War stated angrily.

"I don't know, and it doesn't remember," Death replied. "But it was a part of me during the war, and it has kept me alive all those lonely years. It has a thirst for life that keeps me from ending mine, and in times of need it gives me certain….abilities like the ones we all witnessed today."

There was a long silence as the three contemplated what he shared with them. It would be turning point in their future. Either they would accept him for what he was, and they would continue as a Legion strike team for hire, or they would turn on him and leave him where he had lived the past four hundred years, in isolation. It remained silent the rest of the way to the docking station in Horizon's orbit. A they docked and began to disembark into the drop platform, Agony was the last to leave the ship of the three. As she reached the hatch, she looked back and held out her hand to him.

"Come on, boss!" she said with a slight smile. "It isn't fair if we cash out the contract without you. We are a team after all, and a great one at that."

"The best there is," he replied, taking her hand.

13

Waypoint Station, Legion Headquarters Tower, Level 3

Death had gone out of his way to contact the Head of the Waypoint Chapter of the Legion, looking to smooth over what was currently a rocky relationship. Truth be told, all of the Horsemen's relationships were rocky, and probably would continue to be so for the foreseeable future. What they needed was an ally, or at least someone who wasn't looking to put a high explosive round in each of their heads when they weren't looking. To Death, it was the logical choice to mend fences with the Legion. After all, he was one of the founding members of the organization.

Across the table from him was a bald headed, white bearded man of Asian heritage. Tinno Yazuna was a profoundly serious, no nonsense man who came from a long line of Legion soldiers and the last remnants of the once powerful Yakuza. It was with that organization that Death had originally proposed the idea of the Legion itself, giving a way for the dying criminal organization to go legit, and become profitable once more. To those in the know, Death was a respected member of the founding fathers, family even.

Dressed in his Stage 2 armor, Yazuna carefully examined an incredibly old membership card in his left hand. There was no reason for him to suspect it was counterfeit, nor would he doubt the identity of the being sitting so casually across from him. Dressed in a simple black trench coat that covered his Stage 2 armor, and wearing his favorite mask from his old armor, Death sat back in the wooden chair and waited for Yazuna to address him. Taking his time deciding his next step, the Head of the Legion simply puffed on his cigarette while staring at the aged plastic badge at length.

"My predecessor spoke of you like a ghost." Yazuna spoke at last. "The skeleton in the closet of our proud ancestors which no one wanted to admit was real. He never laid eyes on you, but he was firm in his belief that the legend of the fugitive Horseman was real."

"As you can see," Death leaned forward, "I am very real. As is my offer."

"Have you shown this card at the bar, I wonder?" Yazuna changed the subject.
"What did they say at the number? It must have been a shock to see 001 for a Legion membership number?"

"I used a different identity, and a more recent number." Death replied.

"Ah yes, the Shadowman." Yazuna smiled. "A more diligent man would have figured out the enigma you portrayed, but my attentions were focused on the issues on Horizon. Business, it seems, kept me from coming face to face with the past."

"I would say I am more a man of the future now," Death commented, holding his uncovered cybernetic hand up and flexing the fingers for Yazuna to see. "And the Horizon issues are no longer, so business can begin to be profitable again."

"Indeed, I must say that I am curious to the nature of such a visit from the likes of you." Yazuna set down the badge and turned to the data pad on the table. "Is it money you wish to ask for? I can't imagine those cybernetics you wear are cheap?"

"Trust me when I say that my family and I have no monetary wants or worries," Death said with his monotone voice. "What we need is a friend."

"You are in the wrong business if you are needing friends, my dear Horseman," laughed Yazuna.

"Let me rephrase that, what I offer you is something long overdue." Death changed the direction of the conversation. "What I offer you is an honor restored, and a treasure returned."

"My honor is intact, and I have more than enough treasures," Yazuna countered. "But you have gone to great lengths to set up this meeting, so I will hear you out."

"I am a four-hundred and fifty-year-old Wetworks asset who has the darkest reputation of any Legion member, and my family are recently pardoned War Criminals. Both companies that hired us want to screw us over by finding loopholes in our contract to keep us in their employment. The rest of the station would see us thrown back in the freezer before celebrating our success. So with you, and the Legion, I wish to secure sanctuary from the storm brewing around us."

"There are whispers of such a contract being prepared already." Yazuna stood up and walked over to the window. "Old allegiances have no hold on these turbulent times. Money is the root of all power, and I can only imagine the riches involved with hunting the likes of you."

"You and I both know where that contract leads," Death pointed out. "And before you ponder the riches and fame of accepting a contract to kill the Four Horsemen, think for a moment on what making enemies of us would be like."

"I am not sure if I follow."

"We are the best trained assets in the field, past or present. Put a contract on us and we would strike first at the source, then at some point we would come for you," Death explained with shocking calmness. "Every night from the moment you accepted that contract, you would lie awake wondering which one of us would it be. Would I send the Viking, let her bludgeon you with her bare hands? Or maybe the Witch Doctor? He could conjure up nightmares that would have you lose your mind long before he ever put you out of your misery. Maybe it would be the Cursed Queen? What irony would it be to send the best assassin the Yakuza ever employed to kill the ancestor of one of their own?"

"You have a point." Yazuna swallowed nervously.

"But maybe it wouldn't be them, though if I came calling you would wish it was one of the others," Death continued. "Compared to the others, I am the true monster. There would be no where to hide, no place in the Republic or her

Colonies for you to run that I wouldn't find you. And when I did, I think I would start with your family, then wipe clean your entire bloodline, then when you have lost everything, I would kill you. Then for spite, I would hang your body from the job board with the contract on us stapled to your broken carcass, warning all others what awaits them to accept."

"So, you have gone from asking a favor to threatening me?" Yazuna stammered, though regained his calm shortly after.

"You brought up the contract, I just enlightened you on the repercussions of such an action." Death mirrored his calm.

There was a short silence as the Head of the Legion pondered things. Staring out onto the Legion and warehouse district, Yazuna pulled drag after drag of his cigarette. Death waited with patience, doing otherwise would sabotage every bit of good will extended during this meeting. Finally, when his cigarette was more hanging ash than rolled paper, Yazuna finally spoke.

"So, tell me this offer of yours." Yazuna turned to Death and offered his hand to shake on it. "After such horrid details, I am anxious to know how you will restore my honor and treasure."

"When I approached your ancestors on the idea of the Legion, they accepted without hesitation," Death explained. "The Republic had come down hard on organized crime, and the heads of the families knew it was time to go legit. But there was one member of the Yakuza who defied the others, remaining fixated on the old ways of crime. It was his very brother that spoke the sorrowful words, sending me to end the life of Hanzo Yazuna."

"My disgraced ancestral line," Yazuna whispered. "His very name is a curse to my family."

"Matsu Yazuna knew my price," Death continued, "I even let him tell his dear brother I was coming so they could remove the women and children of the house before my arrival. He was ready, but he stood no chance."

"The family history books said a demon soldier of more metal than flesh came for him." Yazuna remembered the stories of old. "He was cut down like a dog for his refusal to see the future."

"Hanzo died like a samurai, not a dog," Death explained further. "I gave him a good death, but even he knew the fight was over before it started. I left him lying by the family altar, clutching his weapon with hands drawn across his chest. Then I entered his den, and took what was promised to me."

"The Totsuka-no-Tsurugi," Yazuna whispered.

Without hesitation, Death tugged at the Saya to lose it from the straps holding it to him. Once free, he held the katana out with both hands to offer it to Yazuna with a bow of his head. It had served its purpose, and guided Death in his journey back to his family over the ages.

"This katana has served me well for centuries, never failing when I needed it the most," Death offered. "Its hunger has no hold on me, its curse never strong enough to consume me, yet I still gave it blood when it needed some. It has tasted more in the last week than it has in its existence, so I would say the blade is satiated. At least for now."

"So now you know, Hanzo died a warrior, restoring his honor and his line." Death dropped to one knee before a surprised Yazuna. "His prized treasure is returned to the family forced to give it away for such an awful price. Honor and treasure, for the small price of a continued partnership."

Death watched as the weapon was carefully accepted by Yazuna who used two small daggers to touch the sheathed blade to avoid touching it with his flesh. There was a major sense of accomplishment in that action alone as the Totsuka-no-Tsurugi was set down on the table to be admired by its new owner.

"Honor and treasure," Yazuna spoke softly, "Your offer is more valuable than you can imagine, though I am sure you know that. I accept this with great thanks, my family can erase such an ugly chapter from our history at long last. There will be no contract on you or your family, that is my promise. The Legion may not be ready to embrace you fully, but it will not be responsible for any harm to come your way. That is my promise to you."

Death rose to his feet, bowed one more time in respect for the promise made, then left to attend his next bit of business. The deal was struck and made final; his family was safe from the most lethal threat for now. While it was a shame to part with such a weapon, Death had the advantage of time over his counterpart. Time would see the blade back in the hands of the Horseman, it always did.

Epilogue

Waypoint Station, Nowich-Paris Headquarters, Top Floor

The lift doors opened, and Death impatiently stepped out and into the lobby of the CEO's office. His mere appearance startled the secretary, who struggled to maintain her composure as she looked up at the long striding monster of an armored figure bearing down at her. Fighting the urge to crawl beneath her desk, she did her best to stop the uninvited guest before he barged into her boss's office.

"You.....You can't go in there," she struggled to say. "He's in an important meeting and can't be disturbed."

"I don't care," he growled back at her as he crossed the waiting room and pushed the double oak doors inwards, breaking the locks on them.

"Now that will cost you a fair penny!" Trenton Slovis sneered at him with disgust at the broken doors.

"Put it on my tab," Death replied, sitting himself on one of the chairs facing the Nowich-Paris executive's desk.

"You are interrupting an important business deal." Slovis leaned forward with both his hands on the desk to look down at the intruder in the most menacing face he could muster. To Death, this posture was almost laughable.

To his right, Death had noticed Aida and Ginny sitting on the couch by one of the room long windows that looked down on the city of Waypoint below. Lights of different colors changed as signs and holographic advertisements played out in their never-ending skits, all giving that side of the room a soothing glow to it.

Aida was dressed in a smart green business suit with a white shirt of silk beneath the jacket. Her chosen auburn hair reflected the multitudes of colors reaching high up from far below, making her seem more like a hologram herself. But she was real, and she too was unhappy at his interruption.

"I would kindly ask you to leave, but I know you won't listen to me," she chided him. "We are conducting an important business deal her, none of which concerns you."

"Ah, but it does, and you all know it," Death replied, glancing over to Ginny. "Doesn't it, Miss Agefor?"

Ginny looked at Slovis with a confused expression on her face, then over to Aida as if she was missing something. Aida and Slovis exchanged a quick glance, but not so quick that Death didn't notice it.

"Well if you must know," Slovis stood straight and began to walk around his oversized desk, "Aida and I have decided to go over the contract between DeSa and Nowich-Paris. More specifically, we have decided to renegotiate the contract for the services of the Four Horsemen to keep it open for the foreseeable future."

"The contract was fulfilled," Death countered. "We eliminated the threat of hostile lifeforms, thus ending the contagion and making New Athens habitable again."

"And in that part of the contract, you and your team performed admirably," Slovis went on. "But there were some unforeseen damages to certain areas of Horizon as the result of your actions; damages that need to be repaid to Nowich-Paris as they affected valuable mining deposits that are no longer viable."

"There was no collateral damage clause to the contract," Death reminded them all. "The wording was precise, purge the threats from Company property so business could resume promptly."

"Yet business has not resumed," Aida stood up, adding her two cents to the conversation. "And the only business activities to resume are clean up efforts. The bill for which we have decided falls upon the shoulders of your team, which enables our companies to reopen the contract. Your contract with DeSa did not have such wording, but those of the other three did. And the fact that you have assumed leadership of them, means you have also assumed responsibility for their actions. Am I not right, Ginny?"

"The clauses were there," Ginny nodded with embarrassment to Death as he sat in shock at what was happening, "It leaves Nowich-Paris and DeSa the right to reopen and extend the terms of service for your team until they see fit."

Slovis sat at the edge of his table, directly in front of Death with a sinister smile on his face. The bastard was gloating. If what Ginny was saying was true, then the promise of freedom his team so cherished had been ripped out from underneath them.

"In case you are wondering, we OWN your asses now!" Slovis giggled. "And the way I see it, I think we will make sure you and the rest of the Four Horsemen become our company mules for the remainder of your pitiful lives. You are our personal muscle, and there is fuck all you can do about it!"

Death turned his head to the side, looking away from the pompous asshole who was trying to force a reaction out of him. If he was to strike out physically at one of them, the repercussions would be far worse then the enduring servitude being promised. His family was being threatened with a living hell; broken promises of lawyers and ruthless companies were all part of a game he hated playing.

He hated it, but that didn't mean he wasn't good at playing.

"You're right, there is nothing I can do about it," he sighed, feigning defeat to give his foes a bit of false confidence. "You have an army of lawyers, years of experience in the business field, and the might of your corporations behind you. I am just one person."

"See, you're getting it after all," Slovis clapped sarcastically. "I told you he wasn't too stupid to catch on, Aida."

"I am just one person," Death held his right index finger up to interrupt the mock celebration, "but I am also more than that."

"Oh, do tell," Aida sat beside Slovis on the edge of the desk, eager to hear more.

"Ask yourself, Aida. How did you get here?" Death began. "It was with a loan of funds from me that helped you build what was to become DeSa Armory. Funds that you had helped me invest from my earnings and other procurements during the war. Funds that you managed until you turned your attention to growing DeSa."

"And they were funds I paid back with interest in full." She shook her head at him like he was wasting her time. "So, what of it?"

"Well, after you went off on your little adventure, I turned around and reinvested that money and more into growing technology, medical, and other emerging companies. Investments that made ungodly amounts of money which then I turned into buying into the very companies as they turned public. Add to that my earnings over my long mercenary career and I have amassed quite the wealth."

"And how does the fact you have money help your situation now?" Slovis mocked him. "All it does is make you the richest slave in the Republic."

"No, what it made me was able to buy into a majority shareholder role in a few different companies, such as DeSa Armory and Nowich-Paris," Death replied, calmly looking up at the now startled duo in front of him. "You see, I had the foresight to plan far ahead of this moment, over four hundred years to be exact. And in that time, the returns from your companies' ventures enabled me to use different shell companies to keep buying more and more shares until the last twenty years when I now hold fifty-seven percent of Nowich-Paris and fifty-four percent of DeSa."

Slovis and Aida glanced at each other in near panic, not sure if they could believe what they were hearing. Death enjoyed watching the two that had thought they could manipulate him squirm. Back when he started to plan, he had no idea it would benefit him in this way centuries later. Though as it is, he was rather enjoying the moment.

"And before you object or call me a liar," he continued, "I had the intuition to share all the relevant data with Miss Agefor last week so she could have time to review it along with authenticating my claims. If you wouldn't mind sharing your findings with us, Ginny?"

"It took some time to follow the money trail," Ginny stepped out from her observation place off to the side as all attention now focused on her, "But using financial records provided to me by Mr. Death and cross referencing them with the financials of both involved companies I was able to validate the fact that he is in fact majority shareholder of both companies. I have since filed these records for third party review which too had come to the same conclusion."

"You are so very thorough, my dear Ginny," Death thanked her in his usual unchanging tone of voice. "To summarise all of this, it is in fact I that OWN both of you, or more specifically, your companies. And that means that these negotiations do in fact involve me, which as majority shareholder of both involved companies hereby reject the clause to reopen the contracts with the Four Horsemen. For the record, Miss Agefor, will you please repeat what I have just told them?"

"Certainly, sir." She took up position beside him proudly. "As majority owner, Mr. Death has rendered the contracts of the Four Horsemen fulfilled and closed; the motion to reopen them is rejected as his right as majority owner of both Nowich-Paris and DeSa Armory. This means both companies will not look to recoup monetary losses from any activities on the surface of Horizon from the Four Horsemen in any fashion. They have been given their full pardons and are free to pursue any further contracts as part of the Legion going forward."

"I couldn't have said it better," Death added. "Now if you two will excuse me, I have more pressing matters to attend to."

"And what of us?" it was the cowardly Slovis that first popped the inevitable question as Death began to leave. "I assume you will relieve us of our jobs?"

Death stopped, considered carefully his next words, though he had decided before entering the room what his answer to that particular question would be.

"And why would you assume that, Trenton?" he turned back to both him and Aida who looked all but helpless where they stood. "Both of you have done a fantastic job driving profits for your companies. Trenton, you have a ferocity which has moved forward the Dawn/ Horizon project despite its many setbacks. It was your genius that was able to contract the right team to solve the issues on Horizon to bring production back online, which I can only assume you will get done sooner than later."

"As for Aida, well you have done such a wonderful job that I could only recommend to the board to keep you in place as the CEO. Your ability to advance the company's products, research, and of course profits makes you quite the valuable asset to us. We are grateful to have you aboard for now and well into the future."

"How odd," she replied. "All the data I've compiled on you over the years states that your decision should be to fire us. The fact that you aren't is quite puzzling."

"I've changed, but you've always been too busy to truly look closely at how," Death responded. "Besides, I think keeping you both exactly where I can watch you closely is the best thing for us all. After all, it is wisest to keep one's enemies close."

"You won't get away with this!" Slovis shrieked.

"Get away with what?" Death wondered aloud. "None of this is personal, its just good business. Speaking of which, I have promoted Miss Agefor to be my attaché to oversee my interests in both DeSa and Nowich-Paris. Seeing as I hold majority share in the companies, that would make her now your boss, so I suggest you dispose of any malice or resentment to me or her and get on with your work. I would hate to have to present a motion to the board to replace either of you. It would be a waste of valuable resources."

Death held out his left hand to invite Ginny to join him, which she did promptly after giving Slovis the evilest of smiles she could. But as they were about to leave, Death stopped as he heard the whispers of the schemers behind him.

"We could petition the Legion to expel them," Aida whispered as he stopped. "Or even put a contract out on all of them."

Death closed the broken door behind Ginny so she wouldn't be privy to this last bit of conversation. But instead of saying anything, he reached into his cloak to produce two items, setting them carefully on the desk. One was a child's golden colored teddy bear, the other was a jade statue of a Buddha. The items themselves weren't extraordinary, but where he got them was. And the look of horror on both Slovis' and Aida's faces meant the message was received.

A jade Buddha, taken from the den of Aida's undisclosed home, and a golden teddy bear with the initials L.S. written on the right foot, removed from the bedroom of four-year-old Lynette Slovis, Trenton's daughter. Both items were taken without raising a single alarm, without anyone knowing he was even there. The warning was understood, and by the expression on both their faces they felt the gravity of the threat. He had beaten them at their own game, but worse yet if they decided to play in his world, he had them at checkmate as well. All they could do was go about business as usual; they had no other options.

"Oh, and Slovis?" he added, watching the terrified sleaze jump as he heard his name. "Please do send me the bill for these doors. I will ensure they get repaired to look as good as new in no time flat."

With that, he left Aida and Slovis to wonder exactly how they painted themselves into a corner. Joining Ginny in the elevator, the two remained silent until leaving the building and entering the waiting transport to take them both back to the Horsemen's building. It took a few moments, but finally it seemed Ginny was able to put her thoughts into words.

"So," she began, "that happened."

"You are not wanting the promotion?" Death asked, knowing full well she wasn't talking about that.

"No, I meant you took on the two most powerful businesspeople in the Republic and won," she exclaimed. "Better yet, you beat them at their game."

"What I did was make two very powerful enemies, my dear," he replied as he looked out the window to the city of Waypoint which never slept. "While we won this round, the fight is long from over. But for now, they will be too afraid to make any type of move for fear of intense scrutiny. That fear will soon fade, and when it does, I can't imagine what will be in store for us. That is why we need you, Miss Agefor; they play in your world, not ours."

"Well, if I was to be asked to be a part of any team, I can truly say it is an honor to be a part of yours," Ginny said with a big smile on her face.

"Not a team, a family." He bowed his head to her. "And family is always there for one another. Always."

///
///
///
///
///
///
///

The Horsemen will return,
their story has only just begun

///
///
///
///
///
///

Check out the rest of the works from Damian Shishkin:

The Aen Saga:

Rise of Aen
Ghosts of Lyarra
Thy Kingdom Come
Empire of Ashes
Divided We Fall   (available this fall)

In Human Clothing

Made in the USA
Middletown, DE
02 July 2021

43472800R00191